Alexandra Jordan is the author of **Snowflakes and Apple Blossom** (1st Benjamin Bradstock Tale), **Seasalt and Midnight Brandy** (2nd Benjamin Bradstock Tale), **Stardust and Vanilla Spice** (3rd Benjamin Bradstock Tale) and **High Heels in the Sand,** a Peak District whodunit.
Available on Amazon.
Snowflakes and Apple Blossom was shortlisted for the Writers' Village International Novel Award 2014. **Seasalt and Midnight Brandy** has been serialised on BBC Radio.

Alex practises yoga, walks, reads, eats chocolate, and treads the boards of the amateur stage. She lives in the Peak District with her husband and twin boys.

Contact her on Facebook, Twitter@Alexjord18, and Instagram@alexandrajordan1812

STARDUST AND VANILLA SPICE

A Benjamin Bradstock Tale

ALEXANDRA JORDAN

To Becky —
thank you!

Love, Alex.

Copyright © 2018 Alexandra Jordan
All rights reserved.
ISBN: 9781726766531

For Mum and for Dad –
I love you both.

Also for Chris.
A wonderful man. A loyal friend.

Acknowledgements

A great big **Thank you** to all the people who have encouraged and supported me:

To amazing Liz and lovely Becky, my awesome proofreaders

To (very) patient Dave at International Leisure Products, Doncaster, for my amazing cover design

To my wonderful family, my awesome friends, and my faithful readers - thank you!

I couldn't have done this without any of you.

FOREWORD

In order to illustrate this, my third and final tale, I would like to offer two beautiful quotations:

Men are continually seeking retreats for themselves, in the country or by the sea or among the hills. And thou, thyself, are wont to yearn after the like. Yet all this is the surest folly, for it is open to thee, every hour, to retire within thyself. Therefore betake thee freely to this city of refuge, there to be made new.
Marcus Aurelius, Emperor of Rome, philosopher.

We must develop and maintain the capacity to forgive. He who is devoid of the power to forgive is devoid of the power to love. There is some good in the worst of us and some evil in the best of us. When we discover this, we are less prone to hate our enemies.
Martin Luther King Jr.

Food for thought. But on with our tale ...

My very best wishes
Benjamin Bradstock, Edinburgh

Part One
1995

1

Rose Somerton

Thursday November 9th 1995

It's a load of rubbish, really, all this fortune-telling stuff. Even so, as Justine turns the card, my stomach flutters in excitement.

'The Three of Wands. You'll be travelling abroad some time soon.'

I nod. 'Okay, yes, that *is* quite likely. It'd have to be somewhere cheap, though.'

'Tell me about it.' But as she turns the next card, her face lights up. 'Ten of Cups. My darling Rose, you'll be married within the year.'

I check her out, to see if she's having me on. But no. Justine's so excited for me, she's blushing, right to the roots of her lovely red hair. Tears threaten suddenly and I stand up, ashamed and embarrassed.

'Right. Well. That's not very likely, is it? Jason and I are finished. He's gone. Up and left.'

Olivia, my best friend in the whole world, peers over the rim of her cappuccino. 'What?'

Shit, I think. Shit! I didn't mean it to come out like that.

I mean, I haven't cried in months, haven't felt anything in months. Switched it all off. The heartache, the tension, the churning of my stomach. They say what doesn't kill you makes you stronger.

So I've carried on, as if I hadn't a care in the world.

Suddenly, though, I can't go on, can no longer pretend. Olivia's here now. My long-lost friend, back from New York. I *have* to tell her.

'Jason's gone?' she says.

The tinny sounds of the office canteen drift away. No chairs screeching along the floor, no cutlery scraping against plates, no raucous giggles from the likes of Sarah and Kat. I can feel them staring, their eyes burning into my shoulders.

Indignantly, Justine picks up her cards and places them inside the box. 'The cards never lie,' she says, and moves to another table.

'Sorry, Justine,' I murmur.

Olivia stares at me, her coffee cup still in mid-air. 'Say that again?'

'I don't want to talk about it,' I whisper.

She looks round, her dark corkscrew hair brushing against her jacket. 'Alright! No need to stare!' she hisses, pushing out her hand protectively.

Slowly, the room turns back to its musing, to its tuna mayo sandwiches and frothy coffee.

'Ignore them,' she says. 'Come on. Outside.'

She pulls me into the corridor, to where the ancient Xerox copier moans and screeches its way through the day. Unlike me, I think. I may never have sex again.

We dive into the relative safety of the ladies' loos.

'You never said anything,' she says, her eyes staring accusingly.

I lean across the sink, checking my eyes for smudges. 'You've only been back a few days, Olivia.'

'When did it happen? Why didn't you ring?'

Soft tears roll down my cheeks. Gazing into the mirror, I dab at them. 'I thought he'd change his mind, that we'd find a way through, that it was just a stage. You know, a midlife crisis or something.'

'What?' she screeches. 'How old *is* Jason?'

I shrug. 'Thirty-five?'

She stifles a laugh. 'Sorry, Rose, that's just *so* funny!'

I make to leave. 'Right. Thanks. Great friend you are.'

But she pulls me back. 'After work tonight. Me and you. Wig and Pen. We get pissed first, then you can tell me all about it. Is that the kind of friend you want?'

*

The Wig and Pen is a traditional kind of pub, just along the road from the office. Stained glass windows, games machines, carpets musky with old beer. As always on a Thursday night, it's heaving with twenty-somethings. Solicitor's clerks dressed in black, well-to-do programmers from the bank around the corner, semi-naked girls out to try their luck.

I force my way to the bar, Olivia following on behind. The girl serving has a pierced nose and, as ever, I wonder what she does when she has a cold.

Olivia grins. 'She takes the ring out, silly. Don't you know anything?'

There's an empty table in the corner, away from the rabble, and we sit down gratefully. Olivia waves her Strongbow through the air.

'Come on then, tell me. All about it.'

Holding the black plastic straw they've provided, I down half my vodka and coke in one.

'I don't know, really. It all seemed to kick off in April. After the Arena.'

'The Arena?'

'We saw Oasis. I mean, the concert was amazing, but ...'

I'm finding it hard to continue, the memories too raw, too painful. I pull at the straw until I've reached the bottom.

'But what, Rose? What happened?'

'I think he saw all those young things, smoking weed and getting pissed. Decided he didn't want to be tied down.' I blink back my silly tears.

'But you've only been engaged two minutes. I've only been away two years.'

'He wants to travel, see the world. Doesn't want a mortgage hanging round his neck.'

'Wow. Where exactly does he intend living, then? In a tent?'

'I'd been talking about having children,' I confess.

'What? That's not the reason?'

'Probably.'

'Oh, Rose. He should have thought about that before he bloody well proposed.' She stares at my empty glass. 'Another voddie?'

'I'll get these.' I stand up, but she pulls me down.

'I brought you here, I'll buy the drinks. Let's make it a double.'

I watch as she pushes her way to the bar. Such a bright girl. She actually won a secondment with our sister firm Reddings, and jetted off to New York for two years.

I honestly thought she would never return.

'I'm so glad you came home, Olivia,' I say as she sits down beside me. 'So glad.'

'So am I. I've missed you.'

We hug, great big hugs that make me cry even more.

'Sorry,' I gulp.

'Don't be.'

It's the third double voddie and coke that gives me the idea.

'Olivia?'

'What?'

'What are you doing about somewhere to live?'

'How do you mean?'

'Well, are you renting or buying?'

'Buying. Definitely. But I need to look round first. There's a couple of cottages for sale near home, but I don't want to rush into anything. It's nice living at home, and I love being spoilt, but I really do need my independence.'

'Come and stay with me, just while you look round?' I urge. 'I'm renting out the spare room. Okay, I confess I could do with the money - I'm buying Jason out - but honestly, it would be so much fun.'

She grins. 'What an excellent idea. I'd love to. Thanks, Rose.'

*

We leave the pub just after seven, fastening our coats tightly against the biting wind. In contrast to the bright lights of the pub, the dark night seems to close in, enveloping us, drowning us. Yet at the same time it provides solitude, privacy, isolation. A feeling of quiet detachment makes its way through me, right down to my black leather boots.

Tiny balls of snow litter the pavements.

'Just look at that. Snow at the beginning of November,' I cry.

'Oh well, that's Yorkshire for you.'

'I do love it, though. Did you get snow in New York?'

'Every winter. They get snow there every winter, without fail.'

I pause beside an estate agents' window. The lighting throws out its heat and I warm my hands against the glass.

'Why *did* you come back, Olivia? Was it really because your secondment ended? I bet they'd have kept you on if you'd asked.'

She pulls a face. 'They wouldn't have, and anyway I couldn't stand the place after the thrill wore off. Much too busy. The twenty-four hour city. Taxis rushing round like maniacs, people in your face all the time. And sharing an apartment with three other girls drove me mad. They were all so bloody unhygienic, no idea how to clean. I caught a really bad tummy bug.'

'So it wasn't to do with a bloke, then?' I ask, smiling.

Walking away, she pulls up the hood on her coat. 'Maybe.'

I run after her. 'Maybe? What do you mean, maybe? Olivia! I promise I won't say a word.'

She waits while I catch up. 'It's a long story, Rose. I got hurt, he got hurt, his kids got hurt. It was a disaster.'

'He was married?' I say, shocked.

'Divorced.'

'Oh.'

'Promise not to say anything,' she begs. 'He works for Reddings. It's no big secret or anything, I'd rather just forget about it.'

'I won't, but I'm really sorry. I thought it was just me who was useless with men.'

'It just wasn't right, that's all. But I'm over it now. You and Jason, though – you two were good together.'

My foot touches the edge of the pavement, and I wobble. 'Really?'

'Really.'

I steady myself. 'Obviously not.'

'Men, eh?'

'I don't think I ever want to meet anyone else, ever again.'

She smiles knowingly. 'You'll change your mind. When you meet the right one.'

'There's no such thing.'

'You'll see.'

We're approaching the Peace Gardens by this time, a small green park in the middle of Sheffield. A couple of tramps, wrapped in thick grey blankets, sit on a bench, talking.

'Jason loved you, Rose. He really did.'

My face is wet with tears. 'I know.'

So what the hell went wrong? I ask myself that question every second of every minute of every day. Unable to answer, I cry myself to sleep each night.

7

Tonight, however, I slide smoothly between the sheets with no tears to wet my face, no churning in the pit of my stomach. It feels good to have brought it into the open, to have told my best friend, to have her hold me and say everything will be okay.

I sleep right through, only waking up with the alarm.

2

Claude Jolivet

Saturday December 2nd

December. Fairy lights. Tinsel. The scent of pine trees and cinnamon.

But I have a confession to make. I'm not looking forward to Christmas at all this year.

It can be a devastating time of year for some people, *n'est-ce pas?* People who live on their own, no family, no friends.

I peer out of the lounge window. I really need to go for a jog, clear my head, get rid of this lurking sense of depression. But it's dark, the ground is turning icy, and I'm still tired after all the myringotomies this morning. Lined up in a row, they were. Poor kids.

At least they'll be able to hear now, so they can sing *Jingle Bells* properly. Or *Away in a Manger.*

Christmas …

Maybe a beer.

That's what I need, to stop me thinking about work. And women. If I'm honest.

I definitely need to get out more.

I'll ring Ned.

*

At eight thirty, the Sportsman is nearly empty, no queues at the bar, no murmur of voices or sound of laughter. I can see Ned and Jerry over in the corner near the fire, waving.

Ned stands up, pats me on the back. 'Good to see you, old chap. Thought you'd locked yourself away in that operating room of yours.'

I smile. 'Not a bad idea, sometimes. But no, it's been busy, busy, busy.'

'I know the feeling.'

'My round, then?' I offer.

'A pint of the best, please, Dr Jolivet,' says Jerry, always first in the queue for free beer.

Short and stocky, with an already balding head, he's a university lecturer, but also works part-time at the Real Ale Brewery in Castleton, a village in the depths of the Peak District. He used to often invite me and Caroline to his place for parties, so we could test the new beers and ciders, or the weird concoctions that hadn't yet been given a name. It doesn't happen so much nowadays, though. He's getting old, I think, settling down nicely with Nicki and their Old English Sheepdog. Also, I'm no longer with Caroline.

'How are you, anyway? I hear you and Caroline have split up,' he continues, following me to the bar.

I smile at the bartender and order three pints of *Timothy Taylor's Landlord*.

10

'These things happen, Jerry, I'm afraid. Anyway, how are you? Don't you and Nicki have a wedding coming up soon?'

He grins in that enigmatic way he has, not quite telling you anything, yet telling you everything. 'Ah, now there's a thing.'

'What?' I ask, handing over a ten pound note.

'Well, I haven't quite asked her yet, but I am working on it.'

'About time then, *n'est-ce pas*?'

'It is, Claude, it sure is.' He taps the side of his nose with his forefinger. 'So watch this space, m'dear.'

We carry the beers back to Ned, toasting nicely in front of the fire. Ned's single like me, nicely settled in our ways. After working as a pharmacist all day, he calls at the gym in town, works out for an hour, then drives home to dinner and bed. Confusingly, Sheffield is Britain's fifth largest city, but everyone calls it *town*. Ned's life isn't a bad one, by the looks of it. He has to drive to London for training occasionally, but otherwise it's a nine to five with the occasional Saturday morning.

Unlike me.

But I love my work, it fulfils me, and I feel useful, needed. The sound of a baby crying with earache, or the sight of a child in dreamland because he can't hear. Heart-breaking. So if I can help turn their lives around, that's what I must do. To be honest, most of my work *is* nine to five, but then there's the odd Saturday morning, the admin and the accounts, and the times when I'm asked to be on call so I can help Maxillofacial.

No, Ear Nose and Throat is what I do. And I love it.

Ned takes his beer from me, sipping gratefully. 'Thanks, Claude.'

'A pleasure,' I say. 'And make the most of it. They're saying the price is going up next year.'

'Aren't they always?' he moans.

'You can afford it, Ned,' says Jerry. 'You must be making a packet.'

He shrugs animatedly. 'I'm doing okay. A little here, a little there. I just need to find a little someone to spend it on.'

'So how *is* the old love life?' asks Jerry, a twinkle in his eye.

'Non-existent,' says Ned, miserably.

I pat him on the arm. 'You'll find someone, *mon ami*. There are plenty of beautiful girls around, all looking for that special well-toned pharmacist to enter their lives.'

'That's the problem. You say you're a pharmacist and they think you're boring, you work in a shop. Now if I were a dashing young doctor like yourself …'

I groan. 'Not done me much good, has it? Thirty and still single?'

'How is Caroline? Do you ever hear from her?'

I feel sick suddenly. 'She's got someone else. I've seen them together in town. Didn't bother to introduce myself.'

'Sorry about that, old chap,' murmurs Jerry. 'I thought you two were a team.'

'She was fun, but I couldn't see us getting married. It wouldn't have worked. We argued. A lot.'

'Better than having nothing to say,' says Ned.

'I suppose. But really, it wouldn't have worked. I just couldn't see her as wife material. Not my wife, anyway.'

'*I'd* have taken her on,' he says. 'Any day.'

'Oh, so you fancied Caroline, did you?' I ask, grinning.

Hesitating at my challenge, Ned shakes his thick red hair. 'Not when you were seeing her. Obviously.'

'You sure about that?' asks Jerry.

'Okay,' he admits. 'Okay, I fancied Caroline.'

'It's alright,' I insist. 'She was lovely. Just not lovely enough. You can have her.'

*

An hour or so later, and we're onto the subject of football. The Englishman's favourite topic, other than the weather. After a disappointing few months, Sheffield Wednesday has beaten Coventry City 4-3. And Ned can't get enough.

'They're on their way back, I tell you.'

Jerry snorts. 'Not sure about that. They're at Old Trafford next week. We'll see about that one.'

'Man U!' I exclaim. 'They'll never do it. It'll be a walkover.'

I confess, I don't know much about English football, but I do know about Man U. Everyone in the world knows about Man U.

Ned raises his glass. 'To the Owls. And if they don't win, I'll buy the first round next time.'

'It's a deal,' says Jerry.

Ned looks towards the bar. 'How about watching some of that, instead?'

The Sportsman is filling up now, people heading into town. There's a group of girls at the bar, all of them dressed rather inappropriately for a December evening. Ned can't take his eyes off them. Jerry too, I notice.

'Eyes down,' I say. 'Jerry, you're practically engaged!'

'Did I say that?' he says, gulping down his pint.

'Fancy joining me at the bar, Jerry?' asks Ned.

'Best not. It's Claude's round, anyway.'

I down the rest of my beer. 'I'll come with you. If only to keep you out of trouble.'

I order three more pints. One of the girls smiles at me and I recognise her. A theatre nurse from the Children's Hospital. I smile back and suddenly she's making her way over, pushing through the crowd.

'Aye-aye,' says Ned. 'Looks like you've got a friend.'

'She's a nurse. We work together.'

Moving away with two of the beers, he winks. 'Ask if any of her friends are free.'

Suzanne and I chat for a few minutes, mainly about work. But by this time I've had a bit to drink and am feeling quite relaxed, full of bonhomie. So I ask for her number and we agree to meet up. She's good company, petite, intelligent, very pretty eyes.

'Well done, that man,' says Jerry as I return to the table.

Normally I'd be embarrassed, but tonight I feel good and nothing can faze me. From where I'm standing, life is just going to be one long party.

*

I walk back from the Sportsman. The sky is clear, the air icy cold. But my breath is warm, so I breathe hard onto my hands, rubbing them together. I'm nicely relaxed after my evening out and the future's looking decidedly rosy. Meeting up with Suzanne and getting to know her will be a turning point. I know it.

Crossing the road, I open the wrought iron gate, remind myself once again that it desperately needs painting, and unlock the front door. The house is cold as I walk in, so I pull off my coat and scarf ready to mount the stairs quickly. But there's a red light flashing on the answer machine.

It's Mamie, my grandmother.

'Mon chéri. It's Mamie here. Where on earth are you? I do hope they're not overworking you at that hospital again. If you manage to get home before 10 o'clock, would you please call me?'

I check my watch. Half past eleven. She'll be in bed. And anyway, I'd slur my words and she would not be happy. But the message continues.

'I'm just wondering if you've decided whether to accept my invitation to come over for your birthday. I've told Camille, the sister you never see, and she and Isabelle are so looking forward to seeing you. Please say yes.'

It's been a while since I've seen Camille, admittedly. I miss her. Maybe I should go. I've booked some time off over Christmas, anyway.

I climb the stairs, wash, undress, and slide into bed.

But my mind rolls like a ship at sea. First I'm chatting to Suzanne at the bar, taking in the details of her face. Warm. Kind. Lovely blue eyes. A typical nurse, always smiling. Then I see Caroline's. Beautiful. Funny. But spoilt, selfish, always thinking of number one. She was too controlling, always wanting things her way, never listening. We were together for years, but it was only after she moved in that I truly realised who she was. Oh, it was never about anything major, like what car to buy, where to live, stuff like that. Just the little things. Where to go for the day, what to make for dinner.

I sigh so loudly the bedroom echoes. Part of me still loves her. A pity it never worked out. A pity we had to end it in Paris too, in Mamie's apartment. I've not been back since. Way too many memories.

I turn onto my side, shake the images from my mind, and try to sleep.

But I can't. I can't relax. I need a holiday.

I smile, shake my head.

Okay, Mamie. I will accept your kind invitation.

3

Noelle Angevine

Sunday December 3rd

That there exists such a city as Paris, and that one would choose to live anywhere else, will forever be a mystery to me. I was born here and I will die here.

It is elegance, freedom, expression. A beautiful city. The best.

I've had a good long walk this morning, my breath forming soft clouds in the air, my blood pumping its way to my fingers and toes. The streets are a frosty white, but the sun shimmers and sparkles in the sky, a beautiful wintry blue.

I stop at a little square, just off the *rue Michel-Ange*. There's a *brocante* on and I've agreed to help out. It's in aid of *Vision du Monde,* who help children living in poverty all over the world. There is clothing, *bric-à-brac*, books, records and CDs. The stalls are situated outside, so I'm praying it will stay dry. I've wrapped myself in my cosiest coat and popped on a hat and scarf. My fingers are warm enough in my old ski gloves, although at my age I sometimes need to pat my hands together to stay warm.

Valiant and Marie have been here a while, and have everything ready. Valiant makes me coffee from the espresso machine he's set up. In the cold morning air, the scent is delicious. I take it black, no sugar, and strong.

The stalls have been set out in a semi-circle within the square, just in front of a fountain, its stone fish spouting water. A soothing sound against the background of traffic noise.

I take my place behind the bookstall, sip my coffee, and wait. There's a slow trickle of people at first. But as the aisles of the *Paroisse Notre-Dame d'Auteuil,* the local church, empty, this becomes a flood and we're soon rushed off our feet. Valiant provides good coffee at five francs a time, so people stand around hugging their cups and chatting. Many are elderly, out to catch a bargain, their shopping bags faded and worn. But later on some of the local students appear, boys and girls, breezy and confident.

As I chat to Valiant I watch them, secretly admiring their piercings and *avant garde* clothing. I love their zest for life, their cool nonchalance, their youth. It's such a pity they must be moulded, encouraged to fit in with everyone else. *N'est-ce pas?* Why can't they always be the way they are now? Why do they have to adhere to everyone else's way of seeing the world? What would they do if we gave them *carte blanche* to do whatever they liked? Would they save the world from poverty without having to sell *le bric-a-brac* on silly little stalls? Would they end war, terrorism, the awful bombings we've seen recently? Would they find peace for us all?

A teenage girl comes up to me, and smiles. Clutching her purse with fingerless gloves as if it might be snatched from her, she wears a thick woollen scarf that nearly covers her face. Her eyes are a deep brown. They peer at me through round spectacles.

'*Bonjour, Mam'selle.* Can I help you?' I say.

Her eyes smile. '*Bonjour, Madame.* How much are the books, please?'

I move to the other end of the stall and prop up the cardboard sign that's fallen over. *Les Livres - 4f.*

'It's for a good cause,' I say, encouragingly.

She reaches out to a book, a hardback by François Maspero, full of glossy photographs depicting Roissy, a suburb of Paris.

'This one – only four francs?' she asks, incredulously.

I nod.

She opens her purse, counts the money into her hand, and hands it over.

'*Merci. Bonne journée, Mam'selle,*' I say, and pop the coins into my money bag.

'*Bonne journée, Madame.*' Picking up the book, she goes, leaving behind a lingering scent of geranium. In France, even poor students must still have perfume.

It's a good thing we're not in the sixteenth century, I think. Rumour has it a French parfumier at the time decided the various classes should each have a different scent. So he concocted a royal perfume for the aristocracy and a bourgeois one for the middle classes. Having spent time on this, he then had the cheek to decide that the lower classes, the poor, were only worthy of disinfectant.

Disinfectant! I shudder to think.

As one o'clock approaches, we begin to pack away. Valiant pulls out his car keys and dashes off to collect his Citroën from near the *Bois*.

I find some boxes hidden beneath the stalls, and start to fill them. We've actually sold quite a few books. I suppose people have more time to read during the winter, through those long dark nights.

Marie sidles up to me. 'So how is Pascal?' she asks, grinning through coral red lips.

How she keeps her lipstick on all morning still amazes me. She's much younger than I am, by about twenty years, and is Valiant's second wife. You can see he thinks the world of her.

'Pascal is fine,' I reply, passing her the second box to fill. 'But he's had to go away for a few weeks, to Amiens.'

'Amiens? That's quite a way …'

'It's a special commission, some kind of hotel complex. It's quite a big job, so he's employing lots of local people. Which is good.'

'He's doing well then, yes?'

'Yes,' I agree. 'He's doing well.'

'Has he always been a gardener?'

I make sure to correct her. 'It's garden *design* that he does. And yes, he has.'

'So how much younger is he?'

She knows very well Pascal is nearly fifteen years younger. Knowing her next question will be something like, 'Has he ever been married?' or 'Is he good in bed?'

I change the subject by picking up a book, a tome of a thing about Marilyn Monroe.

'This looks interesting, doesn't it?'

She takes the bait. 'Poor woman. They're still saying it was a set-up, aren't they?'

'They are.'

Hearing Valiant's car pull up behind us, I hurry to fill the boxes.

*

Pushing open the door to my apartment, I hang my coat on the stand and saunter into the kitchen. Sunshine pours through the window, highlighting the dust motes as they swirl in and out, around and about. Stardust, I call it. I always call it that, I don't know why. It's an English word, I know, but it somehow fits with what I see. It comes from a song I heard once, way back in the Seventies.

Sunday afternoons are usually a stroll through the *Bois de Boulogne,* or coffee with friends, or painting. I only began painting after Louis died. It helped somehow, gave me something to focus on during the long days alone. It was winter then, too. Dark and long and lonely. Even though I had friends around, and family, I still felt very alone. Nothing can replace the love of a wonderful man.

But now I have Pascal, who is also wonderful. Caring, passionate, and kind.

I often meet Lucienne or Josephine for lunch or coffee when Pascal's busy. But today Lucienne is poorly, some kind of throat infection, and Josephine has family visiting. So I've been left to my own devices.

After a lunch of *potage* made from chicken broth, potatoes, onion and avocado, I enter my studio, fasten on my apron, pull the cloth from my easel and stand back. I've begun a seascape, a long beach with a young woman walking into the distance. It's from a photo I took of Bandol Beach one evening as the sun went down. I have a house there, on the Côte d'Azur.

It's taking me a while, this painting. I began it in July, but after a week or so decided to abandon it, dispirited at not getting it quite right. I'd been trying to make it look 'painterly', where the brush strokes can be seen. But I overworked it, it was too perfect.

So I need to start again.

Squeezing some oils onto my palette, I push on my reading glasses, pick up my brush, mix cadmium yellow with a touch of zinc white, and compare it with the colour I've already used.

Perfect.

I take over an hour to paint the sand in short sharp brushes, so each stroke stands proud, so that your fingertips want to run across it, feel it, become it.

I stand back and admire.

Much better.

The next bit is trickier, and I need to let the paint dry anyway.

So I clean my brush and palette and leave them to dry in the kitchen. Removing my apron, I switch on the radio and make camomile tea.

Again, the news is depressing. Chirac's new prime minister, Juppé, has been coming up with the most dreadful austerity plans. After we were good enough to elect him in May as well. A foolish decision. He's now decided to announce a pay freeze for the public sector, so of course they're all talking about going on strike. The news is full of it. At Christmastime, too.

Drinking my tea, I sit and read my book for a while. It's a ghost story, set during the Revolution. Quite good, actually.

My skin is crawling quite nicely when the phone rings. It's Pascal. I smile, relaxing suddenly at the sound of his voice. Warm, brown, deep.

'Hi there,' I say.

'Just checking up, seeing if you're missing me at all.'

'Of course I'm missing you. I'm missing our walks and our delicious coffees.'

'Not me, then?' he asks, laughing.

'Of course you. How's work going?'

'Not good. We had a delivery due in this morning – stone, tiles, the big stuff. But there was a breakdown on the Rouen road, so it arrived two hours late. And we can't work much longer today - it'll be dark soon.'

'Oh, that's not good, Pascal.' I feel so sorry for him.

'It'll be fine, don't worry. We'll soon catch up. They're a good bunch of workers. But I'll ring you later on, shall I, once we're finished and I've had something to eat?'

'I'm looking forward to it. Think of me when you sit down to your meal.'

'I always think of you. *Je t'aime, ma chérie.*'

'I love you, too.'

4

Rose

Monday December 4th

Gosh, what a pivotal day the ninth of November was. After my voddie and coke-fuelled night out with Olivia, I slept right through. But when the alarm clock woke me, I was hot and sweaty, burning with fever, and there was blood on my pillow. I rang Mum.

'Sounds like you've got a burst eardrum, love. You must have caught a chill. Get yourself to the doctor's.'

'Bloody hell. Just what I need, time off work.'

'You've got yourself run down, my love.'

'I know. Sorry, Mum. I've not been sleeping properly.'

'No, don't apologise to me. But I can tell you this - Jason wants his head looking at. A lovely girl like you.'

'I'm hardly a girl, am I, Mum? I'm nearly thirty, remember?'

'I can hardly forget, can I? Thirty years. That bloody midwife, all the pain I went through.'

I'd heard it all before. Numerous times. It should have been enough to put me off.

'I was okay, wasn't I, though? You were okay? In the end?' I murmured.

'Of course I was. And I wouldn't be without you, my love. But it should be you that's having the babies now, don't you think?'

*

Doctor Woolaton was very sympathetic.

'An upper respiratory tract infection leading to a rupture of the tympanic membrane. Quite common this time of year. If the antibiotics don't work, come straight back. And you'd better stay off work.'

I left the surgery, prescription in hand. The cold wind hit me with the force of a dumper truck, and I pulled up my hood protectively. But as I turned the corner, hood up, head down, I nearly bumped into James Morgan. My ex-fiancé. Well, okay, my ex-ex-fiancé. Standing there large as life, chatting to this bloke, oblivious to the fact he was taking up half the pavement. Typical, I thought. Self-centred as always, not a thought for anyone else. Trust *him* to be there. Trust him to be there, just when I was at my lowest, just when I couldn't face telling him how bad my life had become.

I sighed heavily.

But he was just as I remembered him. Suave. Debonair. Tall, dark and handsome. Actually no, I realised, he's *wasn't* as I remembered him. He was more like a small grey rat. A small grey rat trying to raid the pantry without being seen.

Because that's exactly what he is. A rat. A traitor. An apology of a man. Able to cheat and lie, then cheat and lie again. With no qualms whatsoever.

But I had no way of avoiding him. I needed to get to Boots. So, head up, smile painted on, I walked straight past, nodding as I did so. He seemed taken aback, to say the least, and I could feel him following me with his eyes. The way he does with all women.

It's quite funny, I realise now, how fate has a way of dealing with these things. Because that lack of concentration made me bump into someone else. Another bloke. Not tall, dark and handsome. But tall, kind of strawberry-blonde, smiling and kind. My elbow caught his arm as I passed, forcing him to an abrupt halt.

I stopped, mortified.

'I'm so sorry. Are you okay?' I asked.

He smiled, rubbing his forearm. 'I'm fine, don't worry. And you?'

If his soft smile hadn't caught my attention, the French accent definitely did. I was *not* expecting a French accent, not in the middle of Sheffield on a blustery Friday morning. But it changed the bitter wind into a warm breeze, and a huge grin formed upon my lips.

'I'm okay. Thanks.'

His eyes were the colour of the grey trench coat he wore, and I found myself staring.

'You're sure?' He was still smiling.

'I'm sure. And I'm sorry. Again.'

'Don't apologise, it's not a problem. So, bye then. And be careful next time.'

With another smile, he dashed off, nearly crashing into another bloke in his hurry. So it wasn't just me, then.

I watched as he sped away. His brown tweed cap made him look more Yorkshire than French. Maybe he's trying to blend in, I thought. Maybe he thinks we all live on farms and shout *'ow's tha doing, chuck?*

But as he turned the corner, I saw Shipface had gone. That's my nickname for James, my ex-ex. It was Olivia who started it all, saying he looked like a steamship coming in. All hot air and trumpy noises, destroying everything in his wake.

So the name stuck. It did in fact morph into something else, but I won't even go into that.

We were engaged to be married, in the throes of arranging the big day, the church, the reception, the dress. Or so I thought. I believed all the stories about working late, about visiting clients 'down South' or 'up North'. For whole weekends. Just how gullible can you get? It was Olivia who saw him with Sienna Wickham in Bertucci's.

Sienna. What kind of name is that, I wonder. Sounds like a bathroom suite. Anyway, when Olivia said she'd seen them together, I completely believed her. Because the bastard had lied before.

Why do I always choose the wrong one, the cheat, the coward? Okay, so I'm twenty-nine, getting on a bit. But I'm still attractive, or so I'm told. A little on the plump side maybe, but still *damned* attractive.

So why the hell have I wasted so much time on the wrong blokes?

I rushed to Boots, grabbed my antibiotics like they were the panacea to all my problems, and walked home.

My apartment, the top floor of an old house just off Psalter Lane, is near the city centre, convenient, perfect in fact, for everything. Open-plan, fresh, clean and spacious, there are two bedrooms, a bathroom, lounge and dining kitchen. Jason and I owned the place for nearly two years, and I loved it. So now I'm buying him out. It will completely skint me, I know. But I have savings put aside, and there's always my cake decorating business. Once it gets going.

And now, of course, there's the rent from the spare room.

So, returning home from Boots, I dumped my bag onto the table and looked around. The place was a mess, so I began tidying up, piling dirty plates into the sink and moving my fancy cake tins (the ones that will make my fortune) to the top shelf of the cupboard.

*

A week later, however, I was back at the doctor's. My other ear had started up and I was nearly deaf.

'I'm referring you,' she said. 'We need the experts.'

She checked availability, but there was nothing until mid-January. I mean, how I was supposed to manage, I had no idea. So okay, she was giving me another week off work, but how would I manage after that?

'Could I go privately, do you think? I'll pay for the consultation. If that's okay?'

'Right, yes. Let me see now ...'

There was an appointment for the fourth of December. Today, in fact.

Marvellous what money can do. Not that I can afford it.

So I called into work to let them know I'd be off another week. Ruby, my manager, dressed in very sleek black, was at the coffee machine as I walked in.

'Hi, Rose, are you okay? How's the ear?'

Ruby's the one who interviewed me for my job, saw me through all the studying I had to do to become a qualified legal assistant, and then saw me through my breakup with Shipface. She'll no doubt see me through my breakup with Jason.

'Sorry, Ruby, I'm nearly deaf.' I covered my ears with both hands to demonstrate.

'What? Both ears now?'

I nodded pathetically.

'You poor thing. Come on, into my office.'

Ushering me in with two cappuccinos, she sat delicately back into the folds of her leather armchair. 'So. What's going on?'

I could just about hear her, but I still didn't understand what she was saying.

'Sorry? How do you mean?'

She folded her hands together. 'Forgive me. I don't mean to upset you. But there are rumours you and Jason have split up.'

My head threatened to explode, my heart raced as if I'd run ten miles, and I burst into tears.

'Sorry, Ruby. I'm sorry I didn't tell you …'

She was at my side within seconds, her arms around me.

'Don't be. I understand. I've been there too, remember?'

'I know.'

Ruby had been divorced for years, had had a few dates, but that was it; she'd never wanted to marry again.

I never want to be like that. I want to be loved. Completely. Utterly.

'Listen,' she said, passing me a tissue. 'Take some time off, get your ears better, sort out your life, then come back feeling fresh and ready to go.'

'Thank you, Ruby.'

'How does three weeks grab you? On full pay. I'll sort it with the boss.' She smiled. 'You can't work anyway, not in that state.'

*

So today I'm at the hospital. It's quaint, stone-clad, must have been built over a century ago. It's been built onto since then, obviously, and is now chic and modern inside, with glass walls and pale floors. And it has a certain charm that makes my nervousness float to the ceiling. I walk up to the receptionist, give her my letter, and she guides me patiently towards the ENT waiting room.

Calm. Uncluttered. Free tea and coffee on tap.

Not that I have time. I hear my name called as soon as I walk up to the machine.

'Rose Somerton?'

Pulling my bag onto my shoulder, I turn.

'Oh.'

The consultant smiles at me, his grey eyes crinkling attractively.

'It's you,' I say.

'It is.' He offers to shake my hand, and I take it.

It's a small hand, a surgeon's hand. Warm and firm. An honest hand. My heart races stupidly, and I smile back.

'Hi.'

'It's nice to meet you again, Miss Somerton. Come on, into my rooms.'

5

Claude

Tuesday December 5th

Is there such a thing as Fate, I wonder? That woman, that Rose Somerton, I've met her twice now. And there's something about her.

It's not confidence, elegance, that decisive charm Parisian women have. No. It's the opposite. A vulnerability, a childlike quality that makes me want to hold her, kiss her, run my hands through her hair as if it could take us to the ends of the universe, as if nothing else would ever matter. At the same time, there's a kind of mystique about her, an aura of something I can't quite reach. As if she's been here before, knows the ropes, knows how to catch me, reel me in.

But, damn it, she's engaged. I saw the ring. Two sparkling diamonds.

Merde! What the hell am I doing? What on earth can I be thinking?

*

It's such a scary business, meeting someone for the first time. It seems to matter so much at our age, as if more is expected. As if the female body clock is nagging away, insisting on procreation before it's too late.

Suzanne *is* fun, though, with a big bright smile on her face. Ethan at work fancies her like crazy, but he's married with a kid. To be honest, I can't decide whether or not I'm the marrying kind. I think I like women too much to become tied to just the one. Or maybe I just haven't met the right girl.

Et bien ...

I need to shower, erase the scent of chlorhexidine from my body, slap on some Chanel, and prepare myself.

*

Suzanne's at the bar as I walk in. Her dark hair is long and shiny, so straight it makes its way down her back like a sheet of cling-film. I make my way over and perch onto the stool beside her. She turns, smiles, and pecks my cheek.

The bartender leans across. 'Can I get you anything?'

I order another red wine for Suzanne, and a pint of *Landlord*.

She smiles. 'I knew you'd be on time.'

'It was touch and go, to be honest. Didn't leave work until six.'

'Me too. But we're here now.'

She snuggles up and we study the menu together. We both order Thai chicken curry with lemon rice. I'm not sure I like the fact she wants the same as me. It's kind of flattering, but in an obsequious way it doesn't become her. Or maybe I'm just being over-critical.

We carry our drinks over to sit beside the huge Christmas tree in the corner. It's not quite the place I'd have planned for a first date, but Suzanne seems happy, it was her idea, so I make the best of it. We chat about her job, her friends, her family.

She jogs, rides horses when she has time, and her parents still take her to Italy once a year for the family holiday. She speaks Italian like a native.

'*Amo il colore dei tuoi occhi,*' she says, showing off.

I speak a little Italian, but my pronunciation is awful, so I reply in English. 'Thank you. I love the colour of your eyes, too.'

'Where do you tend to go on holiday?' she asks, sipping her wine.

'Paris, mainly. My family do the same family holiday thing every year, but I avoid it if I can. It's okay when you're a kid, but bloody boring as an adult.'

'Paris,' she says, dreamily. 'I've never been.'

'You should go.'

'So come on, tell me about yourself.'

Me, I think? I'm the boring one in the corner who did really well in school, then agreed to move away from his friends and family just so it wouldn't be the same old same old.

Our food arrives before I can reply, so I order a bottle of Cabernet Sauvignon and we eat.

'Okay. Here goes,' I say, taking a deep breath. 'When I'm not working I like to keep fit. I go jogging most days, although the gym beckons more often when it's cold. I like to drive through quaint Peak District villages, go to the cinema, and frequent local pubs with my friends. When I have time. Other than that, I'm fairly lazy. Although I am thinking about studying for a doctorate – immunology of some kind. So not very interesting, really.'

She smiles, beautifully. 'Don't put yourself down, Claude. Surely your work takes up most of your time?'

'It can be full on sometimes,' I agree.

'But you enjoy it?'

'Very much. There was a kid in today, two years old. Loss of balance, lack of concentration, speech delayed. They'd got him down as possible Asperger's, but in the end we diagnosed otitis media. No big deal. We'll be fitting grommets, so he'll soon be on his way. A cute kid, too.'

'Ah, bless. They must be so relieved, his parents.'

'Parent. Dad's gone off with someone else.'

'Oh. Poor thing.'

'Well, kids survive. They're tougher than they look.'

'I take it you had a good childhood, then?'

'What makes you say that?' I ask.

'You're confident, easy-going, no trauma going on in the background.'

I'm embarrassed, avoid her eyes by picking up some chicken and eating.

'Well. Thanks, Suzanne.'

'No, I mean it. You're – uncluttered.'

'I didn't realise I was that easy to read.'

She laughs. 'I'm not saying I can read your mind, I'm just saying you're uncomplicated.'

Such pretty blue eyes.

'Would you prefer it if I wasn't? So you could sit there and psychoanalyse me? Is that it?'

'I did study psychology, as a matter of fact.'

'Did you now? Doesn't surprise me. So, come on, analyse.'

'Well, I'd say you're fairly extrovert, but still enjoy your own space.'

'You don't have to study psychology to see that.'

'That you came to study in England to get away from your family because you find them too perfect. You want imperfection, so you can help heal the blemishes. It gives you focus. That's why you're a doctor. You don't do it for the money, but because you want to cure the imperfections.'

Merde! She has me down to a tee.

Her smile grows slowly. 'Well?'

'Okay. You win.'

*

By the end of the evening, there is nothing about Suzanne I don't know. She studied ballet as a child and there was talk of the Royal Ballet, but she didn't make the grade, lost interest and stopped attending. At fifteen she was taken to visit her uncle in hospital and was so taken with the nurses, their uniforms, their smiles and warmth, she decided to become one. She went to Lancaster University, got her degree, and the rest is history. She's had a number of relationships, one long-term, the rest fun while they lasted. She sees life as a bunch of roses that never wilts.

I ask her back to my place for a nightcap, even though I don't expect her to accept; first date and everything. But she does, she does accept. She really doesn't let anything stand in her way.

I live in a quiet part of Fulwood, a small cottage I'm still decorating. The sitting room is cosy after the icy blast outside, so I place a Lionel Ritchie CD into the machine, allow the music to filter through my treasured Bang and Olufsen speakers, and turn up the heating.

'Drink?' I ask, and pour a beer for me, a Drambuie for her. 'Make yourself comfortable – I won't be a minute.'

Upstairs, I visit the loo, gather together Caroline's cosmetics, and throw them into the wash basket. I tidy round the bedroom, plump up the pillows, and saunter nonchalantly back to Suzanne.

Before long we're stretched out on the cream carpet. She's on top of me, kissing me, her hair a curtain from the world outside. As we kiss, her long fingers begin to explore. My head, my neck, my shoulders, my nipples, my stomach. Rubbing in a circular motion. Gently. Seductively.

Sitting up, she pulls off her clothes, one by one. Her jumper, her jeans, her bra and pants. Naked, she sits on top of me. She removes my tee-shirt, then tugs at my Levi buttons.

So now it's my turn. In one movement I wriggle free and roll over so she's beneath me, my legs between hers. She tugs again at my jeans, her hand struggling to get inside.

'Claude,' she moans.

My condoms are in the bedroom, so I pick her up and carry her upstairs. Out of breath now, I lay her gently down to remove my jeans and pants.

I push inside, slowly and rhythmically at first, then faster and faster. Until she, and I, can bear it no longer.

We cry out at the same time.

*

At three thirty I wake up, shivering. It's dark, cold, and my mouth is thick with red wine and curry.

I take a pee, then brush my teeth. Returning to bed, I find Suzanne awake. We make love again, but this time slowly, gently, without the urgency of last night.

Four hours later, we wake up and she showers and dresses. Perched on one elbow, I watch lazily as she pulls on her jeans. She's beautiful, her long hair flowing, her navy jumper setting off her bright blue eyes.

'What are you staring at?' she asks, grinning.

'When will I see you again?'

'I'll let you know, shall I? But on one condition.'

'What's that?'

'You make me breakfast next time.'

'It's a deal.'

Throwing my dressing gown around me, I follow her downstairs.

'I'll call you,' I say.

We kiss and she leaves, a flurry of dark hair and mustard coat.

38

6

Noelle

Wednesday December 6th

It's twelve o'clock, midday. The sky is grey, cloudy, the air warm for this time of year. Pascal arrives just as I'm just watering my herbs beneath the cloche on the balcony.

'*Ma chérie,*' he whispers, kissing me gently.

I hug him close. 'I've missed you.'

'It's been really busy, but we've made some great progress. You should come over, take a look.'

I smile. 'I may just do that.'

'We could see the sights?'

'What – in the middle of December?'

'It's a lovely place. There's the cathedral, and we could watch a show. And there's Christmas shopping?'

I snuggle into him, the warmth of him, the calm aura surrounding him.

'It all sounds lovely. When?'

'In a couple of weeks, maybe. Once we're finished, once I have more time.'

I smile. 'Okay. Lovely. It's a deal.'

He follows me into the kitchen. 'Come on, let's have lunch, then we'll go out somewhere, see my most favourite city.'

He makes *spaghetti bolognaise* and salad with my favourite mustard dressing. I busy myself clearing the fridge and wiping the shelves. It doesn't take long, and I could always ask Fleurette to do it. But I don't mind. She has enough to do, knowing how fastidious I am.

I wasn't always like this, you know. It's since Louis died. I've taken on his ways. Where before I didn't give a damn about cleaning, now I'm practically OCD.

But I've always had a cleaner to do it. Fleurette is the tenth. Even my house in Bandol has someone to look after it. Lucie cleans fortnightly in the winter, and weekly in the summer. I used to take the children there for school holidays, and Louis would join us at weekends. But now we just go in term-time, when no-one wants to hire it, and when it's quieter.

Ah, they had an amazing childhood, my two. Skiing in Switzerland, sunning themselves in Bandol, schooling in Paris. My daughter Valerie and her husband Alphonse are both retired now, living in Geneva. He moved there with his job years ago. He was an orthopaedic consultant at the famous *Hôpitaux Universitaires Genève*.

Yes, Valerie married very well, but I do question whether she was happy, living in Geneva and leaving her children behind with me. I don't think she was, not really. I wouldn't have been. Although she never complains, never grumbles. No.

You see, Claude and Camille, their children, attended the Lycée Fénelon, one of the best schools in Paris. They were at a crucial stage of their education when Alphonse was moved to Geneva, so they couldn't just up sticks and move with him. Besides, it would have unsettled them, moving away from their friends. But Alphonse had no choice in the decision; he was head-hunted, couldn't turn it down. So Valerie had to decide. She could either live apart from Alphonse or move the children to another school. But Claude was sixteen and Camille fifteen, they weren't exactly children. So she decided to leave them here with me in Paris. And she's had a good life.

But still, children need their mothers, and I hope I did a good job of replacing her. She did see them during school holidays, of course, and for the occasional weekend, but I'm sure it must have broken her heart.

Matthieu, my son, spent his entire childhood wanting to become a policeman or a detective like Sherlock Holmes. But no, what did he become? The manager of a hotel. It is a five star in Marseille, so he's done well, but where he gets it from I'll never know. Our families have always been medical, no management material at all.

I'm still very proud of him, though. Although he's never married, which is the greatest disappointment to me. He's forty-nine now, so I doubt it will ever happen. Such a lovely man, too. But he lives for his job, so there's never been room for romance. Apart from that Ingrid he fell for. They had an *affaire* that lasted years, but she was married, so it was never going to end happily. Poor Matthieu. She broke his heart.

Pascal's *spaghetti bolognaise* is delicious, as always, and we're just tidying away the dishes when the phone rings. It's Claude.

'Hi, Mamie, how are you?'

I smile at the phone, envisaging him in his little cottage on the outskirts of Sheffield, with the snow falling outside. It's how I always envisage him these days. I've only been over the once, you see, just after he moved in, and it snowed incessantly. We had to practically dig ourselves out to come home.

'Claude! How wonderful to hear from you. I'm very well, thank you, yes. And you?'

'I'm good, working hard as usual. But I thought I'd ring about my birthday.'

'Oh, yes?'

I pray he says yes.

'I'd love to come over, Mamie – thank you.'

'Oh Claude, I'm so pleased. That's wonderful news. We've not seen you in such a long time, not since you came over with Caroline.'

'I know. But they're bad memories, Mamie. Very bad memories.'

'I understand, *mon chéri*. She was a lovely girl, though. Such a shame you couldn't make it work.'

'I know, Mamie. But we were too much alike.'

'There has to be that spark, yes?'

'You've hit the nail on the head, as they say over here. That's exactly what was missing.'

'But never mind now, it's all in the past. I just hope coming to Paris brings good memories for you, *mon chéri*. You just never know what's around the corner, do you?'

'I'm looking forward to seeing you all.'

'When will you arrive, do you know?'

'I've booked two weeks from the eighteenth, so I'll fly over on the Sunday. Is that okay?'

I smile. 'It'll be so good to see you, Claude.'

'Can't wait, Mamie. *A bientôt.*'

'*A bientôt, mon chéri.*'

Happily, I replace the receiver. But as I turn, I see Pascal leaning against the door, hiding something behind his back.

'What?' I say.

'I have a beautiful gift for my beautiful girl.'

My heart races stupidly. I have visions of lilies. Or lace. Or silk.

But he pulls out a small box, gift-wrapped in shiny purple paper. Excitedly I peel away the edges, to find a plain white box.

'Perfume!'

But it's not just any perfume. It is my favourite. *Chanel 22.* So favourite I've just used the very last drop of my very last bottle. The scent is based on white flowers, vetiver and vanilla, with a little incense. There's jasmine, orange blossom, lilac and sweet rose, too. I've been in love with it ever since Louis bought it for me on honeymoon in Venice, delayed, of course, because of the war. And it's no coincidence it was released in the year of my birth, 1922. Apparently, Coco Chanel was designing white dresses at the time and asked for a fragrance to go with them. Therefore, the white flowers.

All I know is this. It smells just divine.

I kiss Pascal, and he takes me into his arms.

'You shouldn't have,' I whisper. 'Thank you. But how did you know?'

'What – that you had only a few drops left?'

'Yes.'

'*Je t'aime*, Noelle ...'

*

Our walk takes us through the *Bois de Boulogne*. The clouds have cleared now, and a bitterly cold wind has developed. My face aches with the force of it.

'Here, hold my hand,' says Pascal, taking hold of me.

He walks fast, pulling me as he does so. Laughing, I fail to keep up, my legs not as strong as they used to be.

'Pascal - stop - please!' I beg.

He turns, takes my face into his hands, and kisses me.

But I pull away. 'We're in the middle of the park!'

A young couple sitting on a park bench turn to us and laugh. She's beautiful, with an ivory skin and dark eyes, her head wrapped in a red silk scarf. He is African, strong and masculine. Embarrassed, I smile at them. Pascal merely waves.

'Come on, Noelle. Time for croissants dipped in coffee. And I will not take no for an answer!'

*

How wonderful. A birthday party to organise. I must invite Camille, of course, and Florian, her husband. Little Isabelle can come too, although she'll be ready for bed by the time they arrive. I might invite Helena too, and that friend of Pascal's – now, what is his name? Oh, I'm useless at names these days - the joys of becoming old. But Helena is on her own now, and so is - Hugo - that's his name! So you never know, I could play Cupid. Now wouldn't *that* be fun?

So I ring round and make plans and become very excited. Everyone can come, it seems, even Hugo. I've only met him the once, when Pascal and I were in Monoprix, shopping. But he's so charming I'm sure he and Helena will get on like a house on fire.

So what to cook? Hot food, I think.

I pull out my favourite recipe book, decorated in thumbprints of grease, and flour, and egg, and possibly cocoa powder. But I'm so excited I can't concentrate, so Pascal makes me sit down with pen and paper.

Basquaise de poulet.
Spaghetti bolognaise de Pascal.
Ratatouille avec pommes boulangère.
Marquise au chocolat et clafoutis.
Pastis et olives pour l'aperitif.
Wine, cognac, non-alcoholic drinks, juice.
Oh, I'm just *so* excited.

7

Rose

Thursday December 7th

I do not believe it. He's only my ENT consultant! How weird is that?

But he's so lovely, his eyes were so gentle, and he was so careful. And the way he speaks, his accent - wow! He gave me drops to put into my ears and I'm to go back on the thirteenth. I can't wait. But this time I *won't* be wearing my ring.

*

It's not like having a lodger. Olivia doesn't get home until seven most nights, and even then she's so exhausted we never really have time to talk. So she eats, works, then works some more. She hasn't brought too much stuff with her, either. A good job because, let's face it, my flat is not that big.

The night she moved in was really blustery, freezing cold, positively evil. Every time we opened the front door to bring stuff in, the bedroom windows rattled and the doors all slammed themselves shut. Goodness knows what the neighbours thought.

I carried a particularly heavy cardboard box through, dumping it onto the table.

'What on earth's in here, Olivia? It weighs a ton.'

'Only some of my favourite mugs and a juicer. I've left the rest with Mum. But I'm surprised you've got so much stuff around yourself. Didn't Jason take half?'

I shook my head. 'He didn't want anything, said he wanted to travel light.'

'Lucky for you, then.'

'Not really,' I replied, sadly. 'Do you want a coffee or anything?'

'Tea, please. I've going off coffee, can't seem to get used to it again. It tastes different from the stuff in New York.'

I laughed. 'Ooh, not good enough for you now, are we, now you've been to New York?'

'You know it's not that, Rose. I just need to get used to everything again, that's all.'

'Don't worry so much - I'm only joking.'

'What's Jason up to these days, anyway?'

'The last I heard, he was on a plane bound for Sydney.'

'Crumbs, he doesn't waste much time, does he?'

I swallowed hard. 'That's what he said he wanted to do, so he's doing it. Good luck to him, I say.'

'What about his job, then?'

'He's taking a year's sabbatical. It's quite good of them, really.'

'Engineering design can be quite specialist, I suppose.'

Tears threatened. Again. So I changed the subject.

'Don't you need to move the car, Olivia?'

'Oh, yes. Thanks. I forgot.'

By the time she'd returned, I felt more in control, had made tea, and was busy moving boxes of clothes into the spare room.

'Olivia, you're gonna have to shove some of this under the bed. There's not much room, I'm afraid.'

'It'll be fine, don't worry.' Unpacking her clothes quickly, she squeezed them into the tiny wardrobe. 'I forgot to ask you – how are your ears? When do you go back to hospital?'

'They're much better. I have to go back next Wednesday, just so he can check everything's okay. And I can't wait.'

My stomach did a weird up down movement at the thought of it.

'Sorry?' she asked.

'The doctor, Claude Jolivet. He was lovely, so kind and gentle.'

She stared at me as if I was insane. 'Rose, you don't have a thing for the consultant?'

Shrugging, I lied through my teeth. 'He was nice, that's all, and I wasn't expecting it. I expected it to hurt when he cleared out my ears. But it didn't. And he was chatty and thoughtful and …'

She crossed her arms knowingly. 'Miss Rose Somerton has a thing for the consultant.'

'No, I haven't. Honestly. He was just really kind, that's all.'

'Methinks the lady doth protest too much.'

'No, he was *really* kind, Olivia.'

'You can't go falling for every bloke who treats you a tiny bit nicer than Jason or Shipface ever did.'

I really didn't want to listen to this. 'We have met before, you know.'

'Have you?'

'We bumped into each other a few weeks ago. In town. I thought he was just cute at the time. But now I know he's cute *and* a really nice person.'

'They're all really nice people until you get to know them. Believe me.'

I sighed deeply. 'And he's got the sexiest French accent.'

She throws up her hands. 'Okay. You win.'

*

There are definite benefits to being off work with an ear infection. I've baked two tiers of chocolate sponge cake, one smaller in circumference than the other, placed the smaller one on top of the other, and covered the whole lot in pale blue fondant icing. On the top tier, I've placed a baby sitting on a turquoise blanket, all made with modelling paste. I made the head first thing this morning, then the body, arms and legs, and clothed the completed body in a turquoise jumpsuit and bobble-hat. A brown teddy bear peeks out from behind the baby.

It looks amazing, even if I do say so myself.

Finally, I've added the tiny cars I made yesterday, in pink, pale blue and lemon, placing them so they run around the base of the top tier. A row of letters spelling JOSEPH, in the same colours and with spots on, stands upright against the base of the lower tier.

Then I take photos with the old Canon Mum's given me. From every angle, just to be sure.

By the time Olivia arrives home from work, there's a sign on the door. *Enter at your own risk! Cake in progress!* She walks into a complete mess of a kitchen.

'Wow, Rose. That looks just amazing.'

I bristle with pride. 'Thank you.'

'No, it really looks good. Very professional. How did you learn all that stuff?'

'It was something I saw on the telly once. Just thought I'd give it a go, and ended up on a course. That's where I met Jason, if you remember.'

'Oh, yes, the night school thing. So he's into all this as well, is he?'

'Yeah. But he gave it up after the first two months.'

'He does like cooking though, if I recall.'

'Yep. Knowing him, he's probably got a chef's job in Sydney.'

*

Tonight, I'm spending the evening designing a poster. The idea is for Mum to take it into school and produce more on the photocopier. I intend using my best photo of Hayley's christening cake, adding a name and my phone number to the bottom. It's taken a while but I've finally chosen a name. 'Rose's Celebration Cakes.' Sounds pretty good, I think.

But when I open my desk drawer, I realise I've run out of A4 paper. And my thick fluorescent pens are running dry.

'I'll have to get some more,' I moan. 'And I can't be seen in town, or someone might sprag on me.'

Olivia looks up from her work. 'If you can wait, I have some at home. Really nice pens, as well. I bought them in New York, but I've hardly used them. You're welcome to them.'

50

'I couldn't ask you to do that,' I protest.

'I insist. You can come with me and I'll introduce you to my parents. Not a problem.'

'Okay, but only if you're sure. How about Sunday, then? I was going to call on Mum anyway, take some buns round for school.'

'Sunday's fine, yes.'

I click the kettle on. 'You're a good friend – you know that?'

'Well, how about this for being a good friend? I'm visiting my Aunt Helena in December. How do you fancy coming with me?'

I groan inwardly. The last thing I feel like doing is visiting some old aunt I've never even heard of.

'Oh, I don't know, Olivia. I'm not in the right mood to be visiting people at the moment.'

'No, it's fine, don't worry. I'll go to Paris on my own, then.'

I'm so excited I knock over the milk jug.

'Paris? You never said you had an aunt who lived in Paris!'

'You never asked.'

I rush to fetch a cloth from the sink. 'Yes, of course I'll come to Paris. I've always wanted to go to Paris. Oh my God, Olivia, of course I'll come! Thank you!'

'It won't cost much. Aunt Helena is happy to feed us, so we'll just have the train to pay for.'

'And the shopping.'

'Of course the shopping.'

I mop up the milk. 'Actually, I've got to be careful. I've got a huge mortgage now, I need to be responsible.' I rinse the cloth under the tap. 'I get too excited, that's my trouble. No wonder I put men off. I need to start being cool, calm and sophisticated. Like you.'

She looks up. 'What? You are kidding.'

'No. I'm serious.'

'Well, thanks, Rose. What you don't see, though, is all the bits going on underneath. I'm like the proverbial iceberg. You only get to see a tiny part of me, the bit I want everyone to see.'

'No, that's fine, I can understand that. What I'm saying is, maybe that's how *I* should be. Anyway, I obviously need to change something about myself.'

'You're lovely as you are. Otherwise, I wouldn't have you as my friend.'

'Thanks, Olivia.'

She shrugs her shoulders. 'It's okay.'

'Aunt Helena? Really? Does everyone in your family have a Shakespearean name?'

She laughs. 'Hah, you caught us out! No. Pure coincidence. At least, I think it is. I'll have to ask Mum about that one.'

'Paris!' I exclaim, visions of walking along the Seine, climbing a sunlit Eiffel Tower and window-shopping on the Champs Elysees floating before me. But then a sudden realisation.

'You do know they've had bombs in Paris, don't you?'

'Who doesn't? We'll be fine, don't worry. That's what these terrorists want, to terrorise us. Anyway, you can't not go. You did say you had a thing for the French accent.'

8

Claude

Friday December 8th

It's good to get away from the hustle bustle occasionally, so today I'm working from home, just for a change. Once I've finished my paperwork, I'll have time to check out the various conferences I can attend. There are new discoveries all the time in the medical world, and I need to keep abreast.

I peer through the bedroom curtains. A deep frost covers the ground, but I really could do with some air before I start work. So I don joggers, long-sleeved tee-shirt and trainers, and I leave the house. The cold makes the hair on my skin stand proud, so I increase my pace. But oh, it is refreshing. The sun is out, the sky is blue, and all's well with the world.

The cottages along here are rather expensive for semi-detached, considering they're only two bedroomed with *bijou* gardens. I've lived here a few years now, so should maybe think about moving. And it would help brush away the memories of Caroline. The way she'd rush through the door, hair flying, coat half-off, always in a rush. Or the way she'd turn to me as she cooked, screwing up her eyes against the light from the window.

Or the way she'd kiss me, and hug me close. As if she would never let me go.

But I mustn't forget the arguments. The bitter, clawing rows that seemed to go on and on and on. I can't even remember what they were about. All I remember is the hurt, the pain they caused. Deep down inside. Pain that pulled at us, destroyed our love, killed our life together.

So I jog. I jog away the memories, the heartache.

The Redmires Reservoirs are great for jogging. Today, even though the cold air has numbed my face, I feel alive, the blood pounding through my limbs as I listen to Simply Red on my Walkman.

Will we sleep and sometimes love until the moon shines?

Maybe the next time I'll be yours and maybe you'll be mine.

It's then I realise something. That mysterious woman, that Rose Somerton, I've been thinking about her. Again. She pops into my head for no reason. As if there's some connection. But there isn't. She's just a patient. An intriguing patient, admittedly, but still a patient. Untouchable, engaged to be married. And definitely mysterious. Unlike Suzanne, who's open and carefree and *very* loving.

What is it about me? Why can't I fall for Suzanne, someone who understands the rigours of the job, who makes love like there's no tomorrow, and who is drop-dead gorgeous?

But I haven't. She's great fun, don't get me wrong, but she's too easy, too transparent, too *amenable*.

She winked at me over the operating table yesterday. I just smiled and concentrated on my patient, a boy with chronic tonsillitis. Poor kid.

I just don't want Suzanne to get serious or anything, and at her age there is that danger. Damn it!

I'm sure someone will love her. Just not me. The confirmed bachelor. I'll never find the right woman.

So it begs the million dollar question. Do I only want Rose because she's so unattainable?

*

My jog takes an hour. It's turning out to be the coldest December since the winter of 1981, according to the news, and I underestimate the effect it has on my body. By the time I arrive home, my breath is coming in short gasps and my legs and arms are on fire.

I climb beneath a hot shower, thaw out, and dress.

Breakfast is cereal and toast over a pile of paperwork. Patients' reports to their GPs, medical insurers needing clinic letters, or just general correspondence. I dictate so Sarah, my secretary, can type it up on Monday.

Lunch is home-made French onion soup out of the freezer, and a chunk of sourdough. I sprinkle shaved parmesan over the top, but it's still not a patch on the fresh soup Mamie has time to make. Her soup melts the taste-buds and warms the heart.

The afternoon is slightly more fun, as I'm able to spend time researching conferences. I've brought leaflets and handouts home from work, and I sit with a coffee on the lounge floor, working through them. It's important I keep up to speed with the latest developments, the newest findings. So after much deliberation, I choose a conference in London. It's to do with research into Granulomatous Tonsillitis, a rare manifestation of Crohn's Disease. I don't know much about Crohn's at all, so it should prove interesting. I call Simon Westing at the Hallamshire, and he books me in for May next year.

I suddenly realise I've not yet booked my flights to Paris. I ring the travel agents in town and book return tickets from Manchester to Charles de Gaulle. Now I've made up my mind and it's all settled, I'm really looking forward to seeing everyone again.

Dinner is sautéed salmon and frozen chips with a green salad. Quick and easy, but nutritious.

I sit and watch the news while I eat. The headline today is the stabbing of a head teacher outside his school in London. It does make you wonder what's happening to the world. I also learn it's the fifteenth anniversary of John Lennon's death. I remember it vividly – it was all over the papers at the time. Shocking, absolutely shocking.

Despite what's just been on the news, I settle down to watch *Murder She Wrote*, a beer in one hand and a bag of nuts in the other.

But then the phone rings. It's Suzanne.

'I'm at the pub. I thought you'd be here,' she says.

'No, not tonight - it's been a long day. Sorry.' I can hear music in the background, Michael Jackson and *Man in the Mirror*. I suddenly feel bad for not ringing her. 'Look – we could meet up tomorrow if you like? A spot of lunch?'

She sighs loudly. 'I'm working.'

'Dinner then? You could come round here and I'll cook us something.'

'Okay, yes, I'd like that. Thanks.'

'What time's best?'

'I leave work at four, so - six o'clock?'

'Great. I'm looking forward to it already.'

'Me too.'

Grabbing another beer, I sit back down to Jessica Fletcher. But I've turned up the heating against the cold outside, and it's making me sleepy. I find myself relaxing for the first time in weeks. I really don't know what's been on my mind. Probably Caroline. Again.

We met in my last year of university at a party thrown by Colin, a chap on Ned's course. The terraced house I'd been sharing with Ned and Jerry for years was just about big enough for the three of us. Smallish kitchen, three good-sized bedrooms, lounge with a huge TV in the corner. Not that I had much time to watch it. Learning in a second language is hard work, but learning medicine in a second language – no contest. My Latin helped no end, but I was still up past midnight most nights.

Caroline would only come round at weekends so I wasn't disturbed, so I could study, burn the midnight oil and meet every one of my deadlines. She was amazing, actually. She'd cook for us, clean the mildew off the walls, wash and iron my clothes. We didn't even possess an iron; she had to bring her own. She still lived at home, working at the local museum as assistant to the Director of Learning. Actually, teaching kids is right up her street.

57

But she saved me hours so I could study. Then she'd climb into bed beside me and fulfil every one of my carnal desires. What a girl.

But we completely messed up and there wasn't a thing I could do about it. We just weren't right for each other.

Nor is Suzanne, I say out loud.

Nor is Suzanne ...

So why am I stringing her along? Am I that desperate? Should I do that to another human being, because I will definitely hurt her? Taking another swig of beer, I try to think straight.

No, why shouldn't I take her out? It might just lead to something. We certainly have more in common than Rose Somerton and I do. I don't even know her, for goodness' sake. There's just something about her, but I have no idea what. Chemistry? Pheromones? Is she a younger version of Maman, because they say you always marry your mother? I really don't know. I mean, does anyone truly know anyone else? You think you do, but then little things begin to creep in, idiosyncrasies that you either put up with or shout about. We are none of us perfect. I want perfection, that's the trouble. And I'll never find it. Caroline used to say I must have some Libran in me somewhere, wanting the perfect balance. Load of rubbish. I'm Sagittarian through and through. Even though I'm a scientist and don't believe in such things.

Once Jessica Fletcher has caught the killer, a nice chap but with ulterior motives, obviously, I write my shopping list. There's hardly any food in the house and I must wine and dine Suzanne tomorrow. I decide on *Flamiche*, a leek tart, to begin with, then *cassoulet*, made with chicken instead of pork, followed by *mousse au chocolat*. I'll buy a nice bottle of Bordeaux and some excellent coffee. There. All done.

9

Noelle

Saturday December 9th

Saturday. My favourite day of the week. Not that I don't enjoy taking care of Isabelle. I do, I love it. But three days a week with a fourteen-month-old, and I've had enough.

Camille works Mondays, Thursdays and Fridays, you see. A dermatologist, she specialises in acne at the local hospital. To be honest, the Mondays I can cope with, but after taking care of Isabelle for two consecutive days I'm exhausted.

So today I'm going to rest. Pascal has returned to Amiens, Isabelle is back with her parents, and I have the apartment all to myself.

I take my morning coffee into the studio, fasten on my apron, pull the cloth from my easel and stand back. Yes, I decide. The sand does look good. Maybe needs a little light in places, but that can wait. Today I must concentrate on the sea. Pushing on my reading glasses, I pick up my brush and place a little zinc white onto my palette. Then I choose the cerulean blue I bought last week and squeeze some out to sit beside the white. But that would be too deep a blue, so I squeeze out the tiniest bit of viridian, a green-blue colour, and mix them. I love the calming, squishy feel of the oils as they come together beneath my brush, and the scent is just wonderful.

Taking a quick sip of coffee, I dip into the paint and stand poised.

My brush strokes are uneven, curled, but as they reach the horizon they need to be smooth, even. So I concentrate, checking against the photograph I have on the table beside me. My painting doesn't have to be an exact copy of the photo, but it should look recognisable, so that when I show it to Camille or Florian, they'll recognise it instantly.

I hope.

Using a thinner brush, I paint pure viridian over the mixture of blues. My brushstrokes stand out beautifully. I stand back, remove my reading glasses, and admire. The waves at the edge of the beach need highlighting, but it needs to dry first. And the sand definitely needs more. It's nearly there, so I add the tiniest bit of titanium yellow – soft trails of light. There. Better.

Satisfied, I remove my apron, return to the kitchen and clean my brushes and palette. The radio is still on, so I listen to the news. It's all about the strikes. It's always about the strikes. Thank goodness Claude's flying over here for Christmas. The railways are striking, the schools have closed, there's no postal service, and there are demonstrations everywhere. Everyone's backing the poor railway workers, who've been threatened with changes to their retirement age *and* their working conditions. Thousands are going to lose their jobs, and all so Juppé can cut the budget deficit. Misguided, I call it. He'll end up spending all the money he's saving on unemployment benefit, and then where will we be? And there'll be more people living on the streets, more poverty. Best to keep people in work, I say. At least there's no more news about bombs. It makes my blood shiver.

*

So much for my restful day. The phone rang just after lunch. Valerie and Alphonse have driven from Strasbourg and are staying for a few nights. But such wonderful news! I've rung Camille and she's coming over with the baby.

They're pulling up just as I reach the entrance to the car park. It's dark now, and chilly, but I pull my coat around me and run out. Valerie is out of the Porsche and into my arms before Alphonse has finished parking.

'Maman!'

We've not seen each other since July. Far too long, especially at my age. Who's to say when will be the last time?

'Valerie.' I hug her close.

'Is there any food around here?' asks Alphonse, climbing out of the car.

Laughing, I kiss him on both cheeks. 'Lovely to see you, too.'

Two hours later, there is *lasagne végétarienne* and *salade verte* on the table. Camille, Florian and Isabelle are here and we are being very rowdy.

'Such a pity you're away for Christmas,' I say.

Valerie makes a moue of disappointment. 'I know. Claude rang me in August to see if he could come to us for Christmas, but we'd already booked for Vienna, couldn't do much about it.'

'We'll have to arrange a big family party next year,' says Camille. 'Could we use the house in Bandol, Mamie? Please?' She smiles sweetly. As if she has to.

'Of course, *ma chérie,* of course you can. I'm looking forward to it already.'

'When's the best time for everyone?' asks Valerie. 'We have a cruise in July, so it will have to be June or August.'

'That's okay for us,' replies Camille. 'Isn't it, Florian?'

He nods. 'No problem. If we arrange something now, I can book it in at work.'

I smile. Florian is a kind man. Camille is so lucky.

'We'll arrange something for definite,' I say.

Isabelle is sitting on Camille's knee. I watch as her tiny fingers reach out for Camille's wine glass.

'Camille!' I warn.

She grabs it just in time. 'Sorry, Mamie. I think she's a bit tired. '

'Would you like me to put her in the cot, just until you go home?'

'Thank you, yes. Sorry - I've had a really busy day with her.'

I take Isabelle and place her inside the cot. 'There you go, *ma chérie.*'

I sit with her, singing an old lullaby my mother used to sing to me.

There was a little ship
That never on the sea had sailed ...

Ten minutes later, she's fast asleep. I stoop to kiss her tiny nose before sneaking out of the room. But as I do so, she wakes up and whimpers. So I return, pick her up, and sit with her on the rocking chair. I rock back and forth, back and forth, until finally she falls asleep on my shoulder.

I place her carefully inside the cot once more. 'There, *ma petite*. Sleep well.'

Tired now, I cross the hall to my own room. I can hear them all laughing in the kitchen – some inappropriate comment by Florian, no doubt. Yawning, I lay down upon my bed. As my body eases slowly into the duvet, I close my eyes.

And I breathe in, deeply.

I have this ability to meditate at the touch of a button. A few deep breaths, in through the nose and out through the mouth, and I'm in a world of my own, a world of silence, peace, tranquillity.

I learned the technique as a girl. When the uniforms of Nazi soldiers walking up the street, and the constant fear of being somewhere I shouldn't, took over my life. I needed to switch off, push it away, all of it.

I was eighteen years old when they arrived. June fourteenth, 1940. A day no-one will ever forget.

But I try to. I try to forget the anguish on Maman's face whenever Papa was home late, or whenever he was called to a patient in the middle of the night and had to break curfew, climbing over garden walls to avoid the streets.

I try to throw the memories to the back of my mind, to push away the pictures that creep before my eyes in the dark of the night. Even now.

Estelle, her mother and father, her little brother Georges. All gone. Because they were Jews. Just because they were Jews. I cried for weeks, for months, forever. She was my best friend, and there was nothing I could do.

Rien!

So - I meditate. I visualise.

The door. I walk through a door. There's a room on the other side - quite small - and in the corner, always, there's a man. He wears a white cloak and he turns as I enter. Always. Removing his white cloak, so delicate you can see through it, so shiny it reflects all the light around us, he places it onto my shoulders, and turns away.

The cloak fills me with light. Warm, welcoming light that fills my senses. I feel love, peace. Forgiveness. It's my security, my protection against the world. If I need it, it is there. Always.

So I breathe. In and out, in and out. Until I feel calm, rested, safe.

After a while, maybe twenty minutes, I pull myself off the bed and return to the kitchen, to my family.

Alphonse is discussing the conference he's been attending in Strasbourg.

'The study of the human genome *is* fascinating, but it's so bloody expensive. They're saying in a few years we'll be able to use a hand-held device to check our DNA. Which I suppose is quite possible, although how much that will cost is another matter.'

Calm now, and rested, I pour myself a glass of Chablis and sit down.

'Do we have to discuss medicine all the time?' I say. 'What about the rest of the world – the starving, the people fleeing war-torn countries, the illiterate?'

Camille pats my hand patiently. 'Mamie, it's nearly Christmas. I know these things concern you, but sometimes we have to put them to one side and enjoy life a little, don't you think? And anyway, medicine helps everyone in its own way.'

'I know. I just feel guilty sometimes, that we have all this, and they have nothing.'

'It will always be the way, I'm afraid,' says Florian. 'While ever people insist upon killing each other, we will all suffer.'

'That doesn't explain the illiterate,' says Valerie, her greying hair recently styled into a pixie cut, showing off her still very beautiful cheekbones.

'It does,' says Camille. 'If governments spend millions on defence, they can't spend so much on education. Some kids need extra tuition to help out, but it's an expensive proposition. Very often it's only rich parents who can afford it.'

I feel a surge of anger. 'Well, I for one aim to do something about it. No more of these silly little market stalls, I'm going to organise something big, something that will continue long after I'm gone.'

'What's that then, Noelle?' asks Alphonse.

It comes to me. Suddenly. A ridiculous idea, but a stunning one.

'A race! That's what I'll do. I'll set up a race.'

10

Rose

Sunday December 10th

Joseph was christened at Loxley Methodist this morning. The reception's taking place in the church hall next door, so I park up my old Fiesta, pull the cake box carefully from the passenger footwell, and dash inside. The traffic has been horrendous for some reason, so I'm late, and angry with myself. Not a good way to start a business.

The hall buzzes with children as they chase one another round in ever-decreasing circles. Avoiding them carefully, I look for the buffet table. The bouncy castle hinders my view at first, but then I spy it against the far wall, its plates of food covered in cling-film and dotted with paper flags.

I carry the christening cake through, holding the box aloft as I work my way through the children and their parents, sitting with babies on their knee, or keeping a watchful eye. A group of people, whom I assume are Joseph's grandparents, stand at one end of the table, already munching on sandwiches and moaning about the cold. Everyone sips tea from delicate bone china cups.

I see Hayley and her husband Jamie enter from the door nearest the table. Leaving Jamie to chat to his parents, she bounds up to me, carrying Joseph in her arms, her pink dress marked where she's been dabbing it with water.

'Rose – here – I've left a space.'

She supervises as I place the cake in prime position.

'There, all done,' I say, standing back. 'I hope you like it.'

Her face says it all. 'It looks amazing, Rose. You are so clever. Thank you so much.'

I smile. 'It's my pleasure. And sorry I'm late. The traffic's awful.'

'There's an incident on the main road, I think. But well - you know Sheffield drivers. A drop of rain and they go into snail mode.'

Taking my arm suddenly, she pulls me into the corner, lowering her voice. 'Listen, Rose, I've just heard about you and Jason. And I'm really sorry.'

I sigh. This is one of the reasons I've never told people, the reason I've kept it quiet for so long. So I don't end up with the usual platitudes, the embarrassed apologies, as if it's all their fault, meant to make me feel better, but in fact brings it all to the surface and makes it worse.

So I smile and nod, wishing myself hidden beneath the overburdened table.

'It's fine, Hayley. I'm fine. Thank you.'

She nods back. 'But the cake looks amazing, Rose. You really are clever.'

'Thanks, Hayley. I'm hoping to set up a proper business, so if you'd pass the word around?'

'Of course. No problem. I'll tell everyone.'

'So how *was* the christening?'

'Lovely. Mum cried a bit. I cried a lot. Silly, I know.'

'No, it's not silly at all. He's a beautiful child.'

I stand with Hayley, Jamie and the grandparents, and coo over Joseph, who really is a beautiful child, for a few minutes more, then make my excuses.

Dashing outside with the empty box, I brush away sorry tears from my cheeks. Why are other people's lives so perfect? Why couldn't it be me in there, with the perfect husband, the adorable baby, and the doting grandparents?

*

Mum lives on the outskirts of Sheffield, in a misty hamlet overlooking the woods of Strawberry Lee Lane. She takes great pleasure in telling everyone that Harry Brearley, the inventor of 'rustless' steel, moved to a house nearby in 1895 and lived there for many years. Mum's only claim to fame, I think.

After lunch, Olivia and I drive over to see her. Her semi stands well back from the main road, but its rough stone walls are still stained from years of pollution. I knock on the old blue door.

Slim, youthful, content (Dad buggered off years ago), Mum opens it with a flourish. 'You don't have to knock, you know. Just come on in, both of you.'

'Sorry, Mum. I didn't want to just walk in, not with Olivia here.'

'So this is Olivia, is it?' She puts out a hand and smiles. 'I'm very pleased to meet you at last. I've heard a lot about you.'

Olivia shakes it. 'Same here, Mrs Somerton. And I just love your house.'

'Thank you. But call me Carol, please. Yes, I like it. It needs a bit of doing up, admittedly, but it's home. Now then, cup of tea, anyone?' She waves us through to the kitchen, hand-painted in smoky green and smelling of warm toast. 'And I've got some buns in the tin. I ended up with some of my Year Fours here on Friday. Lisa, who runs the After School Club, went home poorly with this awful flu bug that's going round. Katy, the Year Five teacher, offered to stay behind with the kids, so I brought the Year Fours back here. We made chocolate buns and biscuits.'

'Of course you did,' I say, smiling and filling the kettle. 'I'm amazed there's any left.'

'They were absolutely starving, bless 'em. So I made fried eggs and spaghetti hoops, and we had buns and biscuits for pudding.' She pats one of the kitchen chairs. 'Come on, Olivia, sit down, make yourself at home.'

She sits. 'Yum. Fried eggs and spaghetti hoops. I could eat that now.'

'You hungry, love?' Mum asks.

Olivia shakes her head. 'We've only just had lunch, to be honest. It's just kiddie food – it takes me back.'

'Where do you come from, then?'

'Fulwood. Not far.'

I turn from making the tea. 'She lives on a farm, Mum. Cows and sheep and stuff.'

'Yes, I know what a farm is,' she retorts. 'But how lovely. So what made you go all the way to New York? I bet your mum missed you, didn't she?'

'She did, I know. But it was a job opportunity I couldn't afford to miss.'

'Well, I suppose we all have to leave home some time.' She turns to me. 'So how are the ears, love? Your hearing any better?'

'Much better, thanks. I'm back at work tomorrow, then I see the doctor again on Wednesday.'

'The good-looking one?' asks Olivia, smiling.

I nod. 'Yes, the good-looking one.'

'Oh no, love,' urges Mum. 'Give yourself chance to get over the other one first.'

'Come on, Mum. Really! He's not going to be interested in someone like me, is he?'

'Why not? You're a lovely girl. Just because Jason can't see it, just because he wants his head looking at.'

I stir at the tea in the pot. 'He's a complete prat, we know that. But I'm not likely to get asked out by a doctor, now am I?'

'You underestimate yourself, my love.'

'Yes, Mum. If you say so.'

'She's right, Rose,' says Olivia. 'But give yourself a bit of time before you go jumping in.'

Mum puts a plateful of chocolate buns onto the table. 'So, what can I do for you two on this lovely Sunday afternoon?'

'Just thought we'd pop in for a chat,' I say. 'And so I can introduce Olivia. I've also brought butterfly buns for your Year Fours. As a treat.'

*

It's four o'clock, already dark, and very misty. We drive down the narrow lane to Olivia's home, an old farmhouse set back from the main road into Fulwood.

It's warm as we walk through the door, neat and tidy, despite the two sheepdogs that come bounding up to greet us.

'Maisie, no! Don't jump up!' exclaims Olivia, catching hold of her paws and pulling her down. 'Sorry, Rose, she gets a bit overexcited.'

I put out my hand to Maisie, who lifts her paw for me to shake. 'Hello. Nice to meet you, Maisie.'

The other dog follows suit, but more slowly and methodically.

'And this is Donna. Donna's a bit more subdued, aren't you, Donna?' Olivia strokes her fur gently.

'So who is this?' booms a voice from the doorway. An elderly man, tall and grey with receding hair, walks in from the kitchen and hugs his daughter. 'What a lovely surprise. You didn't say you were coming?'

'I've just come to pick up some stuff, Dad. We won't stay long.' She turns towards me. 'This is Rose. Rose, this is my dad Malcolm.'

I smile. 'Pleased to meet you, Malcolm.'

'And you too. You too.' Abruptly, he turns to go upstairs. 'Now then, where's your mother? She was upstairs messing with her broomstick last time I looked. I'll just go fetch her.' And he leaves.

Olivia grins. 'Sorry about that. Family joke. He's a bit shy, my dad, but you'll get used to him.'

'No – he's lovely.'

'We'll just stay for a cuppa, shall we?' she asks, ushering me into the kitchen.

'Of course. No rush, is there?'

Her mum, dressed all in black with rosy cheeks and dark curly hair, dashes into the kitchen, hugging us both. 'What a lovely surprise, Olivia. And this is Rose, is it? How wonderful to meet you at last. Come on, sit yourselves down. Your father's just hiding upstairs, so I'll make us something to eat, shall I?'

11

Claude

Monday December 11th

Well, what a weekend that was. Saturday was an early morning jog, a shower, then a drive to Sainsbury's in the new Mondeo. After that, the whole afternoon was spent messing in the kitchen, music on loud.

Cassoulet always needs plenty of time. Chopping the meat and vegetables takes ages, and then it needs three hours to cook. So I got that into the oven before making the *flamiche*. I made two, actually, one to use as a starter, one to freeze for another time. Well, it's nice sometimes to get home from work and not have to cook.

And of course, the *mousse au chocolat* was dead easy. I had it in the fridge by four o'clock.

Suzanne arrived promptly at six, which should have pleased me. But for some weird, ridiculous reason it didn't. She's too keen, and it's worrying.

'I've brought wine,' she said, waving a bottle of Sauvignon blanc through the air. 'And I'll try not to gulp it down, even though I've had the day from hell.'

'Thanks, Suzanne. We'll have a glass now, shall we, then you can tell me all about it? I don't need to ask if it's chilled.'

Following me through to the kitchen, she laughed. 'Too right. Bloody freezing out there! Mm – that smells really good. What you making?'

Pulling two wine glasses from the cupboard, I set them onto the table. '*Cassoulet*. Chicken stew to you. *Flamiche* to begin with, and *mousse au chocolat* to finish.'

'What's flamiche? Sounds kind of Dutch.' She sat down.

I passed her a glass of wine. 'It's French leek tart. Delicious. So delicious I've made two, so I can freeze one.'

'Mm, my mouth's watering already.'

I began laying the table; knives, forks, small dessertspoons, napkins, candles. 'So – why the day from hell?'

She pulled a face. 'Gordon bloody McCauley. As usual.'

I grinned. 'Don't tell me. He interrupted you halfway through the sponge count.'

'How did you know? Oh, my God!'

'Notorious for it.'

'He thinks he's God's gift, that what it is.'

'No, he just doesn't think about anyone else, doesn't think about what *they* need to get done.'

75

She drank half her wine in one gulp, causing me to stare at her, amused.

'Sorry, Claude. Needed that.'

'It's okay,' I said. 'You can drink the bottle as far as I'm concerned.'

'Look, let's not talk about work. I just want to forget about it. How was your day?'

I sat down beside her, listing everything on the digits of one hand. 'Jog, supermarket, cook, tidy up, you arrive.'

Grinning, she pecked me on the cheek. 'So – dinner, then a film?'

'Okay. I don't have many videos, but you can check my collection.'

'I've actually just bought one.' She pulled it from her bag. 'Apollo 13. Tom Hanks. It's supposed to be really good. You fancy it?'

*

Dinner went down a treat, and the film was excellent, had us both on the edge of our seats. So when it came to bedtime, we just seemed to tumble in together. It seemed like the most natural thing in the world.

Only it isn't. The chemistry isn't there. We like the same things, we work in the same environment, we see things the same way, but it just isn't right.

Maybe I'm still a little in love with Caroline.

Despite all this, our lovemaking was exceptional. She really is a very generous girl.

*

Sunday morning began with a long breakfast. Corn Flakes, toast and marmalade, coffee, orange juice, the news. They're still talking about John Major's speech at the opening of the Bosnian Peace Conference. Let's hope it lasts, this peace, fragile as it is. We discussed it, Suzanne and I, and she agreed with every opinion I had. Again. After breakfast, we snuggled up on the couch in our pyjamas (well, *my* pyjamas – she didn't bring any) and watched The Eleventh Hour with Cheryl Baker – a series about people's hobbies. Yesterday it was decorating. One chap they interviewed insisted on decorating his house non-stop, so as soon as he'd finished he would start again.

'I wouldn't call that a hobby, more an obsession,' murmured Suzanne.

'I hate decorating,' I said. 'Give me a wall to paint and I'll tell you where to put your brush.'

'And I thought you were such a gentleman.'

'Did you now?'

I pushed her onto the floor playfully, and thereafter began an episode I shall not divulge.

*

This morning I find myself walking into the hospital humming, despite the ice-cold wind outside. I smile at Sarah as she hands me a coffee. Real coffee. In a real cup. She has a cafetière on the go all day. I don't know what I'd do without her.

'Morning, Sarah. Did you have a good weekend?'

She glances at me curiously. 'Okay, thanks. You certainly did, by the looks of it.'

'I certainly did, Sarah. But that's good, *n'est-ce pas*?'

'I suppose it is. Here you go, then,' and she passes me my patient files.

'Thanks. Give me five minutes, then you can bring the first one through.'

I enter my domain, my consulting room. It's small, cosy, with a desk and three chairs, one of them beneath the window in case a parent or spouse needs to attend. And there's some equipment in the corner, kept out of the way so as not to make the room too clinical. Nothing worse than a nervous patient.

Today my first patient is a child, seven years old. He's lost his voice and I have a feeling it may be down to selective muteness, a psychiatric condition. But first I've had to rule out any physiological cause. I've already questioned his mother, who insists he can speak at home but refuses to speak in school. It's the school who suggested he see a doctor, so I'm seeing him at the Claremont to save him waiting around at the Children's Hospital and missing lessons.

I've already checked the results of his laryngoscopy and CT scan. They're clear, nothing showing on his larynx. His throat and chest are also fine, so physically there is definitely nothing wrong with him. His mother's relieved, although I sense a certain disappointment. There's a stigma attached to mental health problems, especially in children. Which I fully understand.

I place his test results back into the folder.

'It may just be that he's shy in school. They can be quite scary places sometimes, can't they?' He smiles up at me. 'I'm going to refer you onto a colleague of mine, Emma Houseman. She's a child psychologist, the best in her field.'

'But what shall I tell the teacher, Mr Jolivet?' asks his mother, tearfully.

'If you like, you can tell them you're still coming to see me. It shouldn't be a problem. And hopefully it won't be too long before we've got to the bottom of it. It may just involve a change of school.'

I sometimes wish I had a magic wand, a way of healing people quickly and easily. It would save the NHS a fortune.

But I reassure her, and arrange an appointment with Emma. She's a fine doctor, and I'm sure she'll get excellent results. I'm just glad the school spotted the problem early on.

I grab another coffee before admitting my next patient. This chap has become deaf in his early forties, caused by working as a nightclub bouncer. He's currently suing his employers, past and present, so is able to afford private treatment. There's not a lot we can do, unfortunately, other than a hearing aid, but he needs a full medical report for the solicitors.

My third patient of the morning is a woman in her fifties. She has otitis media that refuses to heal, despite two lots of antibiotics. I perform an aural toilet that clears her ears nicely, and give her drops to insert. She's very chatty, despite her discomfort, and I learn she teaches in a secondary school. Just the right environment for picking up ear infections, she says. I have to agree.

Lunch is a sandwich in the café with the other staff members. The food here leaves a lot to be desired, but I'm starving and can never be bothered to bring something in. But they really should employ a French chef, I think, as I join the queue, someone who can turn a mere baguette and a slab of Gruyère into a feast.

Mamie, my grandmother, says that producing French cuisine is a skill rather than an occupation. And that one is born with that skill. She says anyone who comes to Paris will always remember their first taste of its food, will never forget it. She does loves Paris,

Mamie. Even though, as teenagers, she'd gather us up on a Saturday morning and take us on an outing to Versailles, she only really ever talked about Paris. She seems drawn to Versailles, for some reason. I think she just loves its history, although Paris has its own, of course. But she rarely speaks of that – particularly of the second world war. Growing up through the war is something she rarely talks about. I do know a friend of hers was taken to Auschwitz and died there. But that's only because Maman told me about it.

Poor Mamie. Such terrible memories.

12

Noelle

Tuesday December 12th
This race is growing legs. If you'll pardon the expression. But it's going to be such fun - a fancy dress race. And, more importantly, it's going to aid the children from poor families who need extra tuition at school. There will be one board of people to collect the money, and another to decide who will receive it.

Pascal has offered to help, of course, but he's so busy at the moment. So I've placed a notice in the local paper asking for volunteers, and I've arranged an appointment with Madame Maxime Carel of the *Conseil de Paris* to discuss access and dates. It's all so exciting, and I do feel I'm doing something positive with my life. It will be my legacy to the children of Paris.

But today I'm going to do some more painting, then I'll go into the city and do my Christmas shopping. I don't spend a lot these days. Well, it's not like it used to be, when the children were at home, and after that the grandchildren.

I remember one Christmas, years and years ago, watching as Valerie admired a bracelet in a jeweller's window. It wasn't too expensive, with three-coloured gold links, but it was so pretty and she loved it. So I bought it as a surprise, wrapped the box in bright red paper, and hung it on the tree. I teased her with it for weeks, and I don't think she ever guessed what it contained until she opened it on Christmas morning. She was sixteen at the time, and her face – I will never forget the look on her face.

I have such wonderful memories.

I walk into the studio and pull the cloth from my easel. The sand looks alive, but the sea needs its waves. I squeeze a blob of titanium white onto my palette and add the tiniest touch of ultramarine blue and alizarin crimson. I mix it gently so it's not completely one colour, then take my time, daubing it onto the sea, just where it meets the beach. It creates lovely violet hues, but needs more. So I add more titanium white, concentrate on my brushstrokes, my tongue sticking out in concentration, and produce waves that crash and tumble and roll.

Checking my watch suddenly, I realise I've been so engrossed that two hours have already passed since I entered the studio. Where has the time gone? It's lunchtime already and I need to catch the *métro*.

Standing back, I remove my glasses and squint at my work. Beautiful. Just beautiful. Sighing with joy, I leave it to dry and wash my brushes in the kitchen, stardust swirling through the air.

Today is a lovely day. The sun is out, and my painting is everything I could wish it to be. I'm so happy that if I died right now, right here, I wouldn't mind a bit. I have done everything I came here to do. I am content.

*

The *métro* is exceptionally busy, but I actually enjoy the hustle and bustle of people as I walk along the rue de Passy, stopping to look into shop windows and comparing prices. I pause beside a small toyshop, its window full of soft animals and sparkling decorations. I still can't decide what to buy for Isabelle, though. I need inspiration. But then I smell garlic, and coffee, and spot an awning with *Salon de Thé* embellished across the front. I peer at the menu and realise I am now very hungry.

After a lunch of spicy *bouillabaisse*, followed by a very black *double espresso*, I wrap my coat around me and return to the toyshop. It's warm inside, and cosy. The grey man behind the counter looks up and smiles with happy eyes.

'*Bonjour, Madame.*'

'*Bonjour, Monsieur,*' I reply. 'I'm looking for something for my baby granddaughter?'

'A baby? How old?'

'Fourteen months.'

'What a lovely age. And she must be very beautiful.'

I blush at the compliment. 'She is, yes. Thank you, *Monsieur.*'

'So, *Madame*, what about a musical book? One that plays tunes when you press the page?'

He takes me to a corner, replete with shelves of brightly coloured books, the velvet noses of animals and funny faces peering out. Pulling down an A3-sized hardback, he opens it. There are pictures of woodland animals, plants and trees. He presses the picture of a bee, and it buzzes.

'The mouse squeaks, the owl hoots, the fox barks. You get the picture,' he says.

I press the pictures myself, assessing Isabelle's reaction. 'It's lovely. I'll take it, please. Do you mind if I take a look round before I pay?'

'Of course not, *Madame*. Help yourself.'

I wander through the shop, picking up toys and putting them back. I find three shelves of teddy bears. I choose a soft pink one with a pretty face, a red nose, and a flowery dress. Isabelle will love her.

I have a sudden flashback. I see Estelle holding her doll as I open the door to her. I even remember the doll's name. Giselle. Estelle adored Giselle, she went everywhere with her. Except school, of course.

Then I recall her twentieth birthday. Again. How vividly I remember. Going round to their apartment with chocolate and a card. Excited at the prospect of a party, of cake.

I was too late.

She and her family had already been taken. Early that morning, the police rounding them up like cows in a field. It was the sixteenth of July. Giselle was still there, of course, sitting upon a small chair in the hallway. Because, even though we were all grownup, had left school and taken up work, Giselle still had pride of place.

Estelle was an assistant at the *Bureau de Poste* in Paris. Until she had to wear the yellow badge and was sacked. I was a mere volunteer at *l'Hôpital Necker–Enfants Malades*, where Papa worked. The first paediatric hospital in the world.

But I so regret not taking Giselle with me when I went back home. I wasn't thinking straight, obviously. I know she was only a doll, but she was part of Estelle, of her history. I really wish I'd kept her.

We only ever had one doll in those days, you see, not the menagerie of dolls and toy animals that children have now. Valerie had one doll after the other, even though she only ever really loved her first, a baby doll with big blue eyes and a rosebud mouth. Funny, I can remember Giselle's name but I can't remember the name of Valerie's first doll. It was the year Matthieu was born, I do remember that. It's why we bought the doll, so when I came home from hospital she didn't feel left out. Bless her.

Memories. They encircle my mind more and more these days. Some happy, some sad. Some very sad.

It took until the sixteenth of July this year, 1995, for France to apologise for its part in the massacre that took place. Jacques Chirac said it was time the French state admitted responsibility for the complicit role our civil servants and police served in the raid, and the subsequent Holocaust.

Estelle would have turned seventy-three on that very day, the sixteenth of July. If they'd let her live. I watched Chirac's speech on television, then cried and cried. Cold, bitter tears.

So I buy the book and the pretty teddy, and continue on my way.

Next I buy for Valerie and Alphonse, ensuring the items are easy to post; a silk blouse and a pair of ceramic cufflinks. Then I choose beautiful pearl-encrusted earrings for Camille (she's easy, loves jewellery like her mother), and Swiss chocolates and a gorgeous silk scarf in mauves and reds for Fleurette. Again, easy. But the men, as ever, are more difficult. I wander through the shops for ages, while outside the sun goes down and the shop windows light up. But it's Christmassy, nostalgic in a sensitive kind of way, not brash or over-materialistic.

So I continue with my search, despite the sudden drop in temperature. In the end, I buy two shirts for Claude, made from fine poplin cotton, one in pale blue for his birthday and one in pink for Christmas. Very nice. For Matthieu I buy a beautiful fountain pen, gold-nibbed. He'll love it. For Florian I choose a good bottle of Cognac and a box of Havana cigars.

So there's just Pascal. Difficult. He means so much to me these days I'm afraid of spoiling him. Or of disappointing him. I turn into a small outdoor shop that has no Christmas lights, so looks dull in comparison to the others. But here I find the most perfect present. A Barbour waterproof coat in a lovely fawn colour. The coat he wears now is black and makes him look so old. I'm very pleased with my purchase; it will suit his complexion much better.

Satisfied, I pause at the *Café de Victoire* for a *vin chaud* and to rest my feet, before hauling my wonderful purchases home.

13

Rose

Wednesday December 13th

I can't stop thinking about him. Oh my God, I should be thinking about Jason, what he's up to, whether he's enjoying life in Melbourne. Whether he's thinking about me.

But I'm not. I'm *obsessed*. I mean, I hardly know the man.

So I arrive at the hospital with my stomach in a complete flutter. The kindly receptionist again guides me towards the ENT clinic, but this time I have time for a cup of tea. Which calms my stomach nicely, and I try to ease my mind by flipping through the pages of *Vogue*.

But I can't, I can't ease my mind. I need to show him I'm no longer engaged. He must have seen my ring, the two diamonds, chosen so carefully to represent the two of us. So now I've removed it, left it in the bathroom, don't know what I'll do with it. Sell it like the last one, or keep it as a memento? I stroke my bare finger nervously.

'Rose Somerton?' calls a voice.

The way he pronounces Rose makes me tingle, right down to my toes. It's kind of a roll of the r and a slight touch on the e.

I look up, my heart thudding ridiculously, stupidly. But I smile, put down my magazine, and go to him. His grey eyes crease wonderfully as he shakes my hand.

'It's very nice to meet you again.' He indicates for me to follow him into his room. 'We need to just check the ears, to ensure the drops I gave you last time have cleared the infection.'

'They do feel much better,' I say. 'I can hear at last.'

'That's good, but we'll just check. So how are you, Rose?'

I smile. My very best smile. 'I'm very well, thank you.'

'And how is the hearing?'

'It's good, thanks. Completely back to normal.'

'So I'll just check everything is as it should be.'

His nearness makes the insides of my stomach dance and tingle and somersault. But I manage to sit still as he probes my right ear with the auroscope. His fingers are supremely gentle, and my imagination wanders wickedly. But as he moves to check my other ear, I catch a trace of some kind of after-shave. Is that from last night, I wonder? Does he have a girlfriend already? My God, I haven't even thought about that one. He could even be married.

Suddenly chastened, I stay quiet and allow him to check the other ear.

'Okay,' he says. 'A little more suction is needed in the left ear, but the right one is good, with the tympanic membrane intact. That is good. Very good.'

He performs the same aural suction he did before. I sit very still while he proceeds, and wait for him to check the eardrum again.

He smiles. 'It'll be better when the warm weather returns, I think. We have too many of these problems, especially in this country. People need to cover their heads more often, with hats and scarves.'

I smile back, pleased he's becoming chatty.

'The problem is, I've been doing a lot of crying,' I say. 'I think it's blocked everything up.'

He stops smiling. 'I'm sorry to hear that.'

'I split from my fiancé, you see.'

'I'm very sorry to hear that.'

He concentrates on his notes, his pen scribbling away. I need to distract him.

'What made you come to work in England?' I ask.

He looks up. 'I studied here. My parents moved to Geneva with my father's work, but I had to stay in France to continue my education, so I went to live with my grandmother. It was she who suggested coming to England to study medicine. So I came to Sheffield, and I stayed. It's a very nice place, lots of countryside nearby.' He puts down his pen as if to say, *enough about me*. 'Okay. The steroid drops have done their job. The left ear is fine and the tympanic membrane is whole. Wonderful. All done. We can sign you off.'

Snow is falling as I leave the hospital. Soft, gentle petals of white. Crossing the car park gingerly, I climb into my car.

'That went well, then,' I say to the steering wheel. 'Signed off. So that's that. Over before it's begun.'

I drive to work, park up, and rush through the door, heading straight for the coffee machine. Ruby's there.

'Hi, Rose. How are the ears?'

'All clear. He's signed me off.' I wait for her coffee to finish pouring.

'You don't sound too happy about it.'

'I'm fine.'

She pulls her coffee from the machine. 'You know you can always tell Auntie Ruby.'

I cross my arms defensively. 'It's nothing. Really. I'm fine.'

She smiles knowingly. 'Okay. But my door's always open.'

I feel awful now. 'I know. Thanks, Ruby.'

'Look – I was wondering – I know you're a bit starved of cash at the moment. So how would you like to work for Simon Osborne? Emma, his PA, is on maternity leave after Christmas. It would also be valuable experience for you.'

Simon Osborne's a senior partner dealing in high-end aviation claims, and is very well respected. I can hardly believe my ears.

'Really? That would be amazing! Thanks, Ruby!'

'Obviously, you'd have to put some work in, extra training, that sort of thing.'

'No – it's fine. I can do that. Thank you so much.'

'Well, it should help you on your way. Sorry about the pay rise thing, it just wasn't possible. Anyway, from what I hear, you're turning a few heads since you've become young, free and single.' Smiling, she walks off.

Confused, I pour myself a cappuccino and head to my desk.

I'm determined to prove myself. If I can advance beyond legal assistant status I could manage financially, wouldn't have to rent out the spare room, could hold my head high and deal with whatever comes along.

I check the unopened mail on my desk. One is an internal note from Accounts in connection with unpaid estate agents' fees, and do I want them to chase? The next, however, is inside an envelope, from Christopher Walker in Accounts. Asking if I'd like to call at the Wig and Pen for a drink after work tonight.

So that's what Ruby was talking about. I scribble a reply on the bottom, change the destination on the envelope to *Christopher Walker, Accounts*, and push it into my Outbox tray. *No. Thank you. It's very kind of you, but I won't be able to make it, I'm afraid.* (Also, I'm putting everything into my career and won't have time for a private life.) Not that he knows the meaning of the word private, I muse. Half the office must know about his little invitation.

*

Tonight we're having chicken curry. I measure out the spices and throw them into a pan of browned chicken pieces.

Olivia, sitting at the table with a pile of files in front of her, breathes in deeply. 'Mm, that smells delicious.'

'Thanks.' I continue to stir, adding chopped onion, peppers and carrots.

'I've organised the tickets for Paris, by the way.'

'Brilliant.' I pour in coconut milk. 'You did okay it with Ruby, didn't you?'

'Of course. She's pleased you're taking a break.'

'She is nice, isn't she? I don't know why she never got married again. And she's really attractive, you'd think men would be queuing at the door.'

Olivia looks up, surprised. 'You don't know?'

'What?'

'You haven't heard the rumours?'

'Go on.'

'She's living with another woman.'

'That's nothing. So are you.'

'No. She's *living* with another woman. She's gay.'

I turn, shocked. 'Are you sure? I mean, I've never seen that. I mean, she's never made any advances on me or anything.'

'Maybe you're not her type.'

I nod thoughtfully. 'You know what? Now I think about it, she may just have something. I mean, men are just shits, aren't they? At least women wouldn't tread all over you, eat you up, then spit you out for the dustman.'

'Don't become all bitter and twisted, Rose.'

'I'm not. I just think she may have a point.'

'I never thought I'd hear you say that.' She leans forward mischievously. 'I always dreamed you might, though. So when would you like to climb into bed, darling?'

Turning round so quickly causes me to drop the spoon. 'No! That's not funny!'

She's laughing so hard she has to hold her ribs. 'Rose, don't …'

Unable to stop myself, I sit down and laugh until I cry.

A few minutes later we've calmed down, and I return to my cooking. But Olivia still has that look on her face.

'What? I ask.

'So how is *your* love life going? Ruby says you've got a nice little following.'

I smile ruefully. 'It's only Chris in Accounts. He's asked me out.'

'And?'

'No way. It's not like I'm over Jason or anything.'

'Just a minute. I seem to remember you were completely over Jason when you fancied that French bloke at the hospital.'

I blush hotly. 'I know, I know. But he's an exception. What I mean is - I'm not going to date someone like Chris, am I?'

'What?'

'Well, I'll only date someone if they're really special. And Chris isn't.'

'So you're only over Jason if someone special comes along. Is that it?'

'Yes.'

'But if someone mediocre asks you out, then you're still madly in love with Jason?'

I hesitate. Is that what I mean? Am I really that shallow?

'Okay. I suppose it is.'

'Right. So when exactly *is* this doctor taking you out?'

'He's not.' It sinks in suddenly, and I feel lost, forlorn, devoid of hope. 'Oh, what shall I do? I don't fancy Chris. And I really like Claude.'

She stands up to console me. But as she does, she turns deathly white and has to sit down again, her head in her hands.

I rush to her. 'Olivia! Are you okay?'

'I feel sick.'

'You're not coming down with this flu thing, are you?'

'Maybe I just stood up too quickly.'

'Look, why don't you relax in front of the telly and I'll bring it through?'

14

Claude

Thursday December 14th

Yesterday, I drove into work as usual, never thinking about what was to come. In fact, I was too concerned about the roads to even think about the day ahead. Sheet ice lay across the road ahead of me. Like ribbons of silk. There'd been no overnight gritting, and Sheffield had been caught unawares, trapped into a slow crawl that made us all late for work. Stop, start, stop, start, stop. So I drove really carefully, pulling into the hospital car park to find it *had* been gritted and the caretaker was still working on it. I waved to him as I passed.

Sarah had my coffee all ready for me. 'Thanks, Sarah. Sorry I'm late. But how come you're here on time?'

'Richard gave me a lift in, and he had to be in Leeds for nine o'clock.'

'But the roads are awful.'

'I am a bit worried about him, to be honest.'

'Why don't you ring him? But I'm sure he'll be fine. The motorways will be clear, it's just the other roads that are bad.'

'Okay, I will. Thanks.'

She handed me the list of patients for the day, and I glanced down nonchalantly.

Rose Somerton. My first appointment.

Sipping my coffee, I checked my notes for the morning, patient after patient. The consulting room was warm after the freezing air outside and I found myself relaxing quite nicely. This hospital is always quiet, though. Calming. So different to the NHS hospitals I work in. If only we could find a way to make them the same without it costing a fortune. Now wouldn't that be something? And how much better for our patients. Who knows, it might actually aid their recovery?

Rose's notes were unremarkable. Twenty-nine. Unmarried (currently). Only medication *Levest*, the contraceptive pill. No medical history of note. Lives near the city centre.

I checked my watch. Nine o'clock. Sarah appeared at the door.

'Your first patient is here.'

'Thanks, Sarah.'

I walked towards the waiting room, suddenly nervous. *What on earth?*

'Rose Somerton?' I called.

And there she was, her auburn hair long and shiny, her blue eyes smiling as though the day had brought the sunshine and melted all the ice.

She put down the magazine she was reading, and stood up.

I shook her hand. 'It's very nice to meet you again.' Her smile was clear and wide as I indicated for her to follow me. 'We need to just check the ears, to ensure the drops I gave you last time have cleared the infection.'

'They do feel much better,' she said. 'I can hear at last.'

'That is good. But we'll just check. So how are you, Rose?'

She smiled. 'I'm very well, thank you.'

'And how is the hearing?'

'It's good, thank you. Completely back to normal.'

'So I'll just check everything is as it should be.'

She sat perfectly still while I probed her right ear with the auroscope. I caught a whiff of perfume, such delicious perfume it made my throat constrict. Swallowing hard, I moved to check her left ear. It wasn't quite clear.

'Okay,' I said. 'A little more suction is needed in the left ear, but the right one is good, with the tympanic membrane intact. That is good. Very good.'

I proceeded to perform the aural suction I'd done before. She sat very still while I carried out the procedure, then I checked the eardrum again.

'It'll be better when the warm weather returns, I think. We have too many of these problems, especially in this country. People need to cover their heads more often, with hats and scarves.'

She sat back, placing her hand over her ear. I noticed suddenly that she wasn't wearing her engagement ring.

She shook her head. 'The problem is, I've been doing a lot of crying. I think it's blocked everything up.'

'I'm sorry to hear that.'

'I split from my fiancé, you see.'

'I'm very sorry to hear that.'

Actually, no, I'm not, I thought. I'm not sorry at all. He doesn't deserve her.

Imbécile!

'What made you come to work in England?' she asked.

I looked up from scribbling my notes. 'I studied here. My parents moved to Geneva with my father's work, but I had to stay in France to continue my education. So I went to live with my grandmother. It was she who suggested I come to England to study medicine. So I came to Sheffield, and I stayed. It's a very nice place, lots of countryside nearby. Right - the steroid drops have done their job. The left ear is fine and the tympanic membrane is whole. Wonderful. All done. We can sign you off.'

*

On my way to the Children's Hospital today, I can think of nothing, no-one but Rose Somerton. I can't believe it. She's *not* engaged. She's *not* tied to someone. She *could* be mine.

But she's a patient. Surely it's unethical. Besides, I'll probably never ever see her again. Why would I? We move in different circles. We'd probably have nothing in common if we did see each other. Damn it! Why does she have to be so attractive, so tantalising? Why can't I just write her off, forget about her?

That's it.

I need never see her again. It's pure coincidence we bumped into each other in town, pure coincidence she was referred to me with an ear infection. I need never see her again. Instead, I need to concentrate on building a relationship with Suzanne, even if it probably isn't going anywhere. But we'll have fun, won't we?

*

The cottage is cold and unfriendly as I push open the door. It's six o'clock and I'm exhausted after seeing what seems like a thousand children, their parents anxiously hovering over them, seeking answers I can't always give. It's the worst time of the year, with coughs and colds fuelling ear, nose and throat problems. I'm ready to put my feet up with a beer and a good film, but I promised Ned and Jerry I'd meet up with them before Christmas, and I fly to Paris on Sunday. So I eat a quick meal of baked potato, parmesan and beans, take a shower, and walk down to the Sportsman in the freezing rain.

Ned's at the bar, his thick red hair damp and curly. 'Claude, old chap! How you doing?'

I nod happily. 'Not bad, but I'll be much better after an evening in the pub. How are you?'

'Fine, I'm fine, thanks. Jerry's just nipped to the little boy's room, won't be long. A pint?'

'*Timothy Taylor's* please, Ned. Thanks.'

Once Jerry returns, we bag seats in front of the roaring fire and somehow get to chatting about girls. Again.

'Did you end up seeing that lovely little nurse, then?' asks Ned.

I smile uncertainly. 'Yes. I'm still seeing her.'

'Well done, that man,' he says, patting the table with both hands.

I hesitate slightly, before revealing my dilemma. 'But I have a slight problem. I think I'm obsessed with someone else.'

'Now come on,' says Ned. 'Two at the same time? Leave some for the rest of us.'

Jerry gulps down some beer. 'You only *think* you're obsessed with someone else? You either *are* obsessed or you're not.'

'Okay. I *am* obsessed. But there's a slight problem.'

'She's married,' says Ned.

I shake my head.

'She's gay,' says Jerry.

It's my turn to gulp down some beer. 'She's a patient. Well, she *was* a patient.'

'Deep waters, Claude. Deep waters,' says Ned.

'Even for a French chap,' says Jerry.

'I know,' I sigh.

'So what are you going to do?' asks Ned. 'Who is she? When did you meet her?'

'Her name's Rose. But what's so weird is I hardly know her. I've only met her three times, but she's taken over my mind so much I can't think straight.'

'He's got it bad,' murmurs Jerry.

'She must be bloody beautiful if you prefer her to Suzanne. She's drop-dead gorgeous,' replies Ned, draining his beer thoughtfully.

'Too right,' says Jerry.

'It's not that. It's more her personality, her demeanour,' I say, in my defence.

'He has *definitely* got it bad,' he says. 'So, have you bedded either of them yet?'

I lie, obviously. 'I've not actually been out with Rose, and I've only seen Suzanne a couple of times.'

He winks. 'Well, that could be the deciding factor, you know.'

Ned stands up, beer glass in hand. 'It's your round, Jerry. Come on, leave the poor chap alone. Can't you see he's in hell?'

Jerry pats my back. 'Sorry, mate. Why don't you just ask her out then, this one you're fantasising over?'

He has a point, I realise. Why don't I? If it is unethical, then surely I can cross that bridge when I come to it. I'll probably find we have nothing in common, anyway.

'You know what, Jerry? You could be right. Thanks.'

15

Noelle

Friday December 15th

I edge my brush along the skyline, just where it touches the sea, dusting it with a pale pink made from rose madder genuine and titanium white. It adds warmth, a touch of romance, depth. Standing back, I screw up my eyes and admire.

'Nearly finished,' I say to myself. 'Just little old me to paint, once it's all dry.' I pick up the glass of Pinot I'm drinking, and smile. 'A long pink dress and sunhat, I think.'

I remember that pink dress like it was yesterday.

The eleventh of April 1943. Sunday. My twenty-first birthday. Maman had made the dress especially. It was a bright sunny day, marred only by the atrocities going on in other parts of the city. Louis was at work in the American Hospital of Paris, Neuilly-sur-Seine, and I was at home with Valerie, still a baby. I was so excited, waiting for Maman and Papa to come over for tea. When they did arrive, full of fun and laughter, they brought gifts for both myself and Valerie. The dress, which I absolutely loved and changed into immediately, was rose pink cotton with a layer of fine white lace covering the bodice. Maman must have spent a fortune on the fabric, but she'd never tell me how she got it. On the black market, probably. She'd also made a small cake, and knitted a white jacket for Valerie. Beautiful.

'We've been saving this for just such an occasion,' said Papa, holding up a bottle of 1929 Bordeaux. 'An excellent year, it cost a fortune at the time. But you're worth every single franc we've ever spent on you.'

That wine was delicious. Ripe, fruity, rich and luxurious.

Papa is dead now, of course. Maman, too. And after Maman's repeated miscarriages, I was their only child, their sunshine girl. Completely spoilt, now I look back.

I do miss them.

But Louis was late coming home, should have been there for three o'clock. I left it an hour before I began to panic.

'Where is he? He knows you're both here, Maman, that we're celebrating.'

'Doctors are always running behind. Don't worry - he'll be fine,' she soothed.

Papa nodded thoughtfully. 'It'll be a last minute case – another injured pilot or someone. I did hear of a plane coming down yesterday, actually. Maybe any casualties have managed to get to the hospital.'

'I do hope so,' I agreed. 'Sorry to panic, it's just every time …'

Taking hold of my hand, Maman smiled gently. 'It's okay. We know.'

*

Louis arrived two hours late, out of breath and with rusty bicycle clips tugging at his trousers. But at least he was home, and we knew better than to ask the reason for the delay.

His present to me was a small diamond brooch in the shape of a bow. It was so beautiful and I loved it so much, I actually burst into tears. I still have it now, tucked away in my bedside drawer.

'But how did you get it?' I asked, wiping my eyes.

His eyes smiled in that delightful way they had. 'For you, *ma chérie*, I can do anything.'

I didn't ask again. There were things happening in that hospital I could never have divulged. Even now, years later, there are still people out there, anti-Semitics, who would refuse my friendship, my charity, if they knew the truth. So I stay quiet.

We'd waited the whole two hours, had refused to touch the food, until Louis came home. There was bread, cheese, and stewed leeks, and of course the cake and wine. So as soon as he walked through the door, we began in earnest. Not an amazing spread, but to us it was heaven. There was very little food in Paris at the time. People were killing street cats to eat. So once Louis was home, we celebrated, we danced, we ate and drank as if there were no war, no Germans and trucks on the streets outside, no starving children begging for crumbs. Only peace and laughter, sunshine and joy.

Just after nine o'clock, we paused, turned, realised the time. Ten minutes past curfew. So even though they had their papers on them and would probably have been alright, Maman and Papa decided to stay the night while Louis and I slept on the sofas. Valerie's cot we pulled into the sitting room so she could sleep beside me.

How I hated the curfew. The Germans would change the time from one week to the next, and I'm sure they did it on purpose to catch people out. If you were caught, even if you had your papers on you, you could be hauled in front of the nearest *Kommandatur* and interrogated. Brutally. A couple of shopkeepers along the road, Monsieur Moreau and Monsieur Delage, they were caught that year, not long after my birthday. Rumour has it Monsieur Moreau was only standing outside his apartment, smoking.

We never saw either of them again.

*

I wash my brushes, turn up the heating, and make dinner. Cracking three eggs into a bowl, I grate Parmesan, add salt and pepper, and beat them together. I chop fresh tarragon leaves and add them to the mixture, too. Then I melt butter in the pan, and cook. The green salad I've already made sits on the table, tossed in mustard dressing and awaiting its fluffy yellow companion. I don't eat much in the evenings these days. I prefer to eat midday, to allow my stomach time to digest. So I eat, finish my wine, and move into the lounge. There's a documentary on about the war, the details Chirac has been so apologetic for, and I want to watch.

I watch the footage, reels of film about the Jews, innocent children sent to the gas chambers, *les pauvres enfants* the Gestapo would willingly have left behind in Paris. But *our* policemen, our own Parisian policemen, insisted on removing them from their homes, to be transferred to those camps, most of them never to return. Why would they do that, I ask myself?

Why?

I have asked that same question for the last fifty-three years. Every July sixteenth. Every time I see a child looking up at me with the same big, brown eyes as Estelle.

I blink away the tears.

I am tired, I decide.

'I am old,' I retort loudly to myself, and I laugh.

At least I *am* old. Estelle has never had the pleasure of growing old, has never had children, never had her own home, her own lover. She was an innocent, a child, even at the age of twenty.

Why, I ask again?

I try to cheer myself by wrapping Christmas presents. I need to post the ones to Valerie, Alphonse and Matthieu, and the last posting date is Monday.

So I curl up on my pale green carpet with the swirly pattern, and I wrap. As I do so, I watch an old film, a comedy about gangsters called *Les Tontons flingueurs*. It's so silly I laugh out loud without even realising. I wrap the silk blouse, a beautiful turquoise colour, wrap the cufflinks in their box, package the whole lot with a Christmas card, and write Valerie's address on the front. Then I wrap Matthieu's pen, enclose another card, and post it to his room at the hotel in Marseilles. How I wish he could come home for Christmas. He's a grown man, I know, but he must be lonely, down there on his own. There again, maybe I'm wrong. Maybe he loves being on his own, or maybe he's living with someone and just hasn't told me yet. I am so looking forward to seeing him in January, though.

*

My evening ritual is just that – a ritual. I remove my makeup with cleanser, I rub toner into my skin with cotton wool, and I massage in my oil. It's cheap vitamin E oil, forty eight francs. Costs nothing. But it's everything. You see, old skin like mine doesn't readily absorb creams, they're too thick. They sit on the surface. Oil is more easily absorbed. So I sit on the edge of the bath and massage it into each and every pore. I add a little jasmine oil, so it smells delicious, and I breathe in and relax. The jasmine oil does that on its own, of course, but the massage helps too.

My oils collection is well-known within the family. I use them for everything. A drop of geranium, a hint of ginger. To relax or stimulate, or just as a tonic. The olfactory senses are amazing, actually. They're related to memory, emotion, our sense of time. They can even influence productivity in the workplace. All you rich manufacturers and bankers out there, take heed.

I always read a little before going to bed. I'm halfway through a novel, romantic yet slightly disturbing, and I'm not at all sure how it's going to end. But I plod on, falling asleep after only a few pages.

I fall asleep dreaming of blue skies with pink edging.

16

Rose

Saturday December 16th

I was so excited when I got back from work yesterday, so looking forward to my trip to Paris. I ended up filling my case practically to the top with clothes and stuff. I did leave my gorgeous royal blue dress until the very last minute, though, so it wouldn't crease too much.

I love that dress. It's the one Jason and I bought in Narberth. I loved every minute of that holiday, will never forget it. But I wish I could. I wish I could forget everything about Jason. The way his hair curls at the back, the way he screws up his eyes against the sun, the way he clicks his fingers in time to the music. Even the bloody brass hook on the back of the bedroom door reminds me of him. He fixed it there so we could hang stuff. But every time I hang something onto it, like my dress …

Sighing, I pulled one of his tee-shirts from the drawer. He'd left it in the wash basket by mistake, so I'd washed and ironed it. But it still smells of him. Sitting onto the bed, I hugged it to me, breathing in his scent.

I cried. Stupid, ridiculous tears. He'll never come back. I'd never take him back.

Wiping at my tears, I returned the tee-shirt to the drawer. It's in the past, I thought, I need to look to the future. Turning back to my case, the one Jason helped me choose, I pushed pants and socks around the inside corners. I can manage, I thought. I'm going to Paris, something I've always wanted to do, and I'm going to have a wonderful time. I've left room for presents and anything nice I happen to find in the shops, and yes, I'm going to treat myself, I deserve it.

Finally, lifting my blue dress from its coat hanger on the brass hook, I folded it carefully, placed it on top of everything else, and lifted the unzipped case onto the floor.

But as I did so, the bedroom door opened, sending the coat hanger flying. I turned, alarmed, as Olivia barged into the room.

'Rose, oh, Rose …'

She was crying as if she would never stop.

'Whatever's happened?'

'I'm pregnant. I'm pregnant!'

'What?'

I was stunned. Olivia wasn't seeing anyone. Was she?

'Sorry, Olivia, I don't understand …'

'No contraception. Well, apart from a bloody leaky condom. Obviously!'

I still didn't understand. 'What?'

'The coffee, the fainting, everything.'

Sitting her onto the bed, I passed her my box of tissues. 'Are you absolutely sure?'

'I went to the surgery last week. I was supposed to be having the coil fitted, but they do a blood test first. And they've just rung me. It's positive.'

'My God, Olivia, I'm as shocked as you are. So who's the father?'

She looks at me as if I've got a light bulb on my head.

'Well, Doug, of course.'

'Doug as in *New York* Doug?'

'Yes.'

She began to cry again, so I pushed her gently out of the room.

'Come on, a cup of tea and some dinner. Then we can talk properly.'

I'd already made cottage pie from a pack of mince I'd found at the back of the freezer. A tin of tomatoes and some Marmite added flavour, and I'd topped it with boiled potato and parsnip, mashed and whisked with milk and butter.

At the table, a cup of tea and a box of tissues in front of her, Olivia was looking slightly more composed.

'It smells delicious. I'm starving. And exhausted. And I've still got my packing to finish.'

'It's fine, I'll help. I still can't believe we're leaving tomorrow morning, I'm so excited.' I scooped cottage pie onto a plate, added peas and carrots, and passed it to her. 'Here you go. I'd offer you a glass of wine, but best not, I suppose.'

She closed her eyes in disbelief. 'Oh Rose, what the hell have I done?'

'Look, the worst case scenario is you have it adopted. The best case scenario is you keep it, bring it up, carry on with your career, and hopefully meet some nice man who will love you *and* the baby.'

Tucking into her food, she nodded mournfully. 'Maybe.'

'How far on are you?'

'Must be nearly two months.'

'So you were seeing each other right until the end, then?'

'We met for one last drink. He took me back to his place. One last time.' She began to sob. 'That's all it took, Rose. For old time's sake, he said.'

'Weren't you on the pill?'

She shook her head. 'I'd had the coil fitted, but it only lasts four years. When it needed replacing, I rang my US health insurers, but they don't pay for contraception. So I left it, thought I could have it done on the NHS once I got home.' She rolled peas onto her fork. 'A bit late now.'

'Are you going to tell him?'

She stared at me over her fork. 'I don't know. What do you think?'

'That's a difficult one. But didn't you know? I mean, didn't you miss your period or anything?'

'That's the thing. I did come on, but it only lasted a day or so, there was hardly anything there. I suppose I should have questioned it when it happened a second time, but I didn't, didn't imagine for one second I might be bloody well pregnant. I mean, I haven't had morning sickness or anything.'

'That's true.'

'To be honest, I thought I was anaemic, what with the fainting and all that. Or that I was overtired from moving back home. It all seemed to fit in, to make sense.'

'You'll get through this, Olivia,' I said gently. 'There are worse things, you know.'

'How do I tell Mum and Dad?' she cried.

*

The 08:37 to London St Pancras is packed, but we've managed to find our seats and are busy chatting, sandwiches and hot drinks on the table between us. I undo the buttons on my coat, ready to remove it once I've warmed up.

'What I want to know is, how come Ruby doesn't talk about her girlfriends? I mean, I've always felt sorry for her because I thought she was on her own, wasn't interested in men.'

Olivia grins. 'She isn't.'

'Very funny. You know what I mean.'

'I don't think she's actually come out yet. At least, not officially, not at work.'

'So how do *you* know about it?'

'I saw them together.'

'Do you see *everyone*? You're the one who spotted Shipface and that tart Sienna.'

She shrugs. 'I get around.'

'You can say that again.'

'Rose …' she warns.

'I know, I know. You were in love with him.'

'And he loved me. Just wrong time, wrong place.'

112

'So have you decided whether or not to tell him?'

She shakes her head. 'I'll make a decision on holiday. Paris, the land of the romantics. Who knows what might happen? I might ring him, tell him he's about to be a father – for the third time – and he might dash over, decide he loves me more than his ex and ask for my hand in marriage.'

'That would be lovely.' Sipping my coffee, I warm to the idea. 'I'll be chief bridesmaid, and the best man will fall in love with me, and we'll get married too, and we'll all live in New York together, happy ever after.'

She sighs. 'Yes.'

I shrug out of my coat. 'I know you hated it, Olivia, but what was New York like, really?'

'That was just my excuse for coming home. I just needed to get away from Doug, really. It was over and I knew it. But New York was actually okay. I loved the shopping, and the theatres, and the restaurants. And the beaches. They were all amazing. But it was noisy, busy, non-stop, twenty-four hour. It took a while to get used to. But Doug loved it. He was born there, had never lived anywhere else.'

I smile. 'What was he like?'

Her brown eyes sparkle. 'He was lovely. Nice-looking. Intelligent. But I don't think he ever got over his wife, not properly. There was always this - this wall – between us. And he never liked talking about her. Just the kids. His life revolved around them. Which is lovely, I suppose.'

'My God. He sounds like the perfect bloke, Olivia. Are you sure you couldn't make a go of it?'

Avoiding my gaze, she looks out of the window. 'I'm sure.'

113

17

Claude

Sunday December 17th

Snow is falling as I pull my suitcase through my cottage gate. Soft gentle flakes that settle like layers of meringue. It's Christmas. And I'm going home.

The taxi driver talks loudly as we drive through the houses of Crosspool, past University roundabout and on, into Sheffield Railway Station. The roads are icy, treacherous, but he drives like Michael Schumacher.

'It's the coldest December since 1981,' he tells me as we pull up.

'I know.' My hand is still gripping the door handle nervously.

He turns to me. 'You going somewhere nice, then?'

'Paris. My home town.'

'Ah – that explains the accent.' Jumping out of the cab, he opens the door for me. 'Will it be warmer there, then?'

I shake my head. 'No. Definitely not.'

'I suppose it *is* Christmas. You visiting family, then?' He opens the boot to retrieve my case.

'That's right, yes.' I hand him a ten pound note. 'Thank you. Keep the change.'

I'm always a little wary of taxi drivers, if I'm honest. Well, they always know when you're going to be away, *n'est-ce pas*? Who's to say they're not in the pay of some gang or other, ready to burgle you as soon as you step onto the plane?

But I smile sincerely, take hold of my case, and catch the 08:14 to Manchester Airport.

*

The flight is uneventful and I read my Colin Bateman novel throughout, landing at Charles de Gaulle just after lunchtime. I take another, more leisurely, taxi and arrive at Mamie's for three o'clock, tired and thirsty.

Mamie lives in the arrondissement of Boulogne-Billancourt. Her apartment, built at the turn of the century, is a lovely old place, with period features, high ceilings and parquet flooring. I find myself relaxing the minute I retrieve the key from Leon the doorman, who greets me like a long-lost son.

Mamie and Pascal are in Amiens for the weekend. They're due back this evening, so she's arranged for Leon to hand me the key. Before he does so, he carries my case into the lift and I tip him thirty francs.

Once upstairs, I turn the key in the lock and push open the door. The place is neat and tidy, just as Mamie likes it. I smile with contentment.

The first thing I do is to spoon ground coffee into the coffee pot, pour water into the lower chamber, fasten it all together, and place it over the gas.

While the coffee heats, I open the door onto the balcony. It overlooks the Seine, one of the reasons Mamie bought the place. I love watching the *bateaux-mouches* as they sail along, their coloured lights reflected in the water around them. So peaceful, so relaxing. I'm glad I'm here.

Suddenly, I hear the water boil and rush back to pour my coffee.

Mamie's apartment has four en-suite bedrooms, a lounge, a spacious and very white kitchen, a small utility room, a cloakroom, and a lovely balcony full of cloches. Not a bad place to live at all.

Carrying my case into the guest room, I throw it onto the bed and unpack quickly. I hate creased clothing and I'm here for a couple of weeks, so there's a lot to unpack. Shirts, trousers and shoes into the wardrobe, everything else into drawers, and my washbag into the en-suite. There's a pure white duvet on the bed, blue velvet curtains up at the window, and a chaise longue in the same shade.

Memories rush through my head. It's been a while …

We ended our relationship in this room, Caroline and I. A huge row, the biggest, the cause of which I can't even remember. Something about her wanting to go home because her brother and his wife were going through a breakup of their own.

I think just the thought of them splitting up brought our own feelings to a head. I'd known we weren't right for a while, had just never acknowledged it. Caroline, too – she admitted it.

She left me, flew home that very evening. When I went back a few days later, she'd moved out, gone back to live with her parents. I rang and rang, but there was never any ringtone, so I guessed their phone was out of order. Then I discovered they'd changed the number. I was distraught, couldn't think straight for months, couldn't eat properly, felt sick, lost weight.

I've not spoken to her since.

I sit on the bed. And I remember. Her hair, soft and thick and warm. Her eyes, huge brown eyes that would gaze at you longingly. That's what I miss the most. And I do miss her. But we couldn't have continued; it would have destroyed us. The fights, the misunderstandings, the bitterness that remained for days afterwards. No. It was bad, very bad.

Tears threaten, and I wipe them away.

We have a saying in France: *Choisissez votre femme par l'oreille bien plus que par les yeux.* It means: Choose a wife rather by your ear than your eye.

Something I should have done years ago.

But there's a saying in England, too: You live and learn.

Hah!

I head for the kitchen. I need more coffee, then a jog. I need to get her out of my system. Again.

I need to make room, so I can think about Suzanne. And maybe Rose.

Merde! Les femmes!

*

It's damp and cold outside, miserable. But as soon as my feet hit the ground, I am alive. I run through the

Parc des Princes, pound along the *Jardin Fleuriste Municipal*, cross the *Avenue de la Porte d'Auteuil*, and continue on, into the *Bois de Boulogne*. I jog for nearly an hour before turning back again.

As I run, my mind is still, intent on listening to U2 on my Walkman. Okay, I pull on my water bottle occasionally and take a quick look at my surroundings. But other than that, I'm in another world. Quiet. Calm. Still.

I need this stillness. I must have this peace.

Leon is there as I reach the apartment building. It's really dark now, and as I push open the door the bright light hits me.

'Monsieur Jolivet, welcome back. Your key ...'

I thank him, enter the lift, wipe the sweat from my brow, and calm my breathing as I ascend.

The shower is hot and welcoming, and I stand there for a long time, eventually drying myself and dressing in jeans and a polo shirt.

In the kitchen I find a *baguette,* some brie, spring onions, tomatoes and lettuce. I spread mustard and mayonnaise onto the bread, pile on the rest, and eat greedily. Satiated, I make more coffee and sit with it in the lounge on Mamie's white leather sofa.

I try to read yesterday's issue of *Le Monde*, the strike action, the speeches. But other thoughts crowd my mind.

Rose. Her eyes. Her soft, calm voice.

Suzanne. Her naked body straddling me on the lounge floor, her hair falling across me ...

I wake up two hours later to the sound of Mamie and Pascal. Their voices are tired, yet excited, and I can't wait to see them. Pulling myself off the sofa, I rush through.

'Mamie! Pascal! How are you? Did you have a good time?'

Mamie smiles her warm, gentle smile, throws her arms around me, and kisses me on both cheeks. 'Claude! It is so lovely to see you. Thank you for coming over, *mon chéri*'.

I breathe in her perfume, soft tones of vanilla spice. It brings me home.

'I wouldn't miss it for the world, Mamie. It's great to see you.'

'So, what have you been up to this afternoon?' asks Pascal, hanging up their coats.

'I went for a jog through the *Bois* - quite a way, really. But then afterwards I'm afraid I just fell asleep.' I grin with embarrassment. 'Sorry I haven't made dinner.'

Smiling, Mamie takes hold of my arm and pulls me into the kitchen. 'We've eaten, it's fine. But come on, let's have coffee, then I can tell you all my news.'

She's so very excited I know there's something special in the air, but assume it's to do with her charity work, the race.

'Okay, Mamie? What are you up to?'

'No!' she exclaims, waggling her finger at me. 'Coffee first. I'm freezing.'

'Okay. You sit down and I'll make it.'

Assembling the ingredients, I place the coffee pot over the gas.

Mamie pulls a tin from the cupboard and opens it. Inside are soft pink *macarons*, sandwiched together with buttercream.

119

'I made these on Friday, especially. Here you go,' she says, offering them to me.

'*Merci, Mamie*. They look delicious.'

Pascal takes one, too. '*Merci, ma chérie.*'

There's a frisson between them that I sensed the minute they walked through the door. I stand beside the cooker, watching the coffee pot. It's only just starting to steam and the aroma is delicious, but I can no longer wait.

'I can't wait for the coffee, Mamie. *Please* tell me.'

She pats the chair beside her. 'Come on then, sit down.'

I sit obediently.

'You're the very first person to know, *mon chéri.*'

Taking hold of my hand, she smiles a huge smile, the smile of a woman in love.

And I know.

18

Noelle

Monday December 18th

Despite my excitement at going away for the weekend, or maybe because of it, I awoke with a sore throat on Saturday, fully expecting to be full of coughs and sneezes upon my return from Amiens yesterday.

But a few doses of paracetamol, and a warm hat and scarf against the weather, made sure I was feeling better again by Sunday morning. Much better. And what a weekend we had, despite the rain, which was a drizzle one moment, a torrential downpour the next. It was good to have Pascal by my side. I'd missed him.

Pascal booked the hotel, *l'Hôtel Miriam*, and it was just what the doctor ordered. Five star, with a huge bath that soaked away the cold weather, and a champagne bar with enough cocktails to make me forget I'd ever felt poorly. We' only had the one, though, a mixture of gin and elderflower. Very tasty, and it set us up nicely for our visit to the *Comédie de Picardie* on Saturday night. It was Shakespeare, *Rêve d'une nuit d'été*. A Midsummer Night's Dream. Typically French, it was extremely over the top, with mischief-maker Puck miming like Marcel Marceau. But I needed a good laugh, and the acting was just perfect. I've seen some of the actors before, on television, and what wonderful performers they were. I laughed until my sides ached.

Before that, though, we'd spent the day trudging from one street to another, dodging the spurts of rain by huddling inside one shop or café after another. It was all *very* romantic.

'Hot chocolate with cream and marshmallows?' asked Pascal as we sat down inside the window of a small bistro on the corner of *rue de Chaudronniers*.

I smiled. 'You're treating me like I'm a schoolgirl.'

'And so he should,' replied the waitress, scribbling in her pad and hustling away.

Pascal took my hand, still inside its damp glove. *'Je t'aime, Noelle.'*

'Je t'aime, aussi,' I replied, suddenly seeing tears in his soft brown eyes. Frightened to death, my heart missed a beat. 'What's wrong, Pascal? What is it?'

He wiped them away. 'There's nothing wrong, *ma chérie*. Absolutely nothing.'

'Then why the tears?'

He shrugged his broad shoulders. 'You make me happy, that's all.'

I was still frightened. Terrified, in fact.

'Is that it? Is that all?'

He nodded. 'That's it.'

I was so relieved I threw back my head and laughed. 'Oh, I thought there was something wrong, seriously wrong. Thank goodness for that.'

The hot chocolate was delicious, and I ate and drank it like the schoolgirl Pascal thinks I am.

*

We had an early lunch in another restaurant, cosy, with a huge log fire and brassware hanging along the walls. Afterwards, we wrapped ourselves up again before walking along the banks of the Somme, towards *St-Leu*, the old quarter. Oh, it was so beautiful, even in the rain. There were canals flowing by, tall narrow houses with shutters, cobbled medieval streets, and art galleries and bookshops that were so enticing we lingered inside for ages.

But as darkness fell, the rain stopped and the atmosphere changed completely. Lights reflected off the water's surface, and restaurants lured you in with glowing orange candles and the aroma of roasting garlic. Suddenly hungry again, we stopped at a lovely place beside the canal that served *moules marinière* in huge ceramic dishes, and mopped up the juices with the most delicious freshly-baked bread.

*

Yesterday we visited Amien's *Cathédrale Notre-Dame*, the largest gothic building in France and nearly twice as big as the one here in Paris. It was awe-inspiring, and we loved it.

But the best piece of architecture we found was the hotel driveway Pascal has been working on for the past few weeks. Not that it's particularly stunning, not in any way. It is more that this is where he proposed.

We arrived at three o'clock, on our way home. The hotel is just outside Amiens, in its own grounds, the entrance a huge affair with pillars and revolving doors. Under the pretence of taking me there for afternoon tea, Pascal pulled into the car park beside a tall pine-scented tree. Locking the car, he took my hand and we made our way towards the entrance. But as we approached, he stopped suddenly, turned, and knelt down. In the middle of the driveway.

I thought he was mad. A car could have come along at any moment.

'Pascal, what are you doing?'

Taking my hand, he kissed it. 'I'm kneeling down, exactly where the idea came to me. Not the most romantic of places, I know. But I have missed you so much, Noelle. And I know you're richer than I am, and I know you have children you wish to leave your money to. But we can sort all that out, and anyway I might die before you do. I hope I do, *ma chérie* - I would miss you so very much.'

Tears filled my eyes. But I was speechless. Was he really saying what I thought he was saying?

He continued. 'Would you do me the very great honour of marrying me, *ma chérie*?'

I could hardly see him for the tears streaming down my face, but I nodded idiotically, pulling him off the ground and holding him close. 'Oh – Pascal …'

'From the bottom of my heart, I promise to take care of you.'

'I know you will,' I replied, gulping back my tears. 'I know.'

*

Today I am busy, floating, humbled. All those things and more.

Claude was astounded at the news last night As was Valerie when she brought Isabelle round this morning. But happy. They're very happy for us.

So we have rings to buy, arrangements to make.

I feel so, so excited. So loved. So content. So *safe*.

Claude wanted to jog through the *Bois* this morning, so I left him to his own devices whilst I visited the local shops. Taking Isabelle in her pushchair, we visited the local *boulangerie* to buy bread and home-made bilberry tart, then *l'epicerie* for oranges and apples. But I so enjoy the walk. It reminds me of pushing Valerie and Matthieu in their prams. How time does fly.

I linger beside the window of *Soucy Fleuriste*, a new florist that's only been open a few weeks. It's owned by a local woman, Adalene Soucy. I peer through the glass. It's an attractive display, full of Christmas decorations, dried fruits, twigs with shiny baubles, and fluffy stuffed animals. But as I stand there, Isabelle wakes up and moans to leave the pushchair. Deciding I should support Adalene's new business, I pick her up and take her inside.

Holding Isabelle's hand now, I wander round, picking out all the white flowers I can find. I have a thing about white flowers. They're so pure, so distinctive. And I want them for my wedding, so it's appropriate I buy them to celebrate my engagement too.

Avoiding the huge lilies in the corner (funeral flowers), I choose white roses, carnations, gardenia, orchids, and stephanotis. A handful of gypsophila finishes them off.

'*Bonjour, Madame,*' says the woman behind the desk, whom I assume to be Adalene.

'*Bonjour, Madame.*'

She takes the flowers from me. 'These are lovely together. What is the occasion?'

'I'm getting married,' I reply.

She looks surprised. 'You could have had them delivered, you know.'

I shake my head. 'No. We've not set the date yet. He's only just proposed.'

She smiles. 'Well, congratulations. So why the flowers now?'

'To celebrate. I love white flowers. I want them for my wedding.'

'Oh, so sophisticated. What colour dress will you have?'

I laugh. 'I haven't decided on the dress, yet. That's something I need to think about.'

'How about antique cream? That would look wonderful with white flowers.'

I beam as the image takes hold. 'That sounds beautiful, *Madame*. Thank you. Thank you very much.'

*

Claude is home when we get back, showered and sitting at the table with coffee and a newspaper. He watches as I unpack my bag.

'Wow. Oranges. Just what I need. Thanks, Mamie.'

I smile. 'I remembered how you always like one after your run.'

Isabelle is playing with toy bricks on the kitchen floor, so I busy myself arranging my flowers into my beautiful glass vase. I place them onto the table.

'There. To celebrate.'

'I've got something for you, too,' says Claude, producing a card and a gift, wrapped in silver paper and a bow.

I'm perplexed. 'Thank you, Claude. But why?'

'Open it and see.'

I pull open the paper to find a small china plant pot – white - with the words *Noelle et Pascal* engraved into the front.

'Oh, it's lovely, thank you. But how did you …?'

'That new flower shop along the road - thought I'd give them some business. They do them while you wait.'

*

This afternoon has been so busy. I've rung Fleurette to ask her to clean on Thursday as well as Wednesday. Thankfully, she can fit me in. I've rung round everyone to let them know when to arrive on Wednesday, and to ensure they can still come. I've sat and chatted to Claude, and played with Isabelle, and made lunch and coffee. Coffee several times. I've also rung to change my doctor's appointment. They can't fit me in until January now, but never mind, she only wants to check my blood pressure. Then after that, Pascal rang. He wants me to choose a ring.

A ring.

The very thought makes my heart flip up and down. Several times.

A ring. At my age.

19

Rose

Tuesday November 19th

Despite the late hour, the *Gare du Nord* was buzzing as we arrived on Saturday. As the all-pervading scent of garlic tickled my nostrils, I breathed in deeply, so excited at finally being here. But the station was so busy. I mean, entire families were standing around, fathers checking the announcement boards, mothers keeping an eye on toddlers, and tiny babies sleeping through it all. Elsewhere, girls flirted with boys, boys waited nonchalantly for girls, and buskers entertained all of us. One busker, his black beret and denim jacket his only protection against the cold, played a soft, haunting lullaby on his saxophone that sent tingles down my spine.

Paris.

Olivia's aunt had promised to meet us at the exit, so we made our way there, pulling our cases behind us. Two armed guards in combat uniform loomed before us, and the sight of their rifles made me clutch at my throat. The exit suddenly looked dark and disturbing.

'Bit scary here, isn't it?' I murmured.

Olivia smiled. 'They're just taking care of us. Don't worry so much.'

Within seconds, we were out in the fresh air, a cold wind whipping at our coats.

'She's over there - look.'

Aunt Helena was waiting beside a small newspaper kiosk. We ran towards her, our cases trailing noisily.

'Helena!' called Olivia.

Her dark wavy hair just like Olivia's, she hugged and kissed us on both cheeks. She wore a green wool coat, soft and loose-fitting, with huge brown buttons.

'*Bonsoir*. It's so lovely to meet you, Rose. Olivia has told me all about you.'

'You, too. And I just love your coat.'

She smiled. 'Why, thank you, Rose. *You* can come and see me again.'

Olivia grinned. 'She probably will.'

'Come on, let's get you home, out of this freezing cold wind. You must be starving.'

*

We drove to *Porte-Saint-Denis*, a lively residential area in the tenth arrondissement, north of Paris. Helena's apartment is lovely, oozing style, with open-plan ivory walls and a pale blue kitchen. The furniture is warm oak, the sofas a blue velour, the ambience relaxed, cool and calm.

'I've made goulash, so I hope you're okay with meat?'

We nodded and smiled gratefully, and as she lifted the lid to stir, I could smell red wine, and again the scent of garlic.

'It smells delicious. I'm absolutely starving,' gushed Olivia, immediately sitting down at the table.

Helena took our coats, hanging them in the entrance. 'You will be, now you're expecting a baby. But what wonderful news, Olivia.'

'Thank you.'

'And your mother will be thrilled, I'm sure, once you've decided to tell her.'

'I do hope so.'

'So we must catch up, but first I need to get this meal sorted. Glass of wine, anyone?' Embarrassed, she smiled. 'I've got alcohol-free for you, my darling.'

Olivia pulled a face. 'It's okay, don't worry. I'm getting used to it.'

Helena poured a glass for me, and one for herself. 'Just make yourself at home, Rose. I'll show you your room in a bit. You're okay sharing?'

I nodded. 'No problem, I'm fine. Thank you.'

'So what did you think to the new Chunnel?'

'We hardly noticed we were going under the sea,' said Olivia. 'It was amazing. So quiet.'

'I've not had the opportunity to use it yet, but I'm sure it'll be a lot easier than the ferry.'

'When's the last time you went back to the UK?' I asked.

'Christmas last year. I couldn't afford the Chunnel, but the prices will come down, I'm sure, once the novelty's worn off. No, I went by coach, which is alright but takes longer.'

We settled ourselves around the table, a blue cloth covering the surface and a chunky red candle at the centre, and tucked in.

'This goulash is delicious - thanks, Helena,' I said.

'It's an old French recipe Chris used to make. He always used too much wine to my liking, but that's the French for you.'

'What happened to him?' I asked.

She looked down at her meal, suddenly still. 'He died. Twelve years ago. Lung cancer, it was.'

'I'm so sorry about that. Didn't you ever think about moving back to England?'

She looked up. 'No, not really. I'd have had to start again. New job. New friends. Not easy at my age. I love my job, and I have some wonderful friends. Most of the people on this street are British, and we have a fabulous social life. But more than that, I love Paris.'

'I can't wait to see it myself,' I gushed, turning to Olivia. 'Do you have any plans for tomorrow?'

'I thought Aunt Helena could show us round. If that's okay?'

'Try and stop me,' she replied. 'And less of the *Aunt*, if you don't mind. You know I hate it. But I'd love to show you round, I've booked time off work especially.'

*

On Sunday we needed to recover from the journey, so we just chilled, hanging around *Porte-Saint-Denis*. Most places are closed on a Sunday in France, anyway, so we walked through the local park and wandered the streets, before returning to the apartment and an early night.

Yesterday we visited the Eiffel Tower. What a glorious day. The skies were blue, the sun was out, and despite the cold wind, Paris was everything I expected. I mean, I just couldn't believe I was actually standing beside the Eiffel Tower, taking photos with Mum's old Canon.

Plus, there seemed to be an air of expectation about the place, everyone looking forward to Christmas, relieved at the lack of explosions, the ending of strikes, the chance to do some serious shopping.

But as we walked around the *Champs de Mars*, the lovely green park surrounding the Eiffel Tower, there was the most delicious aroma, mouth-watering. Roasting chestnuts. We found an old chap cooking them on a small burner, so we bought some and ate them beneath the tall spruce trees, their Christmas bulbs sparkling in the sunshine.

*

Today we're taking a walk around the *Bois de Boulogne*. It's much larger than I expected. There's a small café serving drinks, and long benches where the elderly sit and chat, or watch the young play whilst revisiting their own childhood. Cyclists ride past, and runners race along, their faces fiercely concentrated, utterly focused on their final goal.

'They hold a half marathon here. And a ten kilometre. They take it all very seriously,' explains Helena.

'Very impressive,' says Olivia.

'On the other side of the coin, we have prostitutes hanging out at night. You can't always see them, but you can see their vans. They park them nearby, so they can move quickly when the *gendarmes* arrive.'

I laugh. 'I can just imagine it. Like Keystone Cops, everyone running round, semi-naked, in and out of the trees.'

'I don't think the Keystone Cops were semi-naked,' says Olivia, grinning.

Helena continues. 'And there's a house here that the Duke of Windsor and Wallis Simpson lived in. They lived here for years after he gave up his kingdom.'

I sigh. 'That is such a romantic story.'

'But come on, let's walk,' she says. 'We need to find my restaurant – well, it's not mine, although I go there often enough. But it's just off the *Boulevard Suchet*, not far.'

Chez Gitan is a small restaurant, dark and intimate, with red wallpaper and brown furnishings.

'It seems a pity to leave the sunshine outside,' I complain.

'Believe me, the food is so delicious you'll forget all about the sunshine,' says Helena, removing her coat.

The place is nearly full, but Gitan welcomes Helena as an old friend. Finding us a table in the far corner, he lights a candle to brighten our meal and brings us drinks on the house. We have three courses, a bowl of French Onion soup to chase away the cold, a parmesan omelette with *Boulangère* potatoes and green salad, and a white chocolate *crème-brûlée*. Helena and I wash the whole lot down with a cold glass of *Clairette de Die*, a sparkling wine recommended by Gitan, while Olivia drinks ice-cold Coca-Cola.

'To Paris!' she says, and we clink glasses.

*

The sunshine has gone and the sky is a cold grey as we leave the restaurant. Pulling up our coat collars, we walk along the *Avenue de St Cloud*, returning to the *Bois*. It's quieter now, serene, with the sweet scent of pine trees filling our senses. Two lakes lay ahead of us, a large one with two islands at the centre, and a smaller one.

'Come on, let's walk along, past the small lake,' says Helena. 'I'll show you the *Grande Cascade* first, though. It is so beautiful.'

The waterfall is gentle, tumbling, soothing, and we stand and watch as water glides from one lake to the other. But as the cold seeps into our bones, we continue on our way, until we reach a small forest, thick with tall pine trees. I look down. A mattress of pine needles covers the ground, their scent rising up towards me. There's an unusually large pine cone, and my foot brushes against it. For some strange reason the shape of it, its shadow against the ground, forces a shiver through me. I pick it up, feeling it with my hands, the weight of it, the sensation of the smooth scales upon my fingers. It seems familiar, somehow ...

'That's lovely,' says Olivia.

I smile quietly. 'I know. I'm think I'll take it home and spray it silver, hang it from the tree.' I look up to see Helena a few yards away, talking to a bloke. 'Who's Helena talking to?'

Olivia shrugs. 'No idea. She obviously knows him, though.'

Intrigued, we walk towards her. The bloke's chatting away, gesticulating, laughing, his back to us.

But as we get closer, he turns towards us.

I recognise him.

I tug at Olivia's coat, pulling her back. 'Olivia!'

'What?'

'It's Claude Jolivet!'

'Who?'

My heart beats fiercely. I feel faint. 'Claude! From the hospital!'

20

Claude

Wednesday December 20th

I don't believe it. There is such a thing as Fate.

I met her again, yesterday. Rose. Rose Somerton.

She's actually staying with Helena, an old friend of my mother's. Helena was Maman's secretary when she worked in Paris, knew me as a boy in school shorts. Does she have some tales to tell.

But I really, really can't believe it.

Such a coincidence.

I cannot believe that fate should bring us together in Paris, miles away from where we both live, at exactly the same time.

Mon Dieu. We had the whole world at our disposal.

I decided not to run yesterday as my legs still ached from Sunday, and I was tired. But I needed to walk, to taste the air, to smell the pine trees. So I decided a saunter through the *Bois* would do me good. And then I saw Helena. I thought at first she was by herself, so I stopped to talk, to see how she is. But she turned, introducing me to the two women accompanying her.

'Olivia, Rose,' she said. 'Let me introduce you to Claude.'

And that's when I saw her. Rose. I could hardly breathe, let alone talk.

Helena continued. 'This is Olivia, my niece, from England, and her friend Rose.'

Our eyes met, and then I found my voice. '*Enchanté.* How are your ears doing, Rose?'

Well, what else could I say? That I find her incredibly attractive, and amazingly sexy, with her long auburn hair, as smooth as the surface of the Seine? That I think of her every day? That I couldn't believe it when she said she was no longer engaged?

Her eyes sparkled. 'My ears are very much better, thank you. You did an excellent job.'

'I do my best.' I smiled at Olivia. 'I'm very pleased to meet you, too.'

'How do you know Helena?' she asked.

Helena replied for me. 'I'm an old friend of Claude's mother. I was her secretary when she worked in Paris. Many moons ago. But she lives in Geneva now, so I assume Claude's here to visit his grandmother.'

I nodded. 'My parents are in Vienna for Christmas, so Mamie asked if I'd like to come over for my birthday.'

'When is your birthday?' asked Rose.

'Tomorrow, as it happens. We're having a little party. You should all come.'

Rose smiled. And what a smile.

'Could we? Would you mind, Helena?'

Helena nodded. 'Of course. Why not? *Merci bien.*'

*

It's eight in the evening, and I have had a lovely birthday. We actually woke up to rain, but by eleven o'clock the sun was out, and not only was there a shimmering rainbow, but a silver shroud of mist rising up from the Seine. Nature is a wonderful thing.

I've opened cards and presents, been for a jog through the *Bois*, spent time with Mamie and Pascal in the kitchen, and am now wearing the soft ice-blue shirt they've bought me. I've also drunk three glasses of *Pastis,* and the only food I've eaten since lunch is a small bowlful of ripe black olives. So I may be slightly drunk.

Mamie is tall, slim, graceful, serene. *So* serene. She keeps her silver hair tied back into a chignon, and for my party wears a soft grey woollen dress that clings to her body seductively. No wonder Pascal hangs on her every word. No wonder he's asked her to marry him.

For my party she has arranged the food beautifully, with white flowers and delicate lace napkins that add that Parisian touch to the table. The kitchen smells of garlic and hot red wine.

Helena, Rose and Olivia are the first to arrive. Rose is like a child with a newly opened toy, walking round the apartment as if in a daze. She peers over the balcony towards the Seine admiringly, before returning to the kitchen.

'I just love your apartment, Noelle.'

'Thank you,' Mamie says, her English a little stilted these days. 'My husband, Louis, would also love it. He always said he'd like a place where he could look out over the Seine each morning.'

'How long have you lived here?'

'Nine years. Louis died eleven years ago. But it took me a while to sell our home and find somewhere else, somewhere I felt I could live without him.'

'That's so sad,' Rose says, sympathetically.

'Not really,' I say. 'Mamie's engaged to be married again. Only just last weekend. And Pascal, her very lucky fiancé, is coming along later.'

'Wow,' Rose says. 'Well, congratulations!'

'Thank you,' Mamie says, beaming. 'It will only be a small affair. But we are so very happy. And I know Louis would approve of Pascal.'

Camille and Florian have just arrived, and are being introduced to everyone. Camille and Rose seem to bond immediately.

'I'm very pleased to meet you,' says Rose.

Camille kisses her on both cheeks. '*Enchanté*. I'm very pleased to meet you, also. Mamie says you and Claude already know each other?'

Rose grins. 'Weirdly enough, yes. I mean, I had a burst eardrum and he was my doctor. Can you believe it?'

'I see. So you arranged to meet in Paris, out of the way, is that it?'

'No, no, not at all. I didn't even know he was here. We just bumped into one another in the *Bois de Boulogne* yesterday. You see, Olivia and I are staying with Helena, a friend of your mother's. She recognised Claude and we got talking. So it's pure coincidence, really.'

Rose looks across as I help myself to more *Pastis,* and she smiles. That smile.

Florian busies himself, topping up Rose's glass. 'So what do you do for a living, you two?' he asks.

'I'm a personal injury solicitor,' says Olivia, 'and Rose works in conveyancing for the same company.'

'Interesting. You must hear of some awful things, then?'

'Sometimes, yes. But it's interesting work, and I do feel as if we're helping people.'

Pascal and his friend Hugo arrive at this point, so we sit down to eat. I'm really hungry and quite drunk by this time, but there is *basquaise de poulet* and Pascal's very own *spaghetti bolognaise*, together with *ratatouille* and *pommes boulangère*, all of which look delicious. I choose the *basquaise de poulet* and *ratatouille*. Dessert is *marquise au chocolat* or *clafoutis,* and I have a little of both which makes Mamie tut-tut. As always. But it's all so delicious I can't resist.

After eating, we move into the lounge with glasses of cognac to aid the digestion. Florian opens champagne to celebrate both my birthday and the engagement of Mamie and Pascal.

'To a wonderfully long and happy future together,' announces Florian. We clink glasses and drink. Even more.

Both Hugo and Camille have brought presents for us, and we open them amid much amusement. I open another new shirt, cream this time, and a bottle of *Cointreau.* Mamie and Pascal receive wine, chocolates and flowers.

But all the while I am aware of Rose. She doesn't just laugh at things, she sparkles. She's intelligent, caring, beautiful. She is all I've ever wanted in a woman. And then there's that extra *je n' sais quoi*, that magic ingredient that reels me in, that I can't quite put my finger on. As if she knows me already, knows what to do, what to say, how to laugh.

So I watch her. And I watch her. Her blue dress moves as she talks, it sways as she moves, it matches her eyes so beautifully. Those eyes.

I await my chance.

But ten o'clock arrives and Helena announces she'll have to leave as she has a busy day tomorrow. Everyone nods in agreement; they should all be leaving.

I panic suddenly. It can't end like this. I need to talk to her.

I take hold of her arm. 'Come on, let's go somewhere quiet.'

I pull her out of the French doors and onto the balcony. The mist has gone and we're only a few days off a full moon. But I ignore its hypnotic reflection in the water. I'm too busy gazing into her eyes. My heart flutters, my hands turn ice cold, and my stomach - I really shouldn't have drunk so much

I take hold of her hands. They're soft and warm. 'Can I ask you a question?'

'Yes, of course.'

'It's quite personal.'

She looks unsure now, but agrees anyway. 'Okay.'

I hesitate, suddenly unsure myself, scared of what the answer might be.

But I go for it. 'I need to ask - have you found another lover yet?'

'No,' she says, shyly. 'Why?'

'Would you like to meet up with me some time?'

Her face lights up. 'That would be lovely. When?'

'Friday? I've promised to spend the day with Mamie tomorrow.'

I can't wait. I bend to kiss her before she can reply. She tastes of red wine and chocolate, the faintest hint of perfume.

'Claude ...'

She melts into my arms, and I pull her close.

21

Noelle

Thursday December 21st

It's cold and grey in Versailles. The rain that went away yesterday has returned and is now persistent. Claude and I have come here for the day with Isabelle. So we can entertain ourselves in the dry, touring the rooms. The very ones Marie Antoinette brushed through on her way to choosing yet another unnecessarily extravagant outfit.

It is a pity we have to be inside, though. I do love the gardens here, with their fountains and romantic little bridges, and the Hamlet, built so Marie Antoinette could experience the simplicity of 'peasant life', as she called it.

So I fasten on Isabelle's reins while Claude takes charge of the empty pushchair. We head up to the first floor and Marie Antoinette's rooms.

'So you like Helena's new friend, do you?' I murmur as we reach the top of the stairs, slightly out of breath.

Claude's cheeks are pink, I notice. I'm not sure if it's the result of my question or the exertion of carrying the pushchair. But he's a runner, so it has to be my question.

'Sorry, Mamie?' he says.

'You seemed very happy out there on the balcony.'

He's definitely blushing now. 'Rose? I already know her. We've met before, back home.' He stops, opens the pushchair up, places it onto the floor, and turns to me. 'Okay. I confess. The truth is, ever since I first met her, I've been unable to think of anyone else.'

'Not even Caroline?'

'Not even Caroline.'

I smile. 'Then it must be serious.' We walk towards the queen's bedchamber. 'Is it serious, Claude?'

'I hardly know her, Mamie, but there's something about her.'

'Like you've know her before?'

He nods. 'Possibly, yes. As ridiculous as that sounds.'

'I felt like that when I met your grandfather. I always felt like that, but if I'd told him so, he'd have ridiculed the idea. I'm a scientist, he'd have said. But I did feel as if we'd met before. It's the one thing that makes me believe in reincarnation.'

Pausing, he turns to me. 'Do you?'

The bedspread catches my eye and I just have to go up to it. It's ivory silk, richly embroidered with a design of red and pink roses, green leaves, and a silver thread running through.

'It's beautiful,' I enthuse. 'Just look at that embroidery.'

'Is that your next hobby, then?' he asks, grinning. 'Once you've gone off the painting?'

I shake my head. 'I would never stop painting. It's relaxing. I feel as if I could float sometimes. But I do have a new interest, and I think you'll approve.'

He eyes me suspiciously. 'Oh, yes?'

'I'm trying to set up a run in the *Bois*, maybe even a half marathon, I'm not sure yet. But it's for charity, and I'm thinking about fancy dress. What do you think?'

'Wow, Mamie! That sounds like a *very* ambitious hobby. What made you think of that?'

'I'd like to do something before I die, a kind of legacy. It would be a good way of raising money, don't you think? It needn't *be* a marathon, but a race of some kind. It's to aid children from poor families who need extra tuition at school. But I want it to be fun too, so children will watch, so they'll learn what's happening to other people. What do you think?'

'I think it's wonderful. So what's happening with it?'

'Well, I've placed a notice in the local paper asking for volunteers. And I've arranged an appointment in January with Maxime Carel at the *Conseil de Paris*, just to discuss access and dates and so on. So we'll see where we go from there.'

'If there's ever anything I can do, just let me know, yes?'

I smile. That's my Claude. Bless him.

'Thank you, *mon chéri*. I will.'

I feel I'm becoming slightly obsessed with this fancy dress race. But I do want to leave something behind, so I'll be remembered. Oh, I will be remembered, I know - by my family, my friends. But I want more than that. I want people to remember me for the right reasons. Because I did something positive. Because I helped other people, their children, their future.

*

The rich fabrics, the décor, and the history of Versailles have always fascinated me. But by lunchtime I'm exhausted and thirsty, so we head for the tea room. We choose baguettes full of roast chicken, mustard and salad, and we feed Isabelle with the steamed vegetables and chicken we've brought from home. We chat for an hour while Isabelle runs round, her little red shoes echoing in the near-empty room.

Before continuing our tour, I take Isabelle to the Ladies to change her nappy. The washroom is new, with sinks hewn out of grey marble, and lighting that would have been more at home in the King's dining room. I wash my hands, drying them on one of the small flannels arranged beautifully into a huge basket in the corner.

'Must take someone hours to do all that,' I say to Isabelle, who smiles up at me, her milk teeth all shiny and white.

'*Oui*, Mamie,' she says, cheekily.

'*Oui*, Isabelle,' I reply, laughing.

I reapply my lipstick and spray on some *Chanel* in front of the huge mirror, before returning to Claude, waiting patiently.

'Mm, you smell nice,' he murmurs.

'Thank you, *mon chéri*. It's only my usual.'

'I know - *Chanel*. You do know, don't you, that every time I smell vanilla it reminds me of you?'

I kiss his stubbled cheek. 'That's sweet of you, Claude.'

He grins. 'Come on, let's go play in the Hall of Mirrors.'

Isabelle is a little tired now, ready for her afternoon nap. So we place her into the pushchair and carry on walking.

'Do you remember bringing us here when we were children, me and Camille?' he says.

'Of course I do. In the school holidays. We had such lovely times, didn't we?'

'I used to love the Hall of Mirrors. Camille would take off her shoes and slide all the way along the floor. And I'd chase her, and …'

'And I'd tell you both to stand still, before a guard came and kicked us out.' I begin to smile, but instead it turns into a huge sigh.

'Mamie? You alright?'

'Just thinking of all the years we've had together. All the places we've been to, me and you and Camille, and the times before that, with your maman and Matthieu, and Papy. Where did they all go?' I pause to wipe the sudden tears from my eyes. 'Sorry.'

He puts his arm around my shoulders. 'No need to be sorry. They were happy years, that's all you need to remember.'

I pat his hand. 'I know, Claude. I'm fine, really. Just reminiscing, that's all.'

'Right. I dare you to take off your shoes and slide along the floor.' Taking hold of the pushchair, he runs away, leaving me standing there. 'Come on, Mamie!'

*

Camille arrives just as I'm pulling a sleepy Isabelle from her car seat.

'*Salut,*' she says.

'*Salut, ma chérie.*'

'Had a good day?' she asks, taking Isabelle from me.

Claude pulls the rucksack from the boot. 'We had a wonderful day.'

I lock the Audi and we walk towards the apartment foyer.

'How was it at work?' I ask.

'Pretty busy. I'm glad to be home.' She smiles. 'One more day, then I can take some time off with my beautiful Isabelle.'

'Can you stay for coffee?' I ask, nodding to Leon, who's opening the door for us.

'I can stay longer than that. Florian's working late, so I've no need to rush.'

Claude grins. 'The life of the married woman, aye?'

'I noticed you were quite cosy with Rose last night,' she teases. 'Couldn't take your eyes off her, if I'm correct.'

'Yes. Okay,' he says. 'I do quite like her.'

'She's very nice. And very pretty. So what happens now? Are you going to see her again?'

We enter the apartment and I start to make coffee. But exhaustion suddenly hits me. This damp weather isn't helping.

Camille takes the coffee pot from me. 'Leave this to me, Mamie. You look tired. Why not have twenty minutes, then come back and play with Isabelle while Claude and I make dinner for you?'

So I go, and I lay down. My bedroom is calming, with a white wrought iron bed, ivory bedding, and a couple of old tapestries on the wall depicting the French countryside.

I close my eyes and I breathe deeply. In through the nose and out through the mouth.

I visualise the door. The man is still there, still standing in the corner. Again, he turns to me, placing the white cloak around my shoulders. Again, I feel its protection. I feel safe.

I sleep for about twenty minutes, but I don't get up immediately. Instead, I allow myself to doze a little.

I think about Claude's party. So much fun. And it was good to see Helena, to talk about the times she and Valerie used to spend together. It's a pity she and Hugo didn't hit it off, though, but there's always next time. And her niece was lovely. I'm sure we've met before, but I can't quite remember where, or when. Maybe she just reminds me of her aunt at that age.

Rose was lovely, too. Kind and gentle. I'm glad Claude has found someone.

So I continue with my breathing. In and out. Until I'm rested.

Suddenly, the aroma of fresh coffee drifts into the room. Of all the scents that can ease me from my bed, it is that. I return to the kitchen and Isabelle bounds up to me, all smiles and hugs, and love.

22

Rose

Friday December 22nd

Oh, my God! He kissed me. He actually kissed me!

When we first arrived, he kissed me on both cheeks and I blushed like a schoolgirl. But it's the French way, they all do it, I'm no-one special. Then all evening, all the time I was chatting to people, I was watching him. The back of his neck, the way his shoulders move as he speaks, the way he gesticulates to describe his words. But then I began to wonder why anyone so lovely doesn't already have a girlfriend, or even a fiancée.

Even if there is no-one back home, I decided, he must surely have a beautiful French mistress somewhere in the background, a Parisian who hangs on his every word, can't wait for him to come round and bed her.

I was convinced of it.

But as the evening wore on, as I tucked into the delicious food, and drank more and more wine, I became emboldened, dared to think that maybe I was wrong, that there was no-one else. The fact that I kept catching his eye as I moved around the room had nothing to do with it. It was more an innate sense of *I've been here before - there's something special here, there is no-one else.*

Ever the cynic, I dismissed it with a *Well, yes, I have been here before. Twice before, in fact. Will I never learn?*

Then he kissed me. Out on the balcony, overlooking the Seine. In the middle of Paris.

He was amazing. His kiss was amazing.

I will definitely never learn.

*

Later that evening, as we sat in her apartment with hot cocoa, Helena asked me about Claude.

'There was a little spark, yes?'

Embarrassed, I nodded. 'You could tell?'

Olivia laughed. 'Just a bit! You need to be careful, though, or he'll think you're an easy touch. French men have a different attitude towards women, you know. Don't let him take you in.'

'I won't, don't worry.'

But I didn't believe her. Not for a second. For some reason I could never explain, I thought his kiss was special, that *we* were special.

Helena smiled. 'Let's see what tomorrow brings, shall we? Noelle is lovely, though, and doesn't she have the most beautiful skin? You'd never believe she's seventy three.'

'It must run in the family,' said Olivia. 'Claude is very attractive. I can see what you see in him, Rose, but do be careful.'

Despite her remarks, I felt happy, had a feeling about this, knew it was going somewhere. Those lovely grey eyes. That kiss.

*

It was Helena's Christmas lunch at work yesterday, so Olivia and I decided to go shopping. Well, the weather had nothing to recommend it. It was cold and misty, not exactly the kind of day to make you want to go walking.

We took the *métro* to Sèvres–Babylone, which was absolutely heaving, everyone obviously catching up on their errands after the bombings and the strikes. But we pushed our way through them, to find ourselves outside *Le Bon Marché,* a huge department store. Full of charm and character.

I stood, looking skywards. 'What a lovely old building.'

'It was built in the eighteen hundreds,' said Olivia. 'And there's a nice old café, kind of traditional. We can have lunch there, if you'd like?'

We spent hours walking. Shoes, bags, perfume, lingerie, clothing. I found a gorgeous black mohair sweater, with a crew neck and tiny sparkly beads knitted into it.

'Everything's so expensive,' I moaned, 'but I love it.'

Olivia smiled. 'Well, you can't afford it, so stop looking.'

'But I have to buy something. You can't come to Paris and not buy something.'

'Well, make that the one thing you do buy, then.'

I bought it. Four hundred and eighty francs. Roughly sixty pounds. Ouch!

Lunch, however, didn't go quite according to plan. The café was absolutely, ridiculously expensive – the equivalent of seven pounds for a coffee. So we found a small *pâtisserie* on the street corner. The prices were still astronomical, but cheaper than *Le Bon Marché,* and the cakes in the window were just perfect. In fact, Olivia couldn't pull me away.

I couldn't believe what was in front of me. There, in the window. Only vanilla slices decorated with raspberries, chocolate slabs topped with ribbons of white chocolate, rum babas dripping with sugary juice. Baby pink meringues, pastries dusted in icing sugar, sponge cake topped with crystallised rose petals.

Such inspiration.

The heavy door chimed as we pushed through. A sweet sugary bouquet filled the air, latching onto my senses so much it actually made my mouth water. Still, there was a queue, so we waited in line before the long counter. But all the time, I was itching to take photos of those cakes. So as soon as we reached the counter I pulled out my Canon and pointed at the display questioningly. The ultra-slim waitress smiled and nodded.

'Of course you can take photos,' she said, in perfect English.

Access to the display was through a narrow wooden door, which she opened for me, so I was able to take close-ups. The detail on each small cake was exquisite, flawless. It literally took my breath away.

Once I'd finished, the waitress showed us to a table near the window. It was still misty outside, but we were able to people-watch as we munched on ham salad baguettes. We then shared a very pricey dessert of *Grand Cru Vanille,* a blend of vanilla mousse and sponge.

It was to die for.

'The French really know how to make cake,' I said.

'You could pick up a few tips of your own,' said Olivia.

'I know. I'm doing alright, though, aren't I?'

'You can always learn something new from the experts.'

'Wouldn't that be something, Olivia? To be an expert? Then I wouldn't have to think twice about buying a sweater.'

She pulled a face. 'At least you can fit into it. Everything I tried on was bursting at the seams.'

'Well, why don't you buy some Parisian maternity clothes? I'll bet they're gorgeous. You could start a new wardrobe, make yourself feel better about everything.'

'I'm fine. Really. I'm getting used to the idea now. Except - except I still haven't thought about what you said before. That I should tell Doug.'

'Well, he is the father.'

'You really think I should tell him, don't you?'

'Oh, I don't know. I mean, what good would it do, really? It's not like he lives down the road and can come and visit the child, is it?'

'No.'

'Would you marry him if he asked you?'

'Probably not.'

'Why not?'

'I think if I did, it would be for the baby's sake, not because he's right for me.'

'So he definitely isn't the one?'

She shook her head. 'Definitely. He's too much in love with Pamela. I want someone who just wants me.'

I smiled, encouragingly. 'It'll all come right in the end. It always does.'

What a ridiculous platitude, I thought. Just who was I trying to convince? Olivia? Or myself?

*

All morning my stomach has been awash with butterflies. Claude rang Helena's number first thing, and we've agreed to meet up at Noelle's.

But I'm feeling so, so nervous.

Will he still like me when he knows me properly? Will we have anything in common? Will he ever love me as much as I love him?

Helena's offered to drop me off in her Citroën as it's her afternoon off work, so we arrive just after lunch. I'm wearing jeans and my brand new mohair jumper. I love it.

Helena drives off, and I look up to see Claude standing on the balcony, waving his tweed cap.

'*Bonjour! Ça va?*'

The doorman takes me up in the lift, but I do wonder why Claude hasn't come down to greet me.

He is there at the door, though. 'Come on in, it's good to see you.'

He ushers me in, and I see a pushchair parked in the hallway. Noelle's great granddaughter. So that's why he didn't come downstairs.

'How are you?' he says. 'Did you have an awful hangover yesterday?'

'I drank plenty of water when I got back. Which always helps.'

He smiles. 'You're quite used to drinking, then?'

'Only since I split from my fiancé. But it's not very good of me, is it?'

His eyes crinkle mischievously. 'Don't worry, I'm only joking. And if it helps fight the blues, it can't be all bad.'

We head towards the kitchen, but I pause to admire the child in the pushchair, asleep beneath a pink blanket, her tiny nose and cheeks peeking out.

'She's beautiful.'

'Let me introduce you. This is Isabelle, Camille's daughter. Camille works on Fridays, so Mamie looks after her. But today she's out shopping, so I've taken over.'

'She's so cute. Do you like children?'

'Why shouldn't I? I only don't like them when they're unloved and joyless. But then that's not their fault, is it?'

Isabelle chooses that exact moment to start crying, so Claude picks her up, hugging her to him. She wears a white satin dress and tights, both shamelessly expensive-looking.

For a nanosecond I imagine I'm Isabelle, cocooned by all that love, by Claude's strong arms. I sigh.

'How old is she?'

'Nearly fourteen months. *Hush, silence, ma petite.*' He rocks her gently. 'She's probably hungry.'

We take her into the kitchen, where a sudden pitter patter makes me look outside.

'Look, it's raining.'

Running to the window, Claude peers out. 'There'll be a rainbow somewhere. *Regarde, Isabelle, un arc-en-ciel ...*'

She stops crying, but turns to look at me.

'Hello,' I say, smiling.

'*Elle est Rose*,' says Claude. '*Mon amie.*'

As she smiles back, I realise suddenly that I'm feeling less stressed, much more relaxed, and my butterflies have completely gone. I look out to see a solid rainbow to the right of us, and I follow its curve as it drops down to the Seine in the distance.

'It's beautiful,' I say, awestruck.

I turn back to find the sunlight has sneaked in behind us, highlighting the dust motes as they swirl through the air.

'Look at that,' I say.

'Stardust,' he murmurs.

'What?'

'When we were children, Mamie would say it was stardust, that it was much too special to brush away.' He grins. 'It was her reason for never cleaning. She's always had a cleaner, you see. But she won't be too happy if it settles – Fleurette only cleaned up after the party yesterday.'

'Well, I'm sure it can't be helped. But I like her name for it. Stardust. It's a good name.'

23

Claude

Saturday December 23rd

She's travelling home today. We've only just met, only just got to know each other, and she's leaving. But I'll call her when I get home. I just have to see her again.

Yesterday was amazing, though. I can't believe it. It's a good job Mamie stayed over at Camille's for dinner.

It was the rainbow that started it, I'm sure. Always a lucky sign. We French are like that, I'm afraid. Superstitious. Although I am a scientist, so that negates a lot of it. Of course.

After the rainbow, we began to talk about Mamie, about her calling dust motes stardust, and about her always having had a cleaner.

Rose smiled at that. 'I take it your grandfather was quite well off, then. There's no way my grandma could have afforded a cleaner.'

'I suppose so. He was a dental surgeon, so yes, they were quite well off.'

At that moment, Isabelle began to cry again, so I passed her to Rose.

'Here. Just while I warm up some food.'

Finding a pureed meal of baked tuna and veg in the fridge, I placed it inside the microwave.

'I'll feed her if you like,' offered Rose.

'Okay. Thanks. I'll make us some coffee, and Mamie has made macaroons if you'd like one?'

She looked quite at home there, her hair falling around her shoulders as she fed Isabelle. What a picture she painted, always smiling, always patient. Thoughtfully, I pulled an old towel from the kitchen drawer and carried it over, placing it onto the table in case of spills. Isabelle is not the best of eaters.

'What's that delicious scent?' she asked.

'Mamie's perfume, probably. Chanel 22. She wears it all the time, so it gets into everything. It's weird, but whenever I smell vanilla, I think of her.'

Isabelle chose just that moment to spit out her food, all over the highchair, all over her hands.

'A good job you gave me this towel,' said Rose, laughing.

'Haha! I've seen what Mamie has to do.'

'She's lovely, your grandma. I like her.'

*

We spent the rest of the afternoon walking Isabelle through the *Bois*, returning only when we became hungry.

Half an hour later, I'd prepared a *Salade César* for us both, Isabelle had been fed yet again and was now chewing on a breadstick, and I'd found some *Picpoul de Pinet* and filled two glasses.

'Are you okay with anchovies, Rose?'

'A bit late for that,' she joked.

'I know. Sorry, I never thought …'

She smiled. 'I love them. It's fine.'

'Great. That's great.'

Suddenly, I was lost for words, couldn't still my mind, my thoughts. She was just so perfect, she even liked one of my most favourite foods.

'Is this Caesar salad?' she asked, piling on more shaved Parmesan.

'It's supposed to be, but I've just thrown everything in, really.'

She took a mouthful. 'Mm, delicious, just the right amount of dressing. You're a good cook.'

'Thanks. Do you like to cook, then?'

'I do cook, unless I'm really tired, then I grab a takeaway. But I prefer making cakes. I've just started up in business, as a matter of fact.'

This surprised me. 'Really? What kind of business? A shop?'

'Bespoke cakes, actually. I make 3D models out of paste and decorate them. For birthdays, anniversaries, that kind of thing.'

'I'm impressed. It sounds very adventurous.'

*

After Isabelle had gone to bed, we drank more wine, sat on Mamie's white sofa, and talked some more. About our plans for the future, of the places we'd like to visit, of the things we'd like to do.

'Once my cake business is up and running, I plan to visit New York.'

'Aren't there more exciting places in the world? China? India? Australia?'

She laughed softly. 'They sound wonderful. But I couldn't afford it. I could visit New York for a long weekend and not have to worry too much about the cost.'

Her laugh was the best thing I'd heard in ages. Soft. Warm.

'Where would you like to go, then, if you had unlimited resources?'

She had to think about that one. 'I think I'd go to the moon. Then I could see every bit of the world, all at the same time. Well, over the space of a day, anyway.'

I grinned. 'Right. Yes. I think not.'

'Where would you go, and who with?'

'New Zealand, I think. I've already seen most of Europe, and I think a beautiful place like New Zealand would soothe the soul. Or India, the Himalayas.'

'And who would you go with?' she insisted.

'I'd have to go alone, I'm afraid. I've not found the right person yet, someone I'd want to spend that amount of time with. Maybe I should move back here, to Paris.'

Placing her hand onto my knee, she leaned forward. And kissed me.

'Are you absolutely sure about that?'

Aroused, I took her into my arms and pulled her close. She sighed, nestling into me, kissing me and holding me as if she would never leave.

Suddenly unsure, I pulled away, and she stared at me, disappointed.

'What?'

Swallowing hard, I looked her in the eyes.

'Rose - I want to take you to bed. I want to make love to you, to touch you, to feel you.'

Her eyes shining, she nodded and took hold of my hand.

'But it's not right,' I continued. 'I've only known you for a few days. We really should wait.'

She stared at me, obviously trying to read me. There was such desire in her eyes I could hardly bear to look at her.

After a while she murmured, 'I feel the same. But I don't want to wait. We shouldn't wait. Please, Claude.'

Suddenly I was pulling her into my room, onto my bed, undressing her, kissing her, touching her. Her hands were hot, insistent, making my heart beat fast, my body ache with desire.

'Claude,' she whispered, pulling me to her. Her hair was soft, her skin smooth. As one hand stroked my face, my neck, the other moved down, slowly, seductively, until she knew I could no longer hold back. Until she knew I was hers.

I pulled a condom from the drawer. 'Rose,' I whispered. *'Ma chérie ...'*

*

Today, Mamie and Pascal are in the kitchen, preparing for Christmas Day. I'm on the *métro,* heading for *les Galeries Lafayette Hausmann*. I'm the typical bloke, leaving it until the very last minute to buy presents. But it's so busy, I immediately regret my decision. As I do every Christmas. Although somehow it feels right, the hustle and bustle, the high spirits, everyone looking forward to the big day. So maybe, subconsciously, I am actually enjoying myself.

And yes, the warmth of the air inside *les Galeries* invites me, soothes me, and I admire the candles on display with their scents of orange and cinnamon. I buy a *café crème* and sit down with pen and paper, brought especially.

Mamie: Chanel 22 body lotion.
Camille: chocolates or silk scarf.
Pascal and Florian: 2 x Rémy Martin
Maman: pretty earrings
Isabelle: a toy
Sarah: real French parfum.

What about Suzanne? I haven't thought about her all week, not properly. I should buy her something, she'll be expecting it. Although how I can see her now, I don't know. I can't. We'll have to finish.

Merde! That'll be awkward at work.

But oh, it will be worth it, to be able to see Rose again. To see those beautiful eyes, that lovely smile. I need to buy her something, too. Jewellery or perfume? Or jewellery and perfume?

So I finish the list, put away my pen and sip my coffee. Mm, creamy smooth.

It's funny. I'm sitting here wondering what to buy my family, my loved ones, but all I can really think about is Rose. *My* Rose. For she is mine.

I suddenly see a girl with long auburn hair, a camel coat, and a brown leather handbag. For a fleeting moment I think it's her, that she's changed her mind, been delayed, something, anything. But it's not her; I know that.

Suddenly, though, I want it to be her. Desperately. I want to run to her, take her into my arms, and stay there forever.

I look around. There's a shop window opposite, full of diamonds. Sparkling in the spotlights. Bright, and shiny, and dazzling. That's it, I realise.

That's what I must do.

I push open the heavy glass door, see the saleswoman look up. I smile, slightly embarrassed, and head straight for the display of rings. The first one I see is a single diamond on a band of gold.

It is beautiful.

It's twelve thousand francs. But I have enough in my account.

And she deserves every centime.

*

With the navy blue box safely in my pocket, I catch the *métro* to the *Gare du Nord* and rush inside to an interior that's magical with fairy lights. Pausing for breath, I look round anxiously. Their train leaves at one, and I pray I'm not too late.

I'm not. I see them.

They're still downstairs, just about to step onto the escalator for Eurostar. Sighing with relief, I don't even think about what I'm going to do.

Oblivious to everyone, everything, I run to Rose and pull her back.

'Claude!' she exclaims, her case jarring on the ground behind her.

I take her hand. I kneel down. 'Marry me? Please, Rose, marry me?'

She shrieks in amazement, hugs me, kisses me, and we practically fall over each other with joy.

Part Two
2016

21 years later

1

Rose Jolivet

Thursday June 9th 2016

My mobile rings as I'm emptying the car. It grates sometimes. I mean, it wouldn't have interrupted me when I first started out all those years ago, would it? Didn't have such things, did we? And they're not just phones now, more like pocket-computers. Which I suppose is a good thing. Useful.

Dumping my groceries onto the ground, I pull the phone from my bag and swipe across.

'Hullo? Rose Jolivet speaking.'

The voice on the other end is feminine, young. 'Hi there. Is that Sugar n Spice?'

'It is, yes. How can I help you?'

'Fab. I'm just wondering if it's too late to make a birthday cake for next Friday?'

I smile happily. 'No problem at all, it's never too late. What kind of thing were you thinking of?'

'Well, you know how you've got that 3D stuff on your website? We were thinking about something like that. Maybe a chap on a motor bike?'

'Okay, yes, I can do that. What's the occasion, exactly?'

'It's my Dad's fiftieth.'

Picking up a bag of groceries, I move out of the sunshine, nearer the house.

'Look - whereabouts are you? Maybe we could meet up so I can take some details, go through some ideas?'

'That'd be lovely. You're Sleaford way, aren't you?'

'That's right.'

'We're only in Ancaster, not far.'

'Okay. There's a nice little café in Sleaford marketplace. We could meet for coffee, maybe?'

'Of course, yes. Which one?'

I rack my brain. 'Something like coffee and cake ...'

'I know it. It's Coffee Cup Cake. The Three Cs, my mum calls it.'

'That's the one - thanks. So what time is best for you?'

'This afternoon any good?'

'Is three o'clock okay?'

'That'd be lovely - thanks. See you there.'

I pick up my shopping and carry it into the kitchen. But my mind whirls as I put it all away. I mean, I've done motor bikes before, yes, so that's not the problem. But I really could do with a free weekend. Louis is nearing the end of his A level exams (thank goodness), Violette is at the end of her GCSEs, and Lottie is – well, Lottie. Fourteen years old, going on forty ...

And the kitchen is a complete mess, even though Lottie's been at school all morning and the other two are in their rooms studying. But okay, I suppose I'd rather they studied than washed up after themselves. Louis has his Chemistry tomorrow and Violette her English Lit.

As long as Environmental Health don't do a spot check on the premises.

Louis appears at the door, still in his PJ boxers and tee-shirt. 'Did you buy any apples, Mum?' He searches the bags carelessly.

'Careful of the eggs!' I screech, pulling out the bag of Granny Smiths and opening it for him.

'Thanks.' Grabbing one, he heads back to his room.

'Louis!' I call.

Turning, he gives me that look as if to say, *I'm busy.*

'Please wash it. What have I told you about chemicals?'

Shrugging, he walks back to rinse it under the tap. 'Sorry.'

'I'll make lunch if you like, but then I've got a meeting in Grantham.'

'Thanks, Mum.'

He looks tired, I realise, his eyes red and puffy.

'You are allowed a break, you know.'

'Not if I want four A stars, I'm not.'

'Louis, it's not the end of the world if you don't get four A stars.'

'It is if I want to be a doctor.'

'But you can overdo it. Why not just go for a walk, get a bit of fresh air?'

'God, have you seen the forecast, Mum? It's going to chuck it down.'

169

So he has been doing something other than studying, I realise. Maybe Facebook or Instagram. Some kind of social media, anyway.

'Okay. Fine. But promise me you'll take a break after the exam tomorrow?'

He shrugs nonchalantly. 'What we having for lunch, then?'

*

I've made ham and egg salad with French dressing. Quick, easy, nutritious. The food I picked up from Folksbury this morning cost a fortune, but never mind. Ocado deliver on Saturdays, but with Louis and Violette being off school all week we've run out. At least they're healthy eaters, my three. Salads and fruit, and fish. The occasional bar of chocolate, I suppose, although Violette's skin could do without it. As her Tantine Camille is always telling her. Not that she listens. Obviously.

I push the remainder of the Cos lettuce back into the fridge. The red peppers sitting there remind me of that old woman I bump into sometimes at the veg shop, with her bright red beret and matching shopping bag. I'm not sure about her at all. She just seems to stand around, smiling as if she knows me, and chatting to old Mrs Fleming. Maybe she's lonely, bless her. And why she wears a beret in the middle of summer, I have no idea. Probably feels the cold. But old Mrs Fleming, who runs the shop, doesn't seem to mind at all. She just carries on chatting, wrapped in layers of cardigans, her hands protected by bright woollen gloves as she dishes out the fruit and veg.

I'm not being derogatory when I call her old Mrs Fleming, you know. It's what everyone calls her, what we all know her as. She's friendly, lovely, knows everyone and what's going on with them. And she's recommended my catering business a few times, from what I've heard. Which is really good of her. No, she's lived in Folksbury (the next village along from us) for years. Well, we arrived in Pepingham in 2003 and she worked at the veg shop then, so that's thirteen years at least. A long time to be selling fruit and veg.

We arrived here after Claude was promoted. He works at the private hospital in Lincoln now, spends three days there with the occasional Saturday morning, then two days in Oxford, doing research at the uni. He's a well-known name in his field these days, works hard.

We're hoping Louis will follow in his father's footsteps, but the way he's going he'll probably end up in cardiology. His summer placement at the local Grantham hospital last summer kind of decided him. He only worked in the cardio suite for a couple of weeks, but it really grabbed him. So we'll see.

*

The Coffee Cup Cake is small, cosy, with floral chintz curtains and matching tablecloths. Vintage lamps hang from the ceiling, and there's an old piano in the corner. Music is playing in the background, Bob Dylan with *Mr Tambourine Man*. The aroma of roasting coffee beans hits my senses, but I stand at the door shaking the rain (as predicted by Louis) from my umbrella before ordering anything.

'Hi!' calls a voice from beside the piano. 'Rose?'

Nodding, I fold up my brolly and rush over.

A girl sits there, aged about seventeen or eighteen. I'd expected her to be older, somehow. She's attractive with red hair and brown eyes, and an oversized green hoodie, the sleeves pushed up to the elbows. She reminds me a little of Justine, my old friend from Sheffield. We still meet now and again, and she's agreed to help with our charity garden party in July, bless her.

She has a cappuccino sitting in front of her.

'You've already got coffee,' I say, disappointed. 'I was going to buy.'

'It's okay. I'll get you one.'

'No, it's fine. Thank you.'

Hanging my coat around the back of the chair, I wander to the counter and order a single espresso.

When I return, the girl's studying her phone, but then puts it away quickly.

I shake her hand. 'I'm Rose, obviously. Nice to meet you.'

'And I'm Sam. Good to meet you, too.'

We discuss her dad's birthday cake, going through the various options – fruit, sponge, colours, decorations – and come up with a chocolate cake that has a vintage motor bike on top, the rider sporting the number 50 on his back, in blue.

She's brought some pictures of Harley Davidsons and I place them inside my bag.

'Do you want me to bring the cake to the venue, or to your house beforehand?' I ask.

Her hand flies to her mouth. 'Gosh, I hadn't even thought about that.'

'Well, some people like to see the cake first, just in case.'

'Oh no, I'm sure it'll be lovely. I trust you. In fact, why don't you come to the party? Bring your husband, have a night out.'

'Thank you – that's very kind of you. But it's a Friday - he'll be working away.'

'Well, that's a pity. But you can still come - if you want to? It's the pub on the corner, on the way to Great Gonerby. Look, I'll text you the address.'

'Okay. Thanks. I'll bring the cake along on the night, then.'

'When do you want payment?'

'On the night is fine. I trust you, too.'

*

I bake chicken breast in garlic sauce for dinner. It's just me and the kids. Claude drives down to Oxford on a Wednesday night and doesn't return until Friday. After dinner, Louis and Violette escape to their rooms to carry on revising, while Lottie and I make a list of the ingredients I need for Sam's birthday cake. I draw the design roughly, on paper, until I'm completely happy with it. Lottie helps. She's very creative when she wants to be.

It's funny, I think, as I climb into bed later. When Claude first began to work away, I couldn't sleep without him. Now, it's easy. In fact, if I'm honest, it's easier. No being woken up at three o'clock as he patters to the en-suite, no-one to push the duvet away because it's too hot, no-one tossing and turning at six a.m. because he can't get back to sleep.

Closing my eyes, I snuggle down.

Okay, so maybe I'm just becoming Mumsy and boring in my old age.

Well, Claude obviously thinks so.

2

Claude Jolivet

Saturday July 2nd
It's July. The child before me should be looking forward to school holidays in the sunshine, not losing blood as I stand here watching. But his pressure's dropping badly, damn it. Lorraine's doing the best she can, using suction and swabs, but the dirty swabs are piling up way too fast.

I've had this before, I know what to do. But it's always stressful, shouldn't happen.

There's a sudden murmur from Will, the anaesthetist.

I look up briefly, and he nods.

Gratefully, I glance at the monitor. Pressure's returning, blood loss is slowing. I calm myself, take a huge breath, and carry on.

The kid's okay, the tonsillectomy will be a success.

I wash up, change out of my scrubs, grab my sports bag, and head towards the staff canteen. Lorraine's already there, blonde, pale, exhausted, a latte on the table in front of her, and a huge bar of Cadbury's Dairy Milk broken into pieces and laid out on its foil wrapper. Picking up a piece, she places it delicately between her lips.

I collect a cappuccino from the counter and sit opposite. 'Hi.'

'Hi.'

She nods towards the chocolate and I take a piece.

'Thanks.'

She smiles. 'You look as knackered as I feel.'

Covering my mouth with my hand, I yawn noisily. 'Yep. I am.'

'He's okay, don't beat yourself up. These things happen.'

'I know.' The coffee tastes good, and wipes away the taste of chlorhexidine that seems to invade my whole being today.

'So what you doing this afternoon?'

'Lunch, a jog, then time with Rose and the kids. We're supposed to be sorting out a holiday.'

'Good. You need one, I'd say.'

'We all need one. Louis and Violette have had tough exams this year, and even Rose hasn't been herself just lately. The only one who'll have any energy left is Lottie, although she can be a bit grumpy too, at the moment. No, a break will do us all good.'

Taking more chocolate, she nods towards it. 'Where are you thinking of?'

I help myself. 'Sun, sea and sand. Other than that, I'm not sure.'

'The Maldives are nice.'

'Hmm - bit expensive, aren't they?'

'You can afford it.'

'I do have a huge mortgage, you know.'

She grins. 'Cleethorpes it is, then.'

*

My run takes me along the Peterborough road, through woodland towards Bourne, then left to Spalding. I take over an hour, my mind in turmoil. That shouldn't have happened this morning. I shouldn't have let it happen. But Lorraine's right. These things *do* happen. They can't always be foreseen and we're trained to handle them as best we can, but I do feel the weight of guilt upon my shoulders.

Maybe it's because I have kids of my own.

But I shouldn't let it get to me. I must have helped thousands of children over the years, adults too. There are bound to be some slip-ups. I need to be able to push it away.

On the outskirts of Spalding, I pause to catch my breath, stretch my back, and change the music on my Apple watch. *The Police*. That'll raise my spirits.

So I continue on my way, eventually stopping at the deli. Their vanilla ice cream is the best, and I'm really in need of something cold and delicious.

I sit cross-legged on the grass with my tub of ice cream and a spoon, and watch the ducks sail gracefully along the river. It's peaceful, the water flowing by, and I find myself releasing a deep and prolonged sigh.

I definitely need that holiday.

*

Louis is in his room, on Snapchat or Facebook, no doubt, and there's the faint sound of *Imagine Dragons* echoing along the corridor. As I run inside to shower, I pop my nose around the door to say Hi, but he just nods and smiles, his eyes glued to his phone. At least he's no longer stuck in a book or staring at his laptop, trying to figure out scattered radiation or one of the other subjects they give them to study these days.

I really miss him when he's studying. I miss his chats, his intelligent, thoughtful, caring discussions about the world and all its foibles. But fair enough. I suppose if he wants to be a doctor he needs to put in the work.

Lottie and Violette are both attending birthday parties, so it's just the three of us for dinner. Chicken lasagne and salad. Rose is laying the table as I return from my shower. I eat ravenously, despite the tub of vanilla ice cream. Louis and I discuss his recent studies, and this girl he's met on Facebook. I ask if he'd like to go to the Maldives for two weeks, and he becomes really excited.

After dinner, he disappears to his room again, this time to shower, spray on an inordinate amount of deodorant, and disappear to the pub. The Royal Oak is where all the kids hang out, and it is a lovely summer's evening. Not a cloud in the sky.

Leaving Rose to finish tidying the kitchen, I carry my glass of Beaujolais into the sitting room. Sitting back into the Chesterfield, my free arm stretched out, I gaze at our beautiful and very pricey stone fireplace. I do wonder why we had to buy such an expensive house. We could have lived quite happily in a cheaper one. Although it is an investment, I suppose. These houses are fetching around the one and a half million mark these days. Not bad going, really. It's the garden that does it, I think. A couple of acres, leading onto the nice bit of countryside surrounding Pepingham. Which is a lovely village in itself. Village green, quaint shops, Parish church. Quintessentially English. Not unlike the villages in France, with their *pâtisseries* and their *boucheries*, I'd say.

We do visit home sometimes, to see Camille and Florian and their two girls, Isabelle and Elodie. Lovely kids too.

I gaze at the painting on the wall behind me. It's one Mamie painted just before she died, now set within a huge gilt frame. The picture is of Bandol Beach, a place we used to go each summer as kids. She's drawn herself walking along in a flowing pink dress and sunhat. It's a lovely painting, very well done. She'd only just finished it when she died. It was still on its easel, the paint drying. Bless her.

Rose and I ensure that one of our trips to Paris coincides with the *L'Angevine* in June – the fancy dress race Mamie set in motion. Camille and I finished it for her after she died, all the planning and the setting up. It begins in the *Bois de Boulogne* and finishes at the Palace of Versailles. It's thirteen miles long, a half marathon, and takes you along the banks of the Seine, through beautiful woodland and on, until you reach the Palace. It's named after Mamie, of course, and so far has raised over two million euros for children needing help with their education.

Mamie's death was caused by a myocardial infarction, a massive heart attack. One Sunday morning, it was. Pascal was there, of course, but there was nothing he could do. The ambulance came quickly enough, but she'd already gone.

She would be very proud of her fancy dress race.

It's funny, actually. I sometimes feel as if she is still with me. I feel her looking over my shoulder when I'm concentrating on something, or I catch a glimpse of her if I turn my head too quickly. It's only my imagination, I know. I'm a scientist, for goodness' sake.

It's Camille who does most of the work for the race nowadays, with a little help from Florian. The website, the sponsorship, the tee shirts, the mailing of the numbers and the timing chips – they all take weeks to set up, but she does it selflessly. I just wouldn't have the time, I'm afraid.

So it's just me and Rose sitting down with the laptop tonight. The Maldives looks inviting, and I'm sorely tempted. But the cost for five of us is prohibitive. It would probably mean foregoing our winter holiday in the Alps.

'We could do it on the cheap,' says Rose. 'The Alps, I mean. And it would be nice to go somewhere different, romantic. Wouldn't it?'

Romantic. She's right. We need that. We need candles and roses. Moonlight. I've been so tired, so tied up with work, so absolutely exhausted. We just flop into bed at night and fall asleep.

And it's been like that for months.

Placing her arm through mine, Rose snuggles up. 'There's an ad in the paper. Someone with a Lincoln number is advertising their place in the Alps. Four bed, skiing and boarding, lift pass included. He might be cheaper than a hotel.'

'I could have a look, I suppose.'

Pulling the *Standard* from the magazine basket, she pushes it in front of me.

'Here.'

I push it away. 'Oh, I don't know. I do like Chamonix.'

'It might *be* Chamonix. Anyway, just the once? So we can go somewhere more exotic in the summer? I've got this garden party to organise for the hospital as well, remember. So I'll be in need of a really nice break. Please?'

I ring the number. The woman on the other end says she's quite particular as to the type of person she lets to, and would like us to meet up. Her fees for a fortnight's holiday are very reasonable, plus she does have availability in the Christmas holidays. So we agree to meet.

'There. All sorted,' I say, placing my phone onto the coffee table.

'Can we book it, then? The Maldives? I'd really like to, Claude.'

Her blue eyes gaze beseechingly. How can I resist? I never could.

We book the holiday.

3

Noelle Angevine

Sunday July 3rd

Pascal and I never did get married. So he needn't have been so bothered about the children's inheritance, after all.

He did get married eventually, three years after my death. To a younger woman, a divorcée with a grownup son and granddaughter. And he's very happy, from what I've seen. Old now, but happy. She looks after him, I make sure of that.

I really should have seen the doctor before that Christmas. That dreadful, miserable Christmas. I really should have let him check my blood pressure. What a waste.

But then I have this unshakeable belief. Things are meant to be. *Everything* is meant to be.

There was a reason for my death.

The first few months were confusing though, I have to confess. I was in such a hurry to let everyone at home know I was okay, to make my presence known. I wanted them to stop worrying so much.

So I sent a lorry-load of feathers down to Camille. I know if people see a feather where there shouldn't be one, they think there's an angel about. So I sent loads. They were raining down.

It didn't work, though. Not one bit. Camille thought an animal had killed some seagulls in the back garden and went screaming for Florian. Not for one minute did she think I'd sent them. So I never tried again. Well, not with Camille, anyway.

I could have reincarnated, of course. I was given that option five years ago, after I'd had a nice long rest. But I refused. There's a reason for my being here, you see.

But I can't tell a soul. Not yet.

When it happened, when I entered the tunnel, I was absolutely fine, no pain, no regrets. It was Pascal who was upset. And my family, when they arrived. They were distraught, of course they were. But me - I was okay.

You see, my friend, the lovely friend who had always been there for me, my friend in the white cloak, was at the end of the tunnel to greet me. Smiling serenely, he held out my white cloak, my so delicate and so shiny white cloak, and placed it gently around my shoulders.

'Welcome home.'

My protection against the world. Always there. Ever present.

I merely nodded and pulled it around me. As if it was the most natural thing in the world. As if I did it every day of every week.

*

So I've spent the past twenty-one years waiting. That's why I'm here. Why I had to die when I did. I've been waiting. And watching.

It's quite fun, actually, being able to move from one place to another with just a thought. I merely think of somewhere, and I'm there. As simple as that. So I can travel to the places that would have taken days when I was alive, and all in the blink of an eye.

So I was there at the wedding. They looked so happy, Claude and Rose, and it was all very romantic. They held hands all the way through the service, they were so much in love. I confess now, I was a little worried when he told me he'd proposed. He'd only known her a few weeks, and I'd learned from Helena that she'd been engaged twice before. So, let's be honest, not a good track record. But at the wedding their love shone through like starlight, and I promised myself there and then to look after them, to ensure it lasted and that she'd never break his heart.

Then when Louis arrived two years later, their lives seemed complete. I was there at the birth. In fact I saw all three births. Such a wonderful thing to witness, a new incarnation, an old soul entering a new body. A brand new beginning.

The first time I witnessed a reincarnation, however, was a few weeks after my death. I was just settling in, my spirit guide Albert showing me around. The glass buildings, the beautiful gardens, sparkling waterfalls and blue skies. We were discussing the concept of the evil spirit when suddenly a slim, attractive woman with long brown hair approached.

I turned to her, gasped in amazement, and threw my arms around her.

'Estelle!'

'Noelle.'

'I don't believe it!'

We hugged each other tight, unable to believe our eyes.

She was all ready to reincarnate into a new body, a baby girl who would grow and live many, many happy years. Unlike her birth in 1922.

She had reincarnated once since her death, she said, but she was appearing to me as Estelle so I'd recognise her. But I would have known it was her, from the yellow badge she was carrying. She always carries it when she's here. It's her way of reminding people, of saying, *Don't ever let this happen again.*

She pulled at my arm. 'Come on, let's talk.'

We found a seat by the most amazing waterfall I've ever seen, its clear running water sparkling and glistening like crystal.

I sat beside her. 'I can't believe it's you,' I whispered.

'It is me. It's definitely me.' She pushed the yellow Star of David into my hand. 'Here, take this. I'm going back soon, and I need someone to carry it while I'm gone. We mustn't let anyone forget. Not ever.'

I took it from her, the yellow star that had been her death sentence. I expected it to be brittle and hard, but its coarse yellow cloth was like new, the word *Juif* still haunting, still sickening. Just the way it would have felt when she was taken from me.

'I won't let anyone forget. I promise. But how are you? Tell me what happened?'

'They took us, all of us, the men, the women and children. The men to the *Vélodrome,* the women and children to the *Parc. Les enfants!* No water, no toilets, hardly any food. They treated us like animals, *ma chérie.* Animals.' Tearfully, she shook her head. 'But it's a long time ago. It's over. Let us talk about you.'

'But – your maman, your papa?' I asked.

She gripped my arm. 'They shot Papa. A soldier made moves towards me – you know. And Papa intervened. He was shot down, right there, right before my eyes.'

'Dear God,' I cried, rage rushing through me.

'Maman was sent with me to the *Parc,* and then to the gas chamber.'

She began to cry, sobbing as if her heart would break.

I pulled her towards me. 'It's over now. Don't talk about it, Estelle. I shouldn't have asked. I'm sorry, *ma chérie.* So sorry.'

*

Estelle reincarnated not long after our reunion. To a happier place, a France of liberation and joy and, please God, no more bombs. Her soul is beautiful, her new body a chance to try again. To bring peace.

I also met Louis upon my arrival. Of course. My Louis. Still so proud, so brave, so articulate. No wonder I'd loved him for all those years. We've spent days talking, walking round, easing back into each other's company. He spends his time assisting hospitals - in the background, of course. Helping with new discoveries, providing clarity and inspiration. He says he wants to reincarnate with me again one day, but first we have work to do. As soon as we have finished, though, that is what we shall do.

So today I'm visiting an old farmhouse, the home of a Mrs Matilda Whirlow. I find her house warm, comforting, with its own memories, secreted away in little nooks and crannies, shadows of light and shade. Mysterious movements that shift at the very edge of your vision. But are comforting, nonetheless.

I visit every now and again. Her husband Andrew runs his own estate agency, is busy and sometimes quite stressed, what with the English economy in the state it's in. But he insists upon making time for Mattie and the children. Flowers, kisses, such joy at seeing them. Yes, he knows how much he loves her. And so does she. For they've lived other lives together, and they've not always been as happy as this one. So this time around, they're sealing their love with an unbreakable bond.

But there's a reason I must visit Mattie's house, and why I watch the children as they race around. A boy and a girl, Thomas and Lily. Beautiful children. As lovely as my own at that age. Eyes sparkling, teeth shiny white, arms brown with the sun.

But the reason I visit must remain a secret until the time is right. There are stirrings afoot; certain individuals who would use that knowledge to their advantage.

Mattie has her own guardian spirit, but she only appears when Mattie really needs her. Grandma Beattie was very close to Mattie when she was alive, but died when she was a mere teenager, so it seems natural she should wish to take care of her.

Mattie left university before completing her degree to marry her first husband, she was so much in love. But he was nothing like Andrew, didn't appreciate her at all. So yes, she's definitely had her share of troubles. Beattie was always there, though, always in the background, watching and guiding.

And look at Mattie now. Happily married with two gorgeous children, and that no-good ex-husband of hers living alone, abandoned by everyone.

So I watch. And I wait.

4

Rose

Monday July 4th

Well, what a pivotal day the ninth of June was. Not only did I meet Sam, agree on the design of the birthday cake and arrange to take it along to the party on the Friday night, I also met her uncle.

Because Sam is only the niece of Jason Stewart. My ex-fiancé.

And there he was, large as life. Propping up the bar, a pint of stout in one hand. I hadn't intended staying, was just going to deliver the cake and leave. But he saw me.

'Rose!' he called, bounding over in that unique way he has.

I turned, shocked at hearing my name called, his voice. Even though I'd already spotted him.

'Hi there, Jason.'

'My, you're looking well,' he said, hugging me.

'You, too.' I pulled back, smiling.

'Come on, let's catch up. You got time for a drink?'

I'll admit, I was curious. What had he been up to, who was he with? Did he have kids, a home, a mortgage now?

So I accepted. 'Okay. Thank you. Dry white wine, please.'

So we sat. And we talked.

Jason is Sam's dad's brother, her uncle. Thus the invitation to the party. He's never married, has no children, and is currently not seeing anyone.

He's spent his life travelling the world, by the sound of it. Which is what he wanted to do, I suppose. And after taking numerous college courses, he's made a living out of working as head or sous chef, depending on whatever's available in whichever part of the world he happens to be living in. Currently Enfield, North London.

'Why did you never marry?' I asked.

He looked at me with those soft brown eyes. 'You.'

My heart raced stupidly. What is this, I asked myself? I'm a happily married woman with three adorable children.

'Sorry,' he murmured. 'I didn't mean to embarrass you.'

I looked down at my drink. 'It's okay.'

'I was only being truthful.'

I had no reply to that, other than the question I'd wanted to ask for the past twenty-one years.

'So why did you go, Jason? What made you do it?'

He took hold of my hand. 'I'm truly sorry. I really am.'

I pulled away. 'You've not answered my question.'

'Because I can't, not really. I just wasn't ready to settle down.'

'I was devastated,' I whispered.

'I am really sorry, Rose.'

There was nothing else to say. Wiping at my sudden tears, I swallowed hard.

Uptown Funk was playing in the background, I noticed. I hadn't been aware of the music, just the sound of Jason's voice.

I lifted my eyes to his. 'Sorry I'm upset. It's just – all the memories.'

'It was a long time ago.'

'I know.'

'You're alright now, aren't you? You're married, happy?' and he smiled.

It was the smile that did it.

I hadn't seen Claude smile in ages, months. We'd not made love in months, hardly seen each other in months. He's married to his work. And I'm married to …

No-one. Nothing.

That's what it feels like. Abandonment. Total abandonment. Just me and the kids. What with his job in Lincoln, his work in Oxford, his research always going on in the background, I feel like second best. No wonder I'm miserable.

'How do you know I'm married?' I asked.

'Apart from the wedding ring, you mean?' He smiled. 'I came home from Australia in the January, after we split up. Bumped into Olivia in town. She told me you'd got engaged. A French bloke, I believe?'

I nodded. 'Claude. We have three children, a boy and two girls.'

He smiled again. 'Wonderful. I'm so glad you're happy.'

'Why did you come back, though? I thought you were staying out there?'

'I missed you.'

Tears formed again, soft tears that fell before I could blink them away, before I could run and hide. I brushed at them.

'Sorry. Again,' he said.

'I'm fine. Like I said, just memories.'

'I was an idiot, running scared. But at least you've come out of it unscathed. Three children. I'm happy for you.'

I smiled, suddenly aware of the time. Claude would be arriving home soon. But I couldn't just leave it like this.

'Listen, we should catch up properly,' I said. 'What do you think? Are you here just for the party, or are you staying a few days?'

He shook his head. 'I'm head chef at the Riverside in Enfield. I need to drive back in the morning.'

I was relieved, to be honest. I don't really know why I asked the question. Desperation, probably.

'It's okay. I just thought it would be nice, that's all.'

'It would have been, but I've only booked today off. Well, Rick's not fifty every year, is he?'

His hair still curls at the back, I noticed, although it's turning grey these days. And yes, he still screws up his eyes against the light. But now the lines he creates are permanent.

*

We've left Louis in charge of the girls. The drive to this woman's house takes forty minutes and is an easy enough drive. And we've brought cash to put down as a deposit on the chalet, assuming we're good enough. She rang earlier to check we were still going, and has obviously been doing some googling because she asked to speak to *Dr* Jolivet. Claude never uses that form of address unless he's on business.

The satnav tells us to pull up outside Number 43, a large Edwardian house with a small front garden and driveway. The house is immaculate, with green curtains at the perfect oak windows, and red and white petunias in pristine green planters. We walk up to the matching door, again perfect, with no dust on the step, no marks on the glass.

'No wonder she wants to check us out,' I whisper.

Claude presses the doorbell. 'I was thinking exactly the same.'

The door opens immediately, as if she's been looking out for us.

She's tall, slim, with greying wavy hair and keen eyes. For some reason I feel as if we've met before, but can't quite place her. Maybe she works in a shop somewhere.

She holds out her hand. 'Emilia. Pleased to meet you. Come on in.'

We enter, remove our shoes without being prompted, and follow her into the kitchen at the rear of the house. It's large, sunny, and the long table gleams with polish, despite being a rustic pine. She indicates for us to sit.

'Tea? Coffee?'

I nod. 'Tea, please – milk, no sugar. Thank you.'

'The same - thanks,' says Claude, sitting beside me.

She busies herself at the kettle. 'So where do you come from? Pepingham, did you say?'

We both nod at the same time.

'We've lived there quite a long time now,' I say. 'So we're no longer *incomers*, as they're called.'

She smiles. 'Yes, I've heard that expression. A strange one in this day and age, when we all move about so much.'

'Have you lived here long?' asks Claude.

'Not really. A few years.' Placing three cups of tea onto the table in china cups and saucers, she sits down opposite. 'Now then, to business. You said you'd like the first week in January?'

Sipping his tea, Claude nods. 'If it's still available. But first, could you tell us exactly where the chalet is? Is it convenient for the piste? What I mean is, do you need a bus or anything to reach it?'

We spend a good half hour discussing the chalet, the skiing, Claude's job, and the children.

'They sound adorable, your children.'

'Do you have children?' I ask.

'I never seemed to get round to it.' She passes us a plate of biscuits. 'So what do they want to be when they grow up, do they know?'

'Louis is hoping to study medicine, like his father,' I say.

'Are you at the local hospital?' she asks Claude.

'The private one in Lincoln, primarily. But I work in Oxford too, a couple of days.'

'Really? I have family down there. My sister. I visit every now and again.'

'Do you work?' I ask.

Sipping her tea, she smiles. 'I'm freelance. Advertising. Wherever the work is, really. Obviously I make money from my chalets, too.'

'You have more than one?' asks Claude.

'Just two. One in Engelberg and the other in Sassari, Sardinia. You don't fancy a summer holiday as well, do you?'

'Sorry - we've already booked,' I reply. 'We're going to the Maldives this year.'

'Very nice. I've never been myself, but I've heard it's beautiful.' She begins to collect our empty cups and saucers.

Claude takes the hint. 'The chalet sounds fine, just what we want. So are you happy for us to rent it?'

She smiles. 'Of course. You seem like a lovely couple, and your children sound adorable. I'd be happy to rent to you.'

'Great. So, here's our deposit. Two hundred, wasn't it?'

Placing the crockery onto the side, she accepts his roll of twenty pound notes. 'I'll just make out a receipt, then.'

She dashes into another room while we sit and wait.

'The trouble with owning your own place,' murmurs Claude, 'is that you feel as if you should go there every year. You don't get to see anywhere else. Mamie was the same. She did love Bandol, though.'

I nod sympathetically. 'We should go there again, take the kids. Maybe next year?'

Camille inherited the house in Bandol. I think Mamie knew if she left it to both Camille and Claude, they'd need to sell it in order to split the money. And

Camille was the one who would go there with Mamie every summer after her husband died.

But she's very generous with the house, doesn't charge if we want to visit. And it is beautiful.

But I'm so, so excited about the Maldives. Only four weeks to go.

5

Claude

Tuesday July 5th

I did my ward rounds this morning with a heavy heart. It's something Rose said last night, something that made me stop in my tracks and listen. I know, I'm a terrible listener these days. Too much going on in my head.

But it was important, and I *needed* to listen. Something about a shopping trip to London. By herself.

Rose never goes shopping on her own. Well, not all the way to London, she doesn't. Says it makes her feel like a sad old lady with no family and no friends. She usually takes Lottie and Violette with her, and she's even been with Camille and the girls when they've been over.

So tonight I'm going to ask her about it. Something isn't right.

But I continued my rounds in the usual way, nodding and smiling. As one does. Despite the concerns I carry for my marriage, and for my mother. Camille rang last night after we returned from booking the skiing holiday. Maman fell over in her apartment yesterday and was rushed to hospital. Such a shock. A fractured femur. It's only a simple crack, so they're hoping she won't need surgery. But we'll have to see. Rose is organising flowers to be delivered today, but I do worry about Maman now she's on her own.

Papa died two years ago. Cancer, it was. Very sudden, a complete shock for all of us. I think we're still reeling from it, to be honest. I know I am. There's the guilt as well, the feeling of not having spent enough time with him. Always busy, always got other things to do, never able to just stop, stop and take time out. For the people I love most. For myself.

You spend your life trying to get to the top, only to realise when you get there that it's not quite where you want to be. In the end. It takes too much of your energy, all of your time. Precious time that should be spent with your family, your friends. I really wish I could cut myself in half sometimes. But then, who would my other half spend the time with? My children? My wife? My mother, my sister, my friends?

I haven't seen Jerry and Ned in years. We swap Christmas cards, but that's about it. Jerry did marry Nicki. They had a beautiful service in her home village of Wentworth, and now have two girls. They live in Castleton, in the Peak District, not far from Jerry's beloved brewery. I last met up with him ten years ago. He was completely bald, which kind of suited him, and he had a slight paunch, no doubt the result of living near his beloved brewery. Which kind of suits him, too.

Ned married a beautiful blonde, slim, sparkling and gregarious. Too gregarious. She left him a few years later for some barrister she met whilst visiting her mother in Glasgow. He's never remarried, still lives in Sheffield, and travels round as a locum pharmacist. Well paid and more exciting than working in just the one shop, I'd imagine. But he doesn't seem to mind the bachelor life.

No. I need to cut back, spend more time at home. Which is easier said than done. I'm currently working eight hour shifts at the hospital, private and NHS, and then I'm in Oxford two days a week, researching hair cell regeneration. And there's my paperwork, of course. Emily, my secretary, does most of it, but I still have clinic letters and research notes to write up.

The team down in Oxford are wonderful, though, and I feel elated that we're actually trying to cure deafness, not just placing a sticking plaster over everything with hearing aids and cochlear implants. This study I'm working on is looking at why cochlear hair cells don't regenerate in mammals when they do in other species, such as birds and fish. It fascinates me. These particular cells are crucial in helping us detect sound waves, but they're easily damaged by loud noise. If we can discover why they *don't* regenerate, we could learn to trigger this regeneration and restore people's hearing.

Only last week we began work on researching the lining of the intestine, which does regenerate, every four to five days. We just need to find out why this doesn't happen in the cochlear. Amazing stuff.

This afternoon's theatre was a panendoscopy, an examination under anaesthetic of the aero digestive tract. There was a slight narrowing, so I did a quick biopsy. I don't think there's anything sinister, it was just to make sure, to ensure the clinical outcome is top-notch, as Rob Meakins says. He's the top otolaryngologist for this area, keeps an eye on everything. Nice chap.

*

My run takes me out to Spalding again, and I stop for ice cream at the deli. It's eight o'clock and the temperature's still in the twenties. I sit on the grass beside the river to eat my ice cream, wiping the sweat from my brow with the back of my hand.

The air is so still. I watch as a parade of ducks shimmies along the edge of the riverbank, before silently jumping in. And above the sound of the occasional car passing, there's the faint echo of children playing in the park along the road. Closer still is the sound of beer-drinkers exchanging banter outside the Boat Inn. I turn to look, but a cluster of grasses and poppies, their orange heads nearly fluorescent, blocks my view. So I gaze at the soft clouds hanging in the distance, and watch as they move slowly towards me.

I miss the days of wandering along to the pub and just sitting, taking in the world around me. Maybe that's what's missing in our lives, mine and Rose's. We really should make a concerted effort, wander along to the pub more often, meet up with friends more often, just walk up the road more often. We hardly go out at all. No wonder she's so bored. She's become very quiet, very reserved, just lately. Hardly said a word in the kitchen after dinner last night.

Something's wrong. I know it.

*

I wait until both girls are asleep and Louis is allegedly in bed, but will in fact be chatting via social media to that girl he fancies. Apparently, she's at Lincoln uni, so they'll have plenty to talk about.

I check the clock on the mantelpiece, the one we brought back from Paris, black marble with an ivory face and gold hands. Rose loved it so much we couldn't resist. She was seven months' pregnant at the time with Louis. I remember every single minute of that pregnancy, we were so happy.

It's ten thirty. Rose is ironing in the kitchen, watching a Maggie Smith film on the small TV in the corner. She looks tired after her day, which included having to drive the girls to their music and dance classes. The roads are so busy these days it can be exhausting just driving from one place to another. Then of course she has to sit outside in the car and wait for them. But she's such a caring mother, never complains once.

I make tea for us both and sit down at the table.

'So what was it you were saying last night about going to London?' I say.

So intent is she on the film she doesn't respond immediately. When she does reply, she's cool, calm, avoids eye contact, checks the ironing, watches the film.

'Yes. Thursday. I'm going on Thursday. It's okay, isn't it, Claude? I just need some *me* time - you know, before the kids break up. I mean, I can always take the girls once they've finished for the summer. I know how much they love it. But I really wanted to check out the cakes in Harrods and Fortnums, and do a little clothes shopping. You don't mind, do you?'

She does have a point, I suppose. It's probably easier to do research like that on your own, although we do have the internet these days. It's not like it was when she first started out, back in the nineties, no internet, no smartphones, no information at the touch of a button. *Mon Dieu*, how things have moved on. And the clothes shopping – well, I can kind of understand that, but she usually likes to take Lottie with her. Her fashion guru, as she likes to call her.

Eh bien …

So I agree. I agree to her going. Not that she needs my agreement, she's her own woman. But given the way things have been over the past few months, I am a little worried. Stupid, I know. She loves me, I know she loves me, but I've been so busy I've not had the time to reciprocate, not properly.

Well, let's hope our holiday in the Maldives will give us the time we need. I certainly could do with it, and I know she could.

So we go to bed and we make love. But I'm tired, she's got backache from gardening, and it ends up being a quick fumble with no foreplay and no romance. Frankly, I'm shocked at myself.

I lay there with this feeling of being dragged down, of a heaviness inside my chest, of sorrow and hurt and pain. What's going on, I ask myself? Do I no longer love her? Does she no longer love me?

I turn to her. She's nearly asleep, her arms tucked behind the pillow, her face squashed against it.

'I love you, Rose,' I whisper.

'Mm – me too,' she replies.

A warm tear forms in the corner of my eye, and I turn away.

6

Rose

Wednesday July 6th

That Peggy Fleming does make me laugh. Well, she is the theatrical type, with her scarlet lips and fingernails, and the scent of patchouli that seems to follow her everywhere. She works for the local greengrocer's shop in Folksbury, not too far from where my Claude lives. You can see her outside in all weathers, rearranging the produce on the old barrow, her long fingers wrapped in woollen gloves, chatting to people, watching and listening.

The first time we met was in her kitchen two years ago, on a cold snowy evening. And for some reason we got to discussing the trials and tribulations of relationships, marriage and so forth.

'You're not telling me Louis was the love of your life, then you go and jump into bed with a man twenty-five years his junior!' Peggy exploded.

'Twenty-five years can make a lot of difference,' I replied.

She grinned wickedly. 'Oh. I see it now. So *that's* why you jumped into bed with a man twenty-five years his junior!'

You can see why she makes me laugh. And why she's known locally as old Mrs Fleming. She's an entertainer. Old Mrs Fleming is a bit of a misnomer, really, because even though she's in her seventies she's as sprightly as anything. All helped, I'm sure, by the witchcraft I know she practises. You see, she doesn't just work at the greengrocer's for money. I'm sure the money helps, of course it does, but there's more to it than that. Because working there lets her keep an eye on everyone. You see, Peggy is a legally ordained Wiccan High Priestess - a special white witch to you and me. There's a white witch in every village and at least one in every town.

That's how I've come to know her. Her revered status allows her to communicate with us on the other side, whenever the need arises.

I've also met Peggy's friend, the white witch for Pepingham, where Claude lives. Enid Phelps is a darling, always there to help. She does have trouble with her knees sometimes, but I ease them as best I can, sending warm thoughts and calming air. Her cat Genevieve knows when I'm around, though. My goodness, does she know when I'm around. Walking along with her tail in the air as if to say, *I know you're there, and I'm watching you.*

Hah! Des chats!

Peggy also introduced me, in a manner of speaking, to Mattie Whirlow and Victoria Seaborne, both friends of Enid's. In fact, they're the reason we got together. Now Mattie I've been keeping an eye on for a while, but Victoria's only just come into the picture. A slip of a thing she is, reminds me of myself at that age. Well, apart from the promiscuity and the sleeping around. For, even though I lived in Paris, the city of love, we still had our morals.

But at the tender age of seventeen, Victoria has been around a bit, as they say. *La promiscuité* has affected every part of her life, her self-esteem, her health, her happiness. Or it did, until she met Enid and Peggy.

Peggy was contacted by Victoria's guardian spirit, you see, an old sailor called Johnnie Seaborne. Between them, they helped get her life back on track. If they hadn't intervened, I dread to think what might have happened. Poor Victoria tried to commit suicide.

But no. Victoria, or Tori as she likes to be called, is special, and Peggy's asked me to watch over her. She's working hard at school now, thank goodness. Says she wants to be a politician, to help people, to stop the violence, the bombs, the hatred. I really hope she succeeds.

No, she *has* to succeed.

We're not at war now, of course, not like the terrible goings-on of 1914 and 1939. But the terror is still there. Only in November last year, there was a series of mass shootings and a suicide bombing, all co-ordinated, all over my beloved Paris. They killed one hundred and thirty people, ordinary people who had never harmed anyone in their lives, and injured hundreds more. They'd planned it so everything happened all at the same time – a concert hall, a stadium, restaurants, bars. Awful. Terrible. Words fail me.

And it has to stop.

*

Today, however, I'm more worried about Claude. There's trouble brewing and I need to ensure he comes through unscathed.

He's trying to do his work, trying to help people, just the same as Tori. He wants to help them live normal lives. Yet he's worrying too much about his marriage, concerned at the way Rose treats their relationship, like a soiled rag to be discarded once the cloth's worn through. Bless him.

I'm concerned at the way she's treating their relationship. How dare she? How can she break his heart when he's done nothing but adore her, grant her every wish, and love her with every breath of his body?

Mon Dieu!

She met an old beau on Monday, you know – an old *fiancé*, and I get the distinct feeling she's transferring her affections to him. Just a feeling, you understand, but it's not a good one. I also think there's more to it than sits upon the surface.

The thing with my Claude is, he won't allow himself to make mistakes. He's a perfectionist, has to do well in every part of his life. His studies, his work, his relationships, even his hobbies. And let's face it, they all interact with one another, don't they? When one of them isn't working to full capacity, the others suffer too.

For instance, if he stopped running, his health would suffer, he wouldn't have the energy for his work, his research, his children, his wife. If he didn't do so well at work, his family would suffer. Smaller house, fewer holidays, less money available for piano lessons, dance lessons, and so on. No. Claude likes to keep a tight ship. Much like his grandfather before him.

So what he would do if his marriage floundered, I dread to think. But I have a really bad feeling.

*

So I'm back in Folksbury, contacting Peggy again. She needs to know exactly what's going on. Maybe she can help.

She's cleaning the outside step of her little cottage, a two-up, two-down, dust rising through the warm air as if it's never seen the back-end of a broom before. She coughs, rushes inside and returns with a bucket of warm soapy water.

As the water runs along the path, carrying the dust with it, I make my presence known with my own kind of dust. Stardust, the tiny motes that appear in the sunshine. And I'm only just in time as it's eight thirty, and not too long until the sun sets.

'That you, Noelle?' asks Peggy, leaning her brush against the wall. She's dressed in dungarees and a tee-shirt, her grey hair swept back into the bun she always wears. My, what long legs she has. Apparently, her mother was a dancer in the West End. Very good too, from what she's said.

I smile quietly. 'Here I am again. How are you then, Peggy?'

'Fine. At least I was until you appeared. Is it Tori again?'

'Not this time, no. It's my grandson, Claude. There's trouble about, and I might need a few favours.'

'Now you know I don't deal in anything that's outside of my jurisdiction. I'm assuming, of course, he's over in France?'

'Actually, he married an English girl. He lives just outside Pepingham, not far from Enid's place.'

'Oh? Whereabouts?'

'One of the big houses on the main Grantham road. High Grange, it's called. With the big gates and the dragon's heads on the posts.'

'Dragon's heads?' she queries.

'It was owned by a Chinese bloke before Claude bought it.'

She thinks about that one. 'Ah, I remember. Mr Tsang, the one who ran that engineering firm in Grantham. He sold to a French bloke, some consultant at the Lincoln Hospital. Is that your grandson, then?'

'That's him. That's Claude.'

'It's a nice house. So why do you need my help? Looks like he's doing okay all by himself.'

'There are some things money can't buy, Peggy. You of all people must know that.'

Nodding sagely, she picks up her brush. 'Come on inside, Noelle. The neighbours must think I'm potty standing out here talking to myself.'

*

So Peggy and I concoct a plan. If Claude and Rose live not far from Enid, it should be easy for her to befriend them. Somehow.

'There's a birthday party coming up. Thomas Whirlow, he'll be ten soon. And Enid's been invited. Let's see if we can't get Claude's kids invited too.'

'Oh, I think they might be a bit old for that,' I say.

'Oh. Right.'

'But Rose makes birthday cakes for a living. Would that help?'

The twinkle in her eyes says it all. 'That's just what we need. *Just* what we need, Noelle.'

So I watch. And I wait.

7

Rose

Thursday July 7th

Pulling up beside the Boar's Head in Grantham, I drop off Violette and Lottie so they can walk to the grammar school. Parking is ridiculous around here.

Violette has rehearsals for the school show after her lessons, so she's quite nervous. But she'll be fine. She's so confident and beautiful she'll wow them all. Takes after her Grandma Noelle, I'd say. Violette takes after me, and Louis takes after his father. He's at home now, lazing around, exams and lessons all finished for this year. He'll still be in bed, no doubt, on his phone.

Claude drove down to Oxford last night as usual, so I've been left to my own devices. As I park my car at the station, I'm wearing a linen trouser suit and silk cami, all matching in sky blue, and I carry a neat straw bag upon my shoulder.

I buy my ticket from the machine on the platform and climb aboard the 8:34 to Kings Cross. Placing my cappuccino and Daily Mail onto the table, I remove my jacket and fold it carefully across the seat beside me. Making myself comfortable, I pick up the paper and read. But the news is full of Brexit and the Chilcot Inquiry. What on earth's going to become of this country I don't know, but it's all doom and gloom at the moment. So I turn to the *Femail* page and brush up on denim jackets and off the shoulder tops. Not that I'll be wearing them (well, maybe an off the shoulder would be nice for the Maldives), but I like to study the pictures, keep up with the times.

We change at Peterborough, and I find another table seat for my newspaper.

I awake to the sound of the guard as we approach Kings Cross. Checking my mascara in my hand mirror and reapplying my lipstick, I pick up my bag, leave the paper, and queue at the door.

Suddenly, I have butterflies.

As I jump down from the train, I can see him beyond the ticket barrier. From a distance, he's the same person. Not put on much weight, despite a lifetime of working in kitchens. The same boyish look, the same walk as he ambles towards me. We hug, and he wraps his arm around my shoulders.

Today is supposed to be a catch-up. Two friends catching up on old times. But it doesn't feel like it. It feels as if we're back in 1993. To where we were. Before that stupid Oasis concert turned his head.

I don't feel bad, I don't feel as if I'm cheating on Claude. No. Claude is the love of my life. I'm just meeting an old friend, chatting about old times.

I mean, why not?

'I have until two thirty,' Jason announces. 'Then it's back to work.'

'That's fine. I'll do a little shopping before I go home. I'm picking the girls up from school at seven. Violette's got a show rehearsal, and Lottie's staying to watch.'

He smiles. 'So where shall we go? I thought a coffee, somewhere nice?'

The sunshine hits us as we leave the station and, for the first time in months, I feel alive.

'I need to visit Harrods, and possibly Fortnums. That's my reason for coming here. I want to study the cakes, to see exactly what's trending at the moment.'

'So shall we do coffee out in the sunshine, a nice pavement café, then wander along to Harrods?'

I nod. 'Sounds lovely.'

'You're doing well with the cake-making, then?'

'Of course. I do parties as well now, not just the cakes. It's great fun, I love it.'

'So we've nearly ended up in the same line of business. How weird is that?'

Jason texted me a few days after his brother's party, and we've been in touch ever since. He then suggested meeting up and well, here we are. Outside a small coffee shop where we can sit and watch the people passing by. Everyone's in a good mood, chatting and smiling in the sunshine. We order two cappuccinos and wait.

'Does your husband know you're here?' he asks.

I blush, my heart racing. 'No. No, I thought he might get the wrong end of the stick.'

'So that's why Harrods and Fortnums,' he says, shrewdly.

I bite my lip. 'Yes.'

He shakes his head at me.

I smile. 'I know. Not very good of me, is it?'

'As long as the children don't get hurt.'

'Why would they? We're just friends, aren't we?'

'We are. But someone I worked with in Delhi once told me an old Indian story, and it is this. 'One day, Love and Friendship met in a bar. Love said, *Why do you exist when I already exist?* Friendship smiled and said, *To put a smile where you leave tears.*'

'That's lovely,' I say, 'but Claude and I are fine. Really. He's just busy all the time.'

'And you're feeling left out.'

I change the subject quickly.

'So when on earth did you go to Delhi? How exciting! I'd love to see India.'

The waiter brings our coffees and we busy ourselves, not quite knowing what to say, taking too long to open the small mint chocolate that's been placed upon our saucers.

'Mm, nice,' I say as it melts against my tongue. 'I love mint chocolate.'

'Me, too.'

'So come on then, tell me about Delhi.'

'I lived there for quite a while, actually. I met someone in Melbourne, the typical Australian, wanted to travel, see the world. She was planning on going over to Delhi for work, so I went with her.'

Suddenly I'm jealous. 'Were you together long?'

He nods. 'A while. We worked at the Central Secretariat, which is kind of like our Houses of

Parliament. Wow, such a beautiful building, you wouldn't believe. We only worked in the kitchens, of course, but what an experience. I learned such a lot.'

'So what's it like - India?'

'The first few months we just travelled around, to be honest. Until the money ran out. Taj Mahal, the pink city, the Ganges. Awesome.'

'Wow, wonderful. So how long did you stay there?'

'Three years, just over. It was amazing – the colours, the heat, the people. The cows. The traffic! Which has to be seen to be believed. No such thing as elf and safety in Delhi. They just pile themselves into, or onto, anything that moves. And the Highway Code – forget it. No such thing.'

I laugh. This is the Jason I knew and loved. 'It all sounds a bit too hair-raising for me.'

His eyes light up with his smile. 'It was. Believe me, it was. We travelled round on a scooter, but honestly, you were taking your life into your own hands. And the honking – oh my God, the honking.'

'What?' I asked, puzzled.

'If someone's in your way, you don't wait for them to move. Oh, no - you press your horn and you move into the most convenient space you can find. Whether it's legal or not, whether there's enough room or not. People will always get out of your way. Can you imagine - millions of people all pressing their horns, one after the other, for hours on end? Bloody exhausting, I tell you.'

'So why did you stay so long?'

His eyes gaze into the distance. 'I loved it. The only reason I left was that Shona and I split up. And I needed a change.' Focusing on me now, he shrugs. 'You know me.'

'And Australia?'

'Awesome, too. You practically live outside through the summer. Unless you work in a kitchen, like me. But when I was off, it was just beaches and barbecues. The night-life was amazing. Wonderful weather, lovely people, but the job situation wasn't great. I didn't stay long. It was difficult to find work and I was struggling, to be honest.'

I'm disappointed. 'Oh. I'm sorry about that. It was your dream, wasn't it, to live over there?'

'Don't be sorry, Rose. I've had an awesome life. I wouldn't have had it any other way.' He takes hold of my hand. 'Except for you. I messed up there, good and proper.'

I feel dizzy, my heart pounding. 'Jason …'

'I know. You're happily married, you have three children, and I was a fool to let you go.'

I pull my hand away, to the consternation of the two old women watching us from the next table. 'You're right on all counts.'

Soft tears fill his eyes. 'Sorry. I shouldn't have asked you to meet up. Stupid of me.'

He stands up, pulls a ten pound note from his wallet and throws it onto the table.

My throat aches as I cry out. 'Jason, you can't go. We have too much to talk about, too much to say.'

He smiles. 'I'm sorry. Really. You're sweet, kind and gentle, and I did an awful thing. I'd only end up hurting you again.'

I collect my bag, take his arm, and pull him away, towards Oxford Street, away from prying eyes. Reaching the safety of an empty bus shelter, I turn.

'We're just friends, Jason. I'm in love with Claude. You could have anyone you wanted. How could you possibly hurt me again?'

'It's the way I am. I end up hurting everyone.'

'I don't believe it. You were just immature, you wanted to see the world. You'll settle down at some point, I know you will.'

I expect more self-recrimination, a grumble about how badly life has treated him, jokes on the subject of settling down, of never growing up.

But no.

He turns, pulls me to him, and kisses me.

8

Claude

Friday July 8th

This morning has been so interesting. Sometimes I wish I could just give up medicine and go into research for the rest of my life. But I suppose there's the mortgage, the children, the holidays, the cars. *N'est-ce pas?*

Then there are the children. No, the other children. The ones who wouldn't be able to hear properly, talk properly, communicate, earn a living and live full lives, without my help.

So I continue. But always with the thought that one day - one day my help will no longer be needed. We'll be able to prevent deafness, loss of hearing, with a simple procedure performed by a nurse, or even just a change of diet. Who knows? Approximately one in every thousand babies is born with a severe or profound hearing loss that will affect their whole life.

So if I can do something about it, I must.

I decide to eat lunch at a nearby café instead of the uni canteen. It's much too nice to stay inside. So I walk along Oxford High Street towards Radcliffe Square. The area's teeming with tourists, most of whom are queuing to see the Radcliffe Camera, built to house the Radcliffe Science Library. It is indeed a very imposing, very beautiful building. I keep promising to bring Rose and the kids down here for a long weekend, but we haven't managed anything yet. Life is so busy.

I find a table in a small courtyard café. It's filled with small citrus trees in pots. The ripe lemons and leaves provide a welcoming backdrop to the tables and chairs. As I choose a seat, the warm sun is on my back, the air is alive with the chattering of people and the singing of birds, and I'm happy. To have the ability to do something useful, exciting, at the edge of the future, fulfils me more than words can say.

I order chicken schnitzel and salad from the waiter, and pour water into my glass from the huge jug he's brought. A couple walk by, arm in arm, and I think of Rose. How she would love it here. We really do need to arrange a weekend. I could stay over one Friday and she could drive down with the kids. There are plenty of hotels to choose from; they really would love it.

I'd have liked Louis to come here for his degree, he's clever enough. But no, he doesn't want to mix with the high and mighty of Oxford. Which is such a shame. But it's his life, I suppose, and I've done pretty well myself as a graduate of Sheffield uni. Very well, actually. Can't complain.

So I'm in a complete daydream, sipping water and watching the people pass by, when a shadow falls across my table. I look up. A woman stands there, a grey shawl wrapped around her shoulders, a clip fastening her hair into a knot on top.

Bewildered, I stare at her. And then I recognise her.

'Emilia!' I exclaim. 'How are you?'

She smiles. 'My friends call me Emmy - please. I *thought* it was you. I've been sitting over there, in the shade. Much too hot for me.' She points towards a table beside the café window. 'I've just had lunch with my sister, but she's popped to the shops while I settle the bill.'

'Of course. You have family down here.'

She nods. 'So are you here in Oxford with that lovely wife of yours?'

'Rose is at home, unfortunately. No, I'm working here. I do research. I mentioned it before?'

'Oh. Yes, of course. Sorry.' She looks suddenly confused. 'It's just - I'm sure I saw the two of you in London yesterday, so I assumed …'

'Did you? No.' Then I remember. 'Actually, Rose *was* in London yesterday, but she went by herself. I was here in Oxford, working.'

'Oh. Right.' She smiles quietly.

'I spend two days a week here. Rose was doing her own research, actually. Checking out cakes and so on.'

'Oh?'

'She likes to see how shops like Harrods, and Fortnum and Mason, design their cakes. What's up-to-date, what's trending. Fashions for these things change all the time, don't they? So she likes to see what's going on in the big city.'

She shakes her head determinedly. 'But I could swear I saw her with you yesterday. You were drinking coffee outside a café. Not far from Kings Cross, it was.'

My stomach lurches, but I smile carefully. 'No. You must be mistaken. There are lots of women with dark hair like Rose's. It could have been anyone.'

Even though she has to fake the dark hair these days, I think.

So what else is fake? Her excuses for travelling alone? Her reasons for going to London? Her declarations of undying love?

I feel sick.

'Well, that's a pity,' says Emilia, smiling. 'You looked like you were having such a good time.'

I shake my head. 'Sorry, but she was definitely alone yesterday. And I was definitely in Oxford.'

She turns to leave. 'Well, I'd best meet up with my sister. It is such a beautiful day, isn't it? Enjoy the sunshine, and *bon appetit*!'

'Thank you,' I reply, and she's gone.

The waiter brings my lunch, which looks perfect. But I've lost my appetite suddenly. What had begun as a beautifully sunny lunch break is turning into a nightmare.

Could she be right?

Is Rose cheating on me? Was she with another man yesterday? Oh, my God.

I eat mechanically, the food sits like a lead weight, and I need to walk.

So I walk, along to the shops.

I walk, hoping to see Emilia and her sister. I want to ask more questions, get more information, more detail.

And yet. I don't.

So I return to work, confused, unsure, utterly miserable.

*

My journey home is tiring. The Friday night crawl along the A1 takes hours longer than it should. And my concentration is lacking, having had the most exhausting afternoon where nothing seemed to make sense, my mind a rabble of incoherent noise.

I walk through the door and she greets me as always. But not as always. Something has changed, I can feel it.

We kiss and hug, and exchange pleasantries. But all the while I watch her. The TV is on in the background, she is setting the table for me, and the children are squabbling over some programme or other. I can smell salmon frying and my mouth waters, my stomach never having registered the food I ate at lunchtime.

'Had a good day?' she asks.

I nod, throw my car keys onto the table, and sit. 'Lovely, thank you. How was yours?'

'Busy. I called into town for holiday stuff, did the food shopping, and came home. I managed to get those beach towels I saw. Ten per cent off.'

She smiles as if nothing is wrong.

But it is.

'Great, good,' I reply. 'So we're all set, then.'

'Just about. Cup of tea, darling?' and she returns to the salmon.

'I'll make it.' I put the kettle on, turning to Violette. 'So how's the show coming along?'

She looks up, her long hair so like her mother's, her smile so like Mamie's, serene, composed. 'Amazing. Totally amazing, Dad.'

I grin. 'It's *that* good, is it?'

'Well, no. Like, Mrs Woods was in a really bad mood cos it wasn't going right. But then Ellie, who's got the part of Maria, brought it round, and it was just awesome.'

'So when do we get to see it?'

'Mum's got tickets for Wednesday, the first night. And Granny's coming to see it, too.'

Her excitement is infectious, and I grin stupidly as I pour boiling water into the pot. Maybe Emilia was wrong about seeing Rose in London yesterday. Maybe her eyes *were* playing tricks. Maybe my imagination is playing tricks, too. Didn't she just call me darling, after all? Or maybe I'm just fooling myself.

Rose's mum, Carol, is in her seventies now, but still as youthful as ever. She always visits when there's a school show or a presentation of some kind, wouldn't miss it for the world. I usually enjoy her company, but today …

Today, I wonder if she knows. Whether she knows her daughter's so unhappy she may have travelled to London to meet another man.

Then another thought. One I've avoided, denied, so far.

Did they sleep together?

Did they have coffee, a double espresso, a large cappuccino? Did they kiss? Did they actually check into a hotel and spend the afternoon together?

9

Noelle

Saturday July 9th

As I said before, I was there at the wedding. Rose looked so beautiful, so very, very happy. Her dress was pure ivory silk, draped across her chest and shoulders, falling into a train that fell to the floor in long folds. She held ivory roses, held together with delicate pink ribbon to match the flower girl's headband. Isabelle was the only flower girl she had. But she looked so sweet, throwing pink rose petals onto the aisle and the grounds of the church. They married in Sheffield, of course, near her mother's home. Such a beautiful day.

A pity I could only watch from beyond the veil. But I had a front row seat, and my joy was as real as that of Valerie and Carol.

They chose a small wedding, thinking they could put the spare money to better use. So they sold

Claude's cottage and bought a four-bed in a lovely green suburb of Sheffield. But then Claude was headhunted, so they had to sell up and move to Pepingham, a village in the beautiful Lincolnshire countryside. And what a house *that* is. Originally an old barn with four acres of land, an extension had been added, creating five en-suite bedrooms, a playroom, a pool, a study, a huge kitchen, and a utility room. And the lounge! I have sat in that lounge beside Claude for hours while he works on his laptop. He must find it so peaceful, so relaxing. Such colours – turquoise, reds, pinks.

The house is wonderful, a good place for the children, away from the hustle bustle of the outside world, a place to grow, to study, to become the people they're going to be.

But there is danger afoot. Danger that, if I'm not careful, will take their wonderful marriage and their beautiful children to the brink of destruction.

I have to do something. And soon.

*

I visit Peggy Fleming again. She's in the small scullery adjoining the rear of the house. It used to be an outside toilet, I think, but now houses a washing machine with a tumble dryer on top. A rack hangs overhead and she's removing white pillow cases and towels as I approach. The heavy scent of washing powder hangs in the air, taking me back to when I washed nappies for Valerie and Matthieu, to a time when all I had to do was take care of them, play with them, and take them to visit Maman before dinner. Ah, those days. I will never forget.

Peggy looks round. 'That you again, Noelle? What is it this time?'

'Sorry to interrupt your work, Peggy. I know you're busy on a Saturday.'

'It's okay, I've just about finished. But I *was* going to put my feet up with a glass of red.'

'It's about what we were discussing before – about Claude?'

She folds a towel neatly, corner to corner, and places it into the basket by her feet. 'Let me put this lot away first, then we can talk.'

I watch as she folds everything neatly, filling up the basket. The chirping of swallows fills the air as I wait patiently, taking in the sunshine and the birds, and the joy of standing in an English garden.

Finally, Peggy picks up the basket, carrying it into the house on her hip.

'Could we stay in the garden, Peggy?' I ask.

'Of course, no problem, there's no-one around. I'll just get some wine, then we can talk.'

So we sit. And we talk.

I miss the taste of red wine, but I can still smell its aroma. It reminds me of home, my beloved Paris, of times spent with my parents and Louis. Of meals out on the Champs-Élysées or the restaurant we used to frequent, the one overlooking Bandol Beach. Ah, such times.

I've already filled Peggy in on the detail, the meetings between Rose and the ex-fiancé, and the woman Claude met in Oxford. She's of the same opinion as me. That Rose is being led astray for a reason.

'But why would anyone do that?' I ask.

'I don't know. We need to dig deeper.'

'We certainly do.'

She sips her wine. 'More to the point, why would anyone watch her drinking coffee with another man, then make out she'd thought it was Rose and Claude together?'

'Maybe she genuinely believed it.'

'But isn't it a bit coincidental?' she says.

'What?'

Peggy waves her glass through the air, the huge gold ring on her left hand glinting in the sunshine. 'That woman, that Emilia. She was lying. How come she's in London, in the very same spot as Rose? How come?'

'You're right. You're so right. In the whole of the city of London, she happened to be in the same place as Rose, at the very same time as Rose.'

'More to the point, she was in the same place as Rose *and* in the same place as Claude the following day. Far too coincidental for my liking.'

'Something definitely isn't right,' I murmur.

'Are you able to watch her?'

'Who?'

'That woman – this Emilia. We need to know what she's up to.'

*

Now I have a confession to make. And you'll probably think this quite hilarious. I do, now I look back on it.

The day Claude and Rose were married, I wanted them to know I was there with them, I wanted them to feel my presence. I hadn't been away that long, and I needed them to know I was a guest at their wedding, that they had my blessing.

So what did I do?

I sent feathers. I know I'd already tried it with Camille and she ended up screaming her head off, but I thought if I was more discreet, Rose wouldn't be so upset. Also, I sent them down to the kitchen, an unlikely place for feathers to appear. The first one landed right in the middle of the room, just beside the table Rose was sitting at while her mother arranged her hair. But they were so busy chatting, so excited about the day ahead, and the dinner they'd had with Claude's family the night before, they didn't spot it.

So I sent another. Then another. And another.

It makes me giggle now, just thinking about it. In the end, there was a huge pile of white feathers in the middle of the kitchen floor, and still they hadn't noticed.

It was only when Rose stood up, brushing her blue dressing gown against the floor, that the feathers flew up, high into the air, round and round and round.

She gasped in amazement. 'Where on earth did they come from?'

'You must have left the door open,' replied her mother.

'No – I don't think I did. We'd have noticed.'

Crossing her arms, her mother smiled slowly. 'Well then, it must be an angel, my love. An angel, come to bless your marriage.'

I wouldn't quite describe myself as an angel, but I do need to make sure their marriage is safe. I have other work to do as well. But I shall come to that later.

*

So I visit this woman, this Emilia. She's still in Oxford, still visiting her sister. The sister is older, and I recognise her.

Emilia is in the kitchen, making tea. The window looks out onto a lake, large ornamental gardens, and woodland. The kitchen is light oak, expensive-looking, a large island at the centre of the room.

Emilia calls out. 'You want cake?'

Her sister walks through, dressed in a long crimson kaftan. I definitely recognise her, but her hair is different. When I met her in Paris, she had dark, corkscrew hair. Now, twenty-one years later, she has it straight and long, fastened into the nape of her neck.

'Just a small piece,' she replies. 'I'm still losing all that weight I put on over winter.'

'The six o'clock curfew, that's what you need,' says Emilia, cutting her a piece of sponge cake.

Olivia sits at the table. 'What's that?'

'No carbs after six o'clock. Someone at work tried it. She lost over a stone, looks amazing.'

'I'm fine, really. There *are* other ways, you know.'

'Well, just be careful, doing stuff like that.'

I stand there, beside the window. I know exactly what she's talking about. She's used it before. And yes, she does need to be careful. Very careful.

So I watch. And I wait.

10

Rose

Sunday July 10th

Mum arrived last night. The children came to the station with me, they were so excited. Well, apart from Louis of course, who's so laid-back he's practically comatose. He does love his grandma, of course he does, it's just uncool to show affection at his age.

I usually look forward to Mum coming over, too. There's something about her being around that makes me feel like a child again. Carefree, silly, buoyant. No worries, no cares, no hang-ups.

But today it's different. I am worried. I do have cares.

I mean, how can I forget?

His kiss. Warm, gentle, lingering, as if he had all the time in the world. As if he actually wanted to be with me.

I know. I'm not being fair on Claude. He's the love of my life. But it's like he doesn't see me anymore. His mind's on his work, his research, the *L'Angevine*. Which is all well and good, and I know it brings home the bacon and helps lots of other people. But I need someone I can talk to, sit down with, someone who has time for *me*.

Which Jason has.

Maybe we could just be friends?

Or maybe not. He wants more. I know he wants more. What was it he said? We're from the same place, the same time. We have the same background, working class, the streets of Sheffield, the crags of the Peak District. Not Paris, not the city of Paris, with medicine going back generations and a bloody holiday home in Bandol.

Yes, we talked. We talked about my life, about the children, my business, about Claude and his family. About us.

He definitely wants more.

So now Mum's home, the kids are all excited, and we're walking down to the Royal Oak for lunch. Claude needs to finish his accounts, so he'll join us later.

Which is all well and good, but at three o'clock I have to leave to throw a kid's party in Bamburgh.

Maybe I should give up my job. Then I wouldn't have to dash off all the time, wouldn't have to be up at all hours finishing off cakes and buns and jellies. But I love it. It fulfils me. It makes me the person I am.

The Royal Oak is buzzing. We sit outside in the sunshine, order drinks and ice (at Lottie's insistence - *it's like, so hot, Mum*), and gaze at the menu.

230

Within seconds, Lottie's checking her phone. 'Mum, Jessica's got a puppy, and he looks so cute. Can we have one? Please?'

She looks at me beseechingly, but I tut-tut and shake my head. 'Sorry, darling.'

Louis throws down his menu. 'I'll have the scampi, I think. Thanks.'

Lottie does the same. 'Me too, please, Mum.'

Shaking her head and nodding, Mum answers them all at the same time. 'Your poor mum doesn't have time to look after a puppy, she's enough on her plate. And yes, you can have the scampi, both of you. We just need to know what Violette wants now.'

Glancing at the menu, Violette shrugs. 'I'll have the scampi, too, please.'

'Okay, love,' says Mum, standing up. 'Three scampies it is.'

'We're paying,' I say.

She picks up her bag. 'No, it's my turn.'

'You've only got your pension, Mum. Keep it. Treat yourself.'

She shrugs and winks at Lottie. 'Well, okay, if you insist. We can go and spend it round the shops then, can't we?'

Lottie, my fashion guru, smiles back, dimples lighting up her face. 'Okay, Gran. But I'm at school all week, remember.'

'I've remembered, don't worry. We can go on Saturday morning. Assuming you've got the energy. Gosh, I remember what those school shows are like. Exhausting!'

'They're not, Gran. They're awesome!'

'You try being on the other end of one. Backstage with ninety-odd kids, or directing the show, or up front organising the punters. I've done the lot. Exhausting, I tell you!'

*

I arrive at Mattie Whirlow's farmhouse ten minutes late. My timekeeping has not improved over the years. The door is open, so I make my way inside, looking for her.

Her kitchen is just beautiful. Window seats with cosy striped cushions, a rustic pine table, long patchwork curtains quilted to keep out the cold. There's no-one around, but the back door is open. So I walk through, to the sound of music and children playing.

The garden is something else. Whereas ours is a myriad of flowers - hollyhocks, roses, petunias, poppies and grasses – surrounding a lawn, their garden is an orchard, full of apple trees and pear trees. I have often wondered what it looks like, to be honest. Whenever I walk past the high walls in the Springtime, all I can smell is the scent of apple blossom. Sweet, haunting apple blossom.

But today the garden is awash with children. The bouncy castle appears to be the favourite thing, but there are also wheeled items littering the place. Scooters, bicycles, dolls' pushchairs.

Just as I spot the long trestle table, Mattie runs towards me, her long dark hair piled onto the top of her head.

'Rose! Thank goodness you're here.'

'So sorry I'm late. I had to drop Lottie at her friend's house. She's such a social butterfly, I don't know where she gets the energy. She's got another show on tonight.'

She smiles. 'No, it's fine, don't worry. I was panicking, that's all. But come on, I'll show you where everything goes.'

I've made a Lego cake for Thomas. It's one of his favourite things, apparently, and such an easy design. A big yellow head with the hat tilted, made from sponge and icing. Then various colours of Lego bricks, all made from marzipan, fall from beneath the hat. Simple, but very effective.

The rest of the food I lay out quickly. I've made buns decorated with pirouettes of chocolate or vanilla icing, finished off with cherries, or sprinkled with hundreds and thousands. Then there are huge cookies, ginger, raisin and chocolate. And miniature brownies, cream horns, cheesecakes, and chocolate cornflake bars. Then there'll be strawberry jelly with strawberries and ice cream to follow. The ice cream I've made myself, using vanilla pods. I place the jelly, strawberries and ice cream inside the fridge and freezer until needed. Mattie's insisted on sugary delights only, no slimy ham sandwiches, no pizza, not even cheese and onion crisps. She says it's a thing she has, left over from her childhood. And who am I to argue?

Thomas, who turns ten today, squeals with delight when he sees the cake. Which makes every minute of my hard work worthwhile. He seems such a lovely boy, sensitive and caring. His sister Lily makes up for it, though. A proper tomboy, she is. But they're always smiling, always happy. Like Mattie, I suppose.

*

233

It's seven o'clock and I'm all in. The children have left with their parents, the garden is littered with plates, bowls and plastic cups, and bin bags full of paper from present opening and pass the parcel. And the bouncy castle has been unplugged, ready for the chap to collect in the morning.

Thomas kicks a ball against the wall while Lily chats to some friends of the family, an elderly woman in her sixties and a bloke, tall and jolly, wearing a worn tweed jacket. They're deep in conversation as I approach.

Mattie comes up to me, an empty bin liner in her hand. 'How you doing, Rose?'

Hot and sticky, I brush the hair from my face. 'That bouncy castle looks like how I feel.'

'Me too. Where these kids find all their energy beats me.'

The elderly woman pulls a small brown bottle from her handbag. I recognised her earlier as the lady who hangs around Folksbury greengrocer's, the one in the red beret. It's far too hot for berets today, though. Smiling, she walks towards me, her brown eyes crinkling at the edges and heavy golden hoops adorning her ears. She holds in her hand a small brown bottle.

'Try this, my dear. Sorry, but I couldn't help overhearing. You just put a few drops onto a tissue and breathe in.'

Her voice is warm, kind, with a touch of Cockney. I accept the bottle.

'Thank you. But what is it?'

'Let me introduce you,' says Mattie. 'This is Rose, who made the party food and Thomas's beautiful cake.

And this is Enid, an old friend of the family. Benjamin over here is another old friend, who's come all the way from Edinburgh for our party, and is staying here for a few days.'

Benjamin smiles, his blue eyes soft and friendly. 'It's lovely to meet you, Rose.' His voice has a lilt to it that I can't quite place. Definitely not Scottish.

I nod and smile. 'It's good to meet you, too.'

'Enid's a gypsy,' Mattie continues, 'who has all sorts of powders and potions in her bag. If I were you, I'd keep a watchful eye on her.'

Enid laughs. 'You watch what you're saying, young Mattie, or I'll get my broomstick out!'

'No – it's witches that have broomsticks, not gypsies,' I say. 'Gypsies have caravans and crystal balls.'

She looks at me oddly. 'Here, I'll fetch us some tissues.'

Two minutes later, she lets three drops fall from the bottle.

'Just frankincense with a little sweet orange. It's a pick-me-up, helps you feel better. I mix my own, you know.'

I breathe in deeply. The spicy, peppery scent fills my nostrils. But as it does so, a vision of Claude fills my head, The Claude I met in Sheffield all those years ago, bumping into me on the street corner with his brown tweed hat and the grey trench coat that matched his eyes. I feel again the joy, the overwhelming joy of meeting him for the very first time.

Tears fill my eyes.

'You alright, Rose love?' asks Enid, gently.

I nod. 'Fine. Just tired, I think.'

'I thought it was supposed to make us feel better,' says Mattie, smiling accusingly.

'It makes you feel however you should be feeling, whatever is best for you at any moment in time. It relaxes the mind, so you can think straight.'

I wander away, into the kitchen. I need to be alone.

So I can think straight.

Is Claude best for me, then?

Is that what my mind is trying to tell me?

11

Claude

Monday July 11th

It's really good having Rose's mum around. It makes the house feel more homely somehow, having a mother figure here. Of course, I know Rose herself is a mother, but not to me. And I miss that, even though I'm a grown man. No, it's a good feeling, and I know the children love having her around, too. Just as I used to love Maman and Papa being around. And then, of course, Mamie.

I still get the feeling Mamie's in the room with me. The scent of her perfume, the sparkle of her stardust. The perfume must be my imagination, and the dust motes – well, they're only dust motes, *n'est-ce pas?* But somehow they belong to her. And I find them comforting.

I'm a scientist. I don't believe in spirits. She's dead. Gone.

And I shouldn't need comforting at my age. I'm a grown man. But sadly, I do. I've not been sleeping, can hardly eat, get palpitations at the slightest hint of stress. My God! How on earth do I carry out my work? I should be the cool, calm surgeon, completely in charge of the situation, not the man in the white coat who loses his temper at the slightest inconsistency. Pah!

She's lying to me, I know she is. She's talking about driving Carol home at the weekend, to save her the train journey. But she's never done that before. So why now? Is she meeting that gigolo, that rogue, that stealer of another man's wife? Who is he, anyway? Where did she meet him?

Is she sleeping with him?

*

It's lunchtime. I wander through the corridor to the staff canteen. The aroma of roasting chicken fills my nostrils, but I'm not hungry. As the sound of cutlery scraping against china greets me, I see Lorraine sitting there, an empty chair opposite. But I can't do it. I'm not in the mood for chit-chat, as friendly as she is. Not today.

So I turn on my heels and I walk away, back along the corridor. Dodging the trolley being wheeled carefully out of theatre, I make my way outside. Blinking in the bright sunlight, I find the sun on my head soothing, nurturing, and I relax for the first time since Friday, since the day I met Emilia in Oxford.

Maybe I'm worrying about nothing. Maybe she was genuinely mistaken and it wasn't Rose at all. Maybe I should just ask her. Communication is the key to a good marriage, after all.

So why don't I? Is it because I'm afraid of the answer? In truth, I haven't been paying her much attention just lately. I've been so busy. But she's been rushing around, too. She always is during the heady days of summer. So it's not just my fault.

But we do need to make the effort.

The Maldives should do it.

Definitely.

So I carry on walking, fast, until I reach Lincoln's High Street. I continue, past the proliferation of charity shops that has sprung up over the past few years, past M&S and Next, and on. Until I reach a small café with tables outside. Sitting at the table nearest the door, I breathe in the scent of coffee beans and sugar.

I order a large cappuccino and a cheese and ham toastie. It's the nearest I can get to a *croque monsieur*. There are newspapers set out on a side table, so I go to pick one up, *The Independent*. But as I do so, I sense someone watching me, a woman, seated just inside the window. I turn to look directly at her and she looks away. She looks familiar somehow, but I can't place her. Long, dark hair, fastened into the nape of her neck. Sunglasses that fill her face. Slim. No, I can't place her at all. I must be mistaken. Ignoring her, I sit down and concentrate on the paper. It's full of Brexit, and the reason why David Cameron is resigning. Or jumping ship. However one sees it.

I look up briefly as my lunch arrives. The woman has gone. That's funny; I'm sure I would have seen her leave. I shiver, and a cold, silvery hand runs its way down my back. Get a grip, Claude, I think. You're tired, stressed. No-one is watching you, no-one's interested in you. Paranoia, get thee behind me.

Lunch is enjoyable, although I confess to preferring French cuisine. Obviously. So I pay my bill and walk back to the hospital. It's a pleasant enough walk, but once again I feel unsettled. Suddenly my life is upside down, inside out, fearful. What the hell is happening?

There's only one thing for it. I need to ask Rose for the truth. No matter how much it might hurt. Emilia may be wrong. In fact, it's highly likely she *is* wrong. She's only met Rose the once, and that was only for an hour or so. Sighing, I push through the main door, walk along the corridor, apologise to Emily for my tardiness, and sit at my desk. My next patient has been waiting ten minutes.

He's ten years old, has a history of recurrent sore throats, but is otherwise fit and healthy. His left tonsil swells up every time his throat is inflamed, so his doctor has referred him to me. It's the first time I've seen the child and he looks nervous, his eyes staring, his hands fidgeting. I try to put him at ease by talking about Lottie and the Shaun the Sheep Movie she can't stop watching. Ever. They're roughly the same age, so I can only hope for the best.

But - success. It puts a smile onto his face.

'So, Ryan, is it alright if I take a look at the back of your throat? I promise not to hurt.'

He nods shyly.

I lean forward, tilt his head back, and place my mirror inside his mouth. The tonsil is badly inflamed and looks painful. I sit back.

'Thank you, Ryan.'

He closes his mouth.

I turn to his mother, a woman in her thirties with a large gold handbag and a worried expression.

'It's nothing to worry about, Mrs Simpson. Ryan has tonsilloliths - tonsil stones to you and me. Little bits of debris that form in the crevices of the tonsil.'

'Are they curable then, Doctor?' she asks, anxiously.

'Definitely. It's definitely curable. He'll have to have a procedure, but I'll try to keep the tonsil by just removing the stones. If that's not possible, then it will need a tonsillectomy.'

As I open my appointment book, I see the fear on the child's face.

'It won't hurt one little bit, I promise. Then afterwards, we'll have strawberry jelly and ice cream for dinner.'

*

I sit, a bottle of *Whitstable Bay* in my hand, as the TV fills the room and Louis stares at it, goggle-eyed. The girls squabble over some friend or other, and Rose is in the kitchen baking for a silver wedding anniversary tomorrow.

No, I haven't asked her about London. She and the children were in the kitchen when I got home, and it's not the type of thing one discusses in front of the children. Anyway, where does one start, how does one begin? *A woman saw you in London with another man? Are you cheating on me?* Or – much worse and I'm not sure I want to know - *Do you still love me?*

So I sit, and I watch the film. It's *The Martian* with Matt Damon in the lead. The kids love Matt Damon.

Yet. I don't watch the film. My mind whirls and pushes and pulls, and swirls and sways, until I can no longer think of anything, other than the fact that I must be going mad.

Then I can't see the film at all. A small cloud of dust motes appears, right in front of my eyes. Even though the curtains are drawn and there is no sunlight. I close my eyes, thinking they must be overworked, tired. But no, the cloud is still there when I open them. Stardust, sparkling flecks of dust, hanging in the air before me.

I stare at them.

And as I do so, a warm feeling seems to slide across my shoulders, as if someone's placing a coat around me. Hugging me, enfolding me, calming me. If I didn't know better, I'd think it was Mamie, because I can smell the spicy vanilla notes of her perfume. Again!

Shaking my head, I stand up, walk through the stardust and stride out of the room. I must be going mad. There are no such things as spirits. Mamie is dead.

Even though I could really do with her right now.

12

Noelle

Tuesday July 12th

I really need to be more careful when there are children around. That dark-haired boy at Thomas's birthday party, for instance. I just know he was watching me, unsure if I was supposed to be there or not. I did try hiding behind one of the glorious old apple trees they have, but he'd already spotted me. I'm just thankful he didn't start screaming and pointing. Which has happened before. No. I've learned to keep out of sight when children are around. They're closer to the spirit world than adults, haven't been away that long, so are more sensitive to the vibrations we produce.

I do love them, though. I often hang around Camille's home in Paris, just so I can be with Isabelle and Elodie. Such beautiful girls. Admittedly, Elodie is a little spoilt, being the baby of the family, but at the age of nineteen she's a complete darling. I don't actually think Camille intended having another baby after Isabelle, but after I died she needed something to fill the void. Bless her.

So Isabelle is at the *Université Paris Descartes* studying medicine. Of course. But Elodie has rebelled and is studying fine art at the *Université Panthéon-Sorbonne*. They share an apartment with two other girls in the Latin Quarter near the universities, and are having a wonderful time. I visit occasionally to check up on them. Although I confess to sometimes reliving my own youth as well.

Oh, how different was Paris in my day, the days of restriction and war, uncertainty and fear. The freedom they have now, the gaiety, the absolute surety that life will be good, is so wonderful to see. I do hope it will continue.

*

Today I'm actually visiting Tori's apartment. She lives here with her mother and grandmother, and Peggy has asked me to keep an eye on them all.

Like Mattie, she has her own guardian spirit, an old sailor. He's known as Great Uncle John, but he actually goes back many generations. Peggy says he only turns up at midnight, so he's not here just yet.

It nearly is midnight, however. The bewitching hour. Tori's mother and grandmother are already in bed, and she's sitting on the sofa watching some film on her computer, the kind that sits upon your lap. Looks like the film is something to do with her studies. She does work hard.

The room is dark, apart from a candle she's lit that sits glowing upon the mantelpiece. She has large headphones over her head and is watching the film intently. So intently that she doesn't see the molten wax as it leaks from the candle's cheap paper casing.

The flame follows at speed. Bright and hot. And moving. Suddenly the mantelpiece is ablaze and Tori hasn't even noticed.

I panic. I have no means of putting it out, and no way of warning her.

So I try the only thing I can do. I speak to her.

'Tori, there's a fire! You need to get water!'

She doesn't respond, just carries on watching her film.

I try again, louder.

'Tori, there's a fire! Stand up! Be quick! Fire!'

Suddenly Great Uncle John is beside me. He wears a scruffy flat cap, his shoes drip with salt-water, and he reeks of alcohol. But he's here.

'Tori!' he shouts. 'There's a bloody fire! Get theeself to the tap, girl!'

I join in, screaming at the top of my voice.

'Tori! There's a fire! Get up!'

Within seconds, she's pulled off her headphones, stood up, and has seen the fire. Rushing to the sink, she soaks the tea towel and throws it over the flames.

Ouf!

The fire is out.

She looks a little perplexed, unsure of what just happened. And she'll have a bit of explaining to do in the morning; there's wax everywhere.

But she's alive.

I look round. Great Uncle John has disappeared, like a puff of cloud. Probably gone back to his ship.

I immediately report to Peggy, who's in her own kitchen, a warm dressing gown on. She's reading a book at the table, a large glass of red wine beside her. Sitting down, metaphorically speaking, I breathe in its scent.

She turns to me. 'Noelle? Everything okay?'

'Not really,' I sigh.

Removing her reading glasses, she stares at me, concerned. 'What is it?'

'I've just been to Tori's place, as you said.'

'And?'

'There was a fire. It could have been dangerous. Really dangerous. But we – me and Great Uncle John - we got her to put it out. The damage isn't too bad but, *mon Dieu*, it could have been disastrous.'

Shocked, she stands up, her hand going to her chest. 'My God! Is she alright?'

'Sit down, Peggy. Everything's fine.'

'Did you see any malevolences?'

I shook my head. 'No, no, I didn't. I didn't look, I was too shocked. Why?'

'No. It's fine. As long as she's okay. Thank you, Noelle, thank you for being there.'

I look her in the eye. 'Just who is it who's out to harm her, Peggy? Why am I watching her? Tell me?'

So she sits back down, takes another sip of her wine, and she tells me.

'I – I had a child. Many years ago. Her name was Millie. Beautiful, she was. She ran into the sea at the age of four, and she never came out. Suicide.'

Soft tears bead her lashes, and she blinks them away.

I put out my hand to comfort her. 'I'm so sorry.'

'I was contacted after that, for the very first time. This spirit just appeared as I was coming home from work one night. Said she was a white witch and had something to tell me. I'd never heard of Flora Middlewood before that. An evil, evil woman.'

She's so enraged by the memories, she finds it difficult to continue, so just sits there.

'Go on, Peggy. Please.'

Gulping down the rest of her wine, she pours another glass and sits back.

'She told Millie to kill herself. But the spirit, the white witch I met, never said anything about Millie having killed herself before. In other lifetimes. But she did. For some reason I don't yet understand, this Flora encouraged her to commit suicide in nearly all her previous lives.'

'Oh, Peggy ...'

'You see, Noelle, Tori is the reincarnation of Millie. We found out last year, Enid and I. She has a birthmark that exactly matches the one Millie had. It marks the place where she injected herself with morphine in 1914, the first time she killed herself. We have a hypnotherapist friend called Benjamin Bradstock. He regressed Tori, so we could trace her previous lives.'

I could hardly bear to look at her, I was so upset. 'Peggy. How awful.'

'It's nice to think she's back here with me, even though she's no longer my daughter.'

'You do get to see her, don't you?'

'Sometimes. Enid has stayed in touch with her, so we meet up now and again. She's a lovely girl. But I'm afraid it looks as if this Flora Middlewood is still intent on killing her.'

'What?' I gasp.

'The spirit I met said Millie had lived before, that she was a wiccan, destined to do great things. But Flora Middlewood had stopped her, would carry on stopping her. Tori's had hypnotherapy now, so she's cured of trying to commit suicide. But there are other ways of killing someone.'

'So you think this Flora set fire to the candle on purpose?'

She nods. 'She really is evil. '

I hiss like a cat, I'm so angry.

'We need to set more Duk Rak in place. I'll ring Enid.'

'Duk Rak?' I say.

'It's a form of protection. Enid's a gypsy by birth, and her family used it all the time. It surrounds the home with a powerful force, a psychic energy. Like healers when they lay on their hands to cure people. You can direct this energy into protecting a place, too. But you have to know what you're doing. So we need Enid.'

*

It's after three in the morning. Peggy has gone to bed, so I decide to check in on Claude. He's fast asleep, his arm around Rose, his right leg sticking out from beneath the covers. It's a warm night, I can tell that. The window is open to let in the air.

Only a quarter of the moon is visible after the new moon last week, so it's inky dark. There's not a sound, not a whisper, not a breeze.

I feel anxious for some reason. Something isn't right. Why is everything so still? It's unreal. Has time stopped? Is something about to happen?

I hover at the end of the bed.

I fall to thinking about my own marriage, my own husband. So brave, so strong. All those people he helped. All those brave men he helped escape. He could have been shot. *Mon Dieu!* He could have been shot.

There's a shadow. A shadow falls against the curtain of the open window. Someone is out there.

I move to hide, then realise there's no need. I can't be seen. Of course I can't be seen.

Yet the shadow doesn't move, no-one comes inside. How did they get here, though? The gates have an entrance code.

My first concern is for the children, and I prepare to check their rooms. But something holds me back. Some kind of sixth sense is pulling me back, telling me to wait.

So I watch. And I wait.

13

Rose

Wednesday July 13th

I wake up with the alarm, but then drag my feet getting out of bed. I'm exhausted, agitated, feel as if I've been awake all night. I really need that holiday in the Maldives.

But I manage to shower and dress, plaster enough makeup on to hide the bags, and am making cereal and toast when the others come scrambling into the kitchen. It's Violette's school show tonight, and she's so nervous she can barely eat, anyway. So I pack Caesar salad for her lunch, with lashings of shaved parmesan, her favourite, and tuna sandwiches for tea. They're all staying on after school to get ready for the show. Violette's one of the Jets, so it's not a major part, but still quite good. And despite her nervousness, I'm sure she'll be amazing.

So Mum and I drop the girls off at school with a *Break a leg!* to Violette, and drive on into Grantham. There's a chap selling Tibetan Terrier pups, and after our conversation at the Royal Oak, I've promised to buy one.

Just for the record, the conversation went something like this:

Lottie: *Jessica's got a puppy, Mum. It looks so cute. Can we have one? Please?*

Mum: *Your poor mum doesn't have time to look after a puppy. She's enough on her plate.*

Me, one hour later: *Lottie, stop going on about having a puppy. It's just not do-able, my darling.*

Enid Phelps (the lady with the red beret, sitting at the next table with her bloke, whose name I can't remember, but who seemed very nice): *I'll dog-sit, if you like, my dear. I don't charge much. I can take it for walks while you're at work, and look after it when you go away. It would do me good to get a bit more exercise.*

Me: *Oh no, it's alright. But thank you for the offer, anyway.*

Lottie (now in floods): *Mu-um! Please!*

So that's where we are. The dog seller.

But oh, they are so beautiful. There are three puppies to choose from, and we take ages choosing. In the end, after copious details of our house and our background have been shared (this bloke doesn't sell to just *anyone*) we choose the smallest and the cutest. Like a ball of fluff, she is.

*

It's nearly teatime. We're eating early so we can get to the show before it starts (unlike last time when they had to sneak us in at the back). Mum's made a quick meal of fish, oven chips, peas and carrots, all smothered in parsley sauce, followed by home-made brownies from the freezer, and custard.

Bonnie's asleep, curled up in the brand new bed Mum insisted on buying. There's a small pink blanket in the corner (she is a girly girl, after all) and a squeaky toy shaped like a cricket bat (not very girly) for her to chew. A tray of newspaper sits beside the back door, our attempt at house-training.

Claude has come home on time for once. Marvellous what he can do for the children. But we're all very excited and a little nervous on behalf of Violette, so everyone's happy.

Lottie comes up to me as I fill the kettle, her soft grey eyes pleading. 'Will Bonnie be okay if we leave her by herself, Mum? She's not really used to our house yet, and she might be upset when she wakes up and there's no-one here.'

'It's okay,' I reply. 'I've rung and asked Enid to babysit. You know – the lady at the Royal Oak? She should be here any minute.'

My words are barely out when the doorbell rings and Bonnie wakes up. I gave Enid the code for the gates earlier, so she could come straight through the garden and up to the door. I pull it open, Bonnie at my heels.

'Enid – come on in.'

'Thank you, my dear. It's nice to meet you again.'

I gather Bonnie into my arms as Enid smiles at me, at the children, and then at Claude.

'This is my husband, Claude. Claude, this is Enid, my new friend. We met at the birthday party on Sunday, and she's kindly offered to babysit Bonnie for us.'

They shake hands, smiling and nodding.

'Come on,' I urge. 'I'll introduce you to Bonnie.' I place her back into her bed, which she immediately begins to chew. 'Oh no, Bonnie!' I exclaim.

'You need to give her something to chew on,' Enid says.

'There's a cricket bat thing somewhere,' I insist, searching for it. 'Ah, here it is.'

But Mum interrupts. 'Rose, we need to go or we'll miss the beginning.'

'And they might not let us in this time,' says Louis, fiddling with his hair in front of the mirror.

There must be a girl in school, I realise, smiling to myself. Those were the days.

We drive to school in two cars as Claude has to drive straight down to Oxford afterwards. I wish he didn't have to go. I love us being a family like this, and Mum being here seems to remind me of how things should be.

*

West Side Story is ablaze with colour and song, rhythm and energy. There are tears of joy and tears of sorrow.

Mrs McPherson, the headmistress, introduces it as one of the best shows the school has performed. And even though I'm convinced she says that every year, this year I think she may be right. It's amazing how a few teachers can guide so many children into such a small space and make something so wonderful come out of it.

And Violette. My Violette. My heart swells with pride. Claude, too, has tears in his eyes as we applaud at the end.

We leave the main hall, I kiss him goodbye, and he hugs me close before climbing into his Audi.

The rest of us wait for Violette to change so we can take her home. Her face is flushed, and her eyes shine with so much passion I worry she may be coming down with something.

I feel her forehead. 'You alright, darling? You look a little hot.'

'Oh Mum - you do fuss! What did you think to the show?'

*

Enid is snoozing on the sofa as we walk in. Bonnie's also asleep, snuggled into her lap. The house is quiet, but there's the faint scent of patchouli in the kitchen that disturbs me. Then I realise it's probably just one of Enid's oils. I put the kettle on, then sneak back to the lounge to shake her awake. But Violette has woken her already, and is playing with Bonnie, chasing her round and round.

'You should have come to see the show, Enid. It was amazing,' she's saying, breathlessly.

Enid smiles. 'I'd love to see it. Is it on all week?'

She pauses to nod enthusiastically. 'Every day until Saturday.'

'Come and sit down, darling,' I say, going to undo her lovely long hair; she's had it in a ponytail for the show. 'I don't know if there'll be any tickets left, but I can try. When would you like to go, Enid?'

She looks up, her eyes soft and warm from sleep. 'I can go any evening, really. But I'd need two tickets, if that's alright. Then I can take my friend Harry.'

Picking up Bonnie, Viloette sits down. 'Is he your boyfriend, Enid?' she asks, cheekily.

'I suppose that's what you could call him, yes. We've not known each other long, but yes, I suppose he is.'

'How did you meet?' I ask.

'Well, he's the brother of Bill Mitchell, an old friend of mine. Bill used to live just round the corner from me, and Harry inherited the house when he died. I started to pop in now and then, just as I always had with Bill, and I suppose it began from there, really.'

'That's so sweet!' exclaims Violette, gushing theatrically and releasing Bonnie to the floor.

I smile. 'It *is* lovely, Enid. And I'll do my best to get you some tickets. But I'll pay for them, as a thank you for coming over at such short notice.'

She stands up, the gold bangles at her wrist jangling. 'It was no problem at all. I'm always around, and always happy to help. But thank you, anyway, it's very kind of you.'

'Shall I drive you home? I know it's not far, but it's getting pretty dark out there.'

She nods. 'Thank you. That would be nice. I'm not afraid of the dark, but these old knees aren't what they used to be, especially at this time of night.'

Mum walks in with a tray of tea and biscuits. 'Here we are, everyone. Then it's bedtime. Especially for little starlets who have another amazing show tomorrow.'

Bonnie chooses just that moment to wee on the floor.

*

It's only as I return from dropping Enid off that I notice the loose soil outside the kitchen door. As if someone's been digging the garden. I'm confused at first, but then I remember we now have a puppy in the house. Enid must have let her out. Of course.

Still, before I go to bed I check all the windows are closed. Louis has his opened, but I close it and admonish him. We're all on the ground floor, it's a bungalow, and even though the gates to the road have an entry code, there are fields behind us.

I'm not usually so anxious, but something has taken hold of my mind and I can't seem to shake it off. Maybe it's the thought of Claude driving so late at night.

I ring him, but he doesn't reply. He has Bluetooth in the car, but he doesn't like to answer, says it distracts him.

It takes me ages to get to sleep.

14

Claude

Thursday July 14th

Last night's show was brilliant, amazing, in fact. It really is a talented school. But Violette was the star, as far as I'm concerned. She sang and danced beautifully, and her acting was spot-on. I couldn't take my eyes off her, in her black capri pants and ballet shoes. My beautiful daughter.

It was certainly worth the long drive down to Oxford afterwards. Although it was uneventful with very little traffic, so I arrived at my hotel just after twelve thirty. Not bad going, really.

I am a little tired and groggy this morning, though. I've been drinking coffee to keep me going while I read this report on the 'regeneration of cochlear hair cells in birds after damage'. It's interesting, informative, even though it does occasionally make me yawn my head off.

The findings state that mammalian cochlear hair cells never regenerate, either spontaneously or after being damaged through trauma. But lower vertebrates such as fish and birds have the ability to regrow these cells. We already knew that, but this most recent research confirms that after regrowth of the hair cells, birds can definitely hear again. More to the point, this regrowth is spontaneous. Now if we can somehow stimulate this hair cell regeneration in mammals, we could restore hearing function.

As Louis would say in his teenage vernacular, *this is what we're talking about.*

I'm supposed to read these findings from Professor Anthony's report, then write my own notes on what we should do from here. We need to find a way to stimulate these hair cells, either by 'waking up' dormant stem cells in the cochlear, or by grafting embryonic stem cells onto the cochlear. Plan B sounds the most promising, as it would help the cells differentiate into hair cells to take the place of those missing.

This work is so exciting I've nearly forgotten about lunch. But then my stomach rumbles loudly, reminding me. I fancy a walk to the courtyard café again. It's such a lovely afternoon, and the fresh air should wake me up a bit.

So that's what I've done, and I'm now sitting in brilliant sunshine, *The Independent* in one hand and an espresso in the other. This time, though, there's no Emilia out to ruin my lunch, no weird feeling of being watched. The only upset I have is Rose.

But my mood is such that I determine to talk to her. I need to know the truth, one way or the other. So – I'll ask her. Tomorrow night, as soon as I get home. Her mum can look after things while we go for a drink. And there's little Bonnie now, to keep them occupied.

No, things are going to be different. I'm going to pay her more attention, take her out more, we'll come down to Oxford for weekends. With or without the kids. This is for them, after all. I mean, they don't want to come from a broken home, do they? How would that make them feel? No, we need to work at it.

But then. A thought. What if she *was* with someone else in London? What if they *did* sleep together? What if she's in love with him?

What if I'm already too late?

*

After a fine meal of crab linguine with avocado salad, I spend the evening doing my accounts. So I won't have to do them over the weekend, so I can spend more time with Rose and the kids. Louis is already reading up on anatomy, ready for uni in September, so I can help with that too. His first choice for uni is Edinburgh, with University College London a close second. I'm sure he'll get into Edinburgh, but damn it, I shall miss him. It will just be me and the three females after that. We need to do some serious bonding over the summer, Louis and I.

I'll help with his studies as much as possible once he's there. There's Skype or Facetime. Unlike when I was at uni. Hundreds of miles away from my family and only the phone in the halls of residence for contact. And that cost a fortune. But it did me good, made me strong, independent. And because I had to, I developed my English quickly and easily.

It did make me appreciate my family, though, made me realise what they'd done for me. Even though Maman and Papa went to live in Geneva when I was sixteen. But they only left us behind so we could have the best education, so we'd do well. And we have.

I hope Louis feels the same about us, once he's left home.

It's a warm summer evening, so I open the window to my room. The hotel does have air-con, but I like the fresh air better.

I open a beer from the fridge and sip. My accounts are all done, so I send copies to my accountants and to my inbox. Just in case.

*

It's late, eleven thirty. I can't sleep, thoughts of Rose with another man whirling around my head. Visions of them walking along, hand in hand. Or laughing and joking at some silly little thing that's not really funny. Or in bed together, him lifting up her top and kissing her.

My God! I'm only going on the eyesight of a woman who's met Rose the once. Once. One time. What can I be thinking of? She may be short-sighted, for all I know. She may be imagining things. She may even be making the whole thing up.

But how come she was in London one day, allegedly where Rose was, and then in Oxford the next, standing right beside my table? Is she stalking us for some reason?

The more I think about it, the more I think the whole thing very weird. I mean, you do hear of such things, don't you? People becoming obsessed with other people, googling them, following them.

I throw back the bedclothes, pull myself out of bed, and wander to the window. We're on a main road, but it's peaceful outside. There's a stillness, as if the shops and offices are waiting for something to happen. There's very little moon, so the windows opposite are black, the streetlights stark against them.

A car breaks the silence, zooming down the street at speed, screeching to a stop and emptying its passengers onto the pavement. It's only Thursday night, but the girls are giggling, laughing loudly as they pay the taxi driver. They're drunk, scantily-clad, oblivious to the world around them. Easy prey.

I hope to God my girls don't end up like that.

No – we need to discuss our marriage, Rose and I. We need to ensure our girls have security and a loving upbringing. Louis too, of course, but girls are more vulnerable, to my mind. They need security, or they end up going off the rails. Just my opinion, of course.

I climb back into bed and switch on the lamp. The room floods with light and I notice how clinical it is. Clean, yes, but clinical. If I'm to continue staying over in Oxford I need to find somewhere more homely.

I miss home. I miss the beautiful hand-made curtains, the soft colours, the kitchen always cluttered with cups and plates, the garden with its lovely flowers especially chosen by Rose. Such an appropriate name. I miss the chit-chat, even the bickering, of the children.

I miss Rose.

Sighing, I pick up my novel, the French version, a thriller set in Paris in the 1950s.

But as I begin to read, I notice the flood of dust motes around me. I'm sure I didn't disturb the dust that much. In fact, there isn't any dust. The room is much too clean for that.

My imagination playing tricks, I decide. It's late at night and I'm tired.

Then I realise. Mamie's stardust.

It's Mamie's stardust again.

The scent of her perfume fills the room, that lovely vanilla scent that always reminds me of her. Then the feeling of a coat being slipped around my shoulders.

It's just my imagination, I know. I'm upset, I need comforting.

But it's happened before. I've felt this before.

Is there such a thing as souls living on after death? Could Mamie still be up there looking after me? If so, what's with the coat feeling? Is it there to protect me?

It's a comforting thought. Truly comforting. But a load of rubbish. I should leave it to the mystics, the psychics, the women who sit in tents at the fairground and read your palm.

Placing my book onto the bedside table, I fall into a deep sleep.

15

Noelle

Friday July 15th

My beautiful France. Ravaged again. Last night, while Claude was doing his accounts, people were being massacred on the Promenade des Anglais, in Nice. They were only celebrating Bastille Day, bless them.

I heard the news this morning, as I was sitting with Claude in his Oxford hotel.

Why would anyone *do* such a thing?

We will probably never know the answer. Because the police killed him, the inhuman being who ran his lorry into a crowd of people. Innocent people, out celebrating the freedom of France.

My France.

*

But there appears to be evil everywhere. If I hadn't hung around Claude's house on Tuesday night, I dread to think what might have happened.

That shadow, the shadow that fell against the curtain, it never solidified, never became a person, a solid being. As if it was an extension of someone, or something. There to spy. To cause harm.

So I stayed very still, unsure if it could sense my presence.

Until, finally, it made its move.

Rose stirred suddenly, moved away from Claude and climbed out of bed, her nightie gathering around her knees. She was sleepwalking, I realised, her eyes still closed.

I watched as she moved from the bed towards the open window, towards the shadow, as still and as dark as night.

I sensed its pleasure, its gloating pleasure, as she glided towards it. Slowly but surely, she was walking towards it.

I screamed, couldn't help it. 'Rose! No!'

She heard me. Thank God she heard me.

Opening her eyes, she looked around, saw where she was, and cried out.

'Claude! Claude!'

As he leapt from the bed, I turned.

The shadow had gone.

*

So Enid's placing of the Duk Rak the following night could not have been more timely. Because something had to be done. Peggy helped, of course, but she had to disappear quickly, leaving only the scent of patchouli.

If the Duk Rak is as strong and powerful as they believe, we should have nothing to worry about. But I have a feeling.

I think I know what's going on.

I've always been intuitive. Even when Estelle and Georges were taken, I suspected something, had a feeling. If only I'd taken notice. If only I'd listened to that little voice inside my head. If only I'd warned them.

It was the birthday cake that did it. Her mother had made it, but there were no eggs around, so she'd added grated carrot and sultanas to add flavour. There was no icing, and very few sultanas, as they were a rarity, expensive.

That cake had pride of place on the kitchen table. Yet to me it looked all wrong. Two of the sultanas caught my eye as I walked in, the evening before Estelle's birthday. As if they were following me, as if they were planning something. They were sultanas, for goodness' sake. But they didn't look right. I knew they weren't right.

That was the last birthday cake her mother ever made.

But it's gone now, in the past. We must forgive.

As long as we don't forget.

But haven't we already forgotten?

People are still being jailed, or killed, for speaking out against governments. Women and children still have to prostitute themselves in order to eat. All over the world. How can that be? How can we forget? Why do we choose to ignore it?

I sigh.

I'm back there again. Sitting in the hallway, hugging Giselle and sobbing my heart out. I can even smell the *Gauloises* smoked by the soldiers as they walk by, hear the squeaking of bicycles and the trundling of trams as people make their way to work. As if it's a normal day.

I am one person who will *never* forget.

But I know this – there is definitely something wrong at Claude's house. Something that even Enid's Duk Rak won't put right.

*

Tonight, I'm checking in on Tori. As I promised Peggy. She's fast asleep, her schoolbooks still open on the bed. She is a beautiful girl, her skin brown with the sun, her hair strewn across the pillow as though she's designed it to fall that way. But she seems fine, so I check through the rest of the apartment and leave.

All is well.

How I remember being that age. Oh, how I remember. But times were hard, we had very little. I was just Tori's age, seventeen, when the Nazis invaded Poland and the war on Europe began. The First World War had left us with rationing and shortages, but after I was born the economy began to boom. We even hosted the Olympic Games. But by the early 1930s the Great Depression hit and then, of course, with the German Occupation, we went back to rationing.

It was an awful time to be alive. Sandbags littered the streets, prostitutes made a fortune, selling themselves and other, black market, commodities, and rows of cheap velo-taxis lined the streets for the poor to use.

Even though there was very little food around, Maman made sure we kept our self-esteem. We'd use olive oil on our skin and hair, rubbing it in, then rinsing it off. She knew a man who knew a man, so there was never a shortage as far as we were concerned. I'm sure that's why I always had lovely skin. Maman too. Always.

As for clothes – well, Maman would give me clothes from her vast wardrobe and I'd alter them in such a way they looked as if they'd been made for me. Some clothes we shared, though; we were nearly the same size.

It still amazes me that, even though there was a war on and a shortage of everything, Parisian women insisted on retaining their chic, their charm. When there was a shortage of shampoo, we wore turbans on our heads, the brighter the better. When we could no longer scrape lipstick from the bottom of the tube, the common old beetroot was there to lend a hand. And if there were no nylons to wear, we'd use stinky old gravy powder.

After all, if Mr Hitler hated cosmetics, which he did, what was the best way of upsetting him? And of making ourselves feel better? So we did, we did everything we could to cheer up that dark, miserable world.

I was wearing a dress Maman had given me when I first met Louis, you know. The third of July, 1939, it was. Cream with double-breasted buttons and a small green collar. I loved it. And after it caught Louis' eye, I absolutely adored it.

I was outside old Monsieur Bernot's shop, waiting for the arrival of the tripe he'd promised us. We'd all heard the rumours, so the queue stretched down to the

Tuileries. Even little Colette Paquet was queuing, saving a place for her mother.

Suddenly, however, a man pushed into the queue, much to the annoyance of Madame Harvey behind me. But he ignored her, instead asking if I was going to be queuing for long, as he had to get to work and wanted to arrange a date. Blushing, I asked where he worked and he told me, his cigarette forming curls of smoke in the air. Then he smiled. That lovely, warm smile.

And yes, I confess it. I was impressed. A doctor. Already. And he wanted to take me to dinner, so could I please tell him when.

I was standing there in Mum's dress and white cotton socks, my hair tied into a ponytail, barely out of school. What could he possibly have seen in me? But he did. We were married six months later, he in his dinner suit and me in the most beautiful dress, hand-made from parachute silk.

But he took care of me. He always took care of me.

Such days.

*

So now it's my turn to look after Claude. And Rose and the children, of course. But Claude seems more susceptible, somehow. Or maybe that's because he's my grandson, was my responsibility all those years ago. When he needs me, I go to him, place my precious cloak around his shoulders, and stay. Just for a while. Just so he knows he's not alone.

Could Peggy be right, though? Is someone trying to hurt Claude? This Flora Middlewood or whatever she's called - if she can kill Tori, what might she do to Claude? Oh, my God. Is she trying to get him to commit suicide too, by harming his marriage? After all, there's more than one way to skin a cat.

He has become very short-tempered lately, blaming the children for things that at one time would never have bothered him, shouting at Rose in his frustration. He doesn't take care of himself, either, as he used to do. That trench coat of his has definitely seen better days, yet he never has it cleaned, never bothers if he spills onto it, shoves it into the boot of the car so Rose can't get to it.

That's not the Claude I know. Not at all.

So I watch. And I wait.

16

Rose

Saturday July 16th

It's early. Nearly six o'clock. I can't sleep.

It's Claude. He knows about Jason, about my trip to London, about the kiss.

He asked me, so I told him.

He came home last night, waited for me to return with Violette from the show, took me by the arm, and suggested a drink at the Royal Oak. We had a couple of quite pleasant drinks, bumped into one of our neighbours (John Wittingham, a civil engineer from up the road), and chatted for a while. Mundane stuff.

It was on the way home that he told me. Apparently, that Emilia (the woman who's renting us the chalet) says she saw me with Jason near Kings Cross.

So it all came out. About him not paying me enough attention. About me sleepwalking because I'm so stressed. About him always being involved in his work, even when he's not actually at work. About me having to run the household, ferry the kids around, do the shopping, cooking and cleaning, even though I have my own business to run. And, if I'm honest, about Louis, my gorgeous clever son, leaving home in September. Which is breaking my heart.

Claude actually accused me of taking advantage, of being unfaithful, of sleeping with Jason, of all sorts of awful, horrible things. How could he?

We argued bitterly, said too many things, things we've bottled up for far too long. I cried so much, couldn't believe we were even having this conversation, saying these words. He's the love of my life.

The children were already asleep when we got home, so we climbed into bed quietly, not hugging, not talking. Just lying there like wounded animals.

Afraid.

*

I climb out of bed, trundle along to the kitchen, and boil the kettle.

The radio mumbles softly in the background as I sit cross-legged on the stone floor, stroking Bonnie's head and drinking tea. I need to lick my wounds. I need to decide what to do.

I need to make it up to him.

But today we'll be too busy. School broke up yesterday, it's Lottie's final show tonight, I've promised to make cupcakes for the after-show party, and I need to ring round and finalise plans for the garden party next weekend.

I've not even bought the ingredients for the cupcakes yet, so that will be a trip to Tesco. Then I need to bake, take Mum to the station (I was going to drive her up there, but she's insisted), clean through the house as I've not had a minute, and help set up the party with the other mums at school.

But we really need to talk.

I sigh loudly, every inch of me needing to hug him, to make him feel better.

Bonnie licks my hand in sympathy.

*

It's ten-thirty, and the kids are still in bed. I'm making fresh coffee in the Nespresso and chatting to Mum when Violette comes running through, her hair flying.

'Mum! Gran!'

'What, my darling?' I say.

'Louis isn't here! He's gone, Mum! He's not even slept in his bed, I don't think!'

'Are you sure?' My stomach tumbles with fear. Grabbing my phone, I rush to his room. It's empty, the bed still immaculate from when I made it yesterday. I ring him.

No answer.

Claude's in the garden, sitting with an empty coffee cup and the newspaper.

'Claude!' I scream. 'It's Louis! He's not answering!'

Confused, he throws down the paper. 'What? Where is he?'

'He's not here, he's not slept in his bed. I don't know where he is.'

We race round, all of us, checking each room in turn; the house, the garage, the old stables, the garden. It's a big house.

As we finally assemble in the kitchen, I can't think straight. Mum sits at the table, grey with worry.

Suddenly a text comes through. I grab my phone so fast I nearly drop it.

Please don't worry about me, Mum. I'm with Juliet. We want to be together, so I'm not going to uni. I'll take a year out, maybe two. Don't get in touch, I'm changing my number.

My world falls from the sky.

My boy.

My funny, clever, gorgeous boy.

Turning to Claude, I burst into tears.

'What? What's he said?' he asks, taking the phone from me.

'He's gone. He's left. Oh, my God! What do we do?'

He pulls me to him, hugging me tight. 'We can't do anything, *ma chérie*,' he says, from somewhere far, far away. 'He's eighteen. He can do whatever he likes.'

My body stiffens with panic. 'But we can try and find him, can't we? We can make sure he's alright?'

'Mum?'

Violette takes my phone from where Claude has left it on the table, enters my PIN and reads the text.

I wait for the tears, the screams, the entreaties.

Instead, she just stands there, shaking her head.

'No. That's not right.'

I turn to her, confused. 'What?'

'That's not Louis. He never calls her Juliet, he says it's too posh. He'd have put Jules. He would have put Jules, Mum.'

273

I feel sick.

'I don't understand,' I murmur.

'Something's not right, I can tell. It's not right. Something's happened.'

*

The police sergeant in Sleaford fills out a report. But he's not really interested. Legally, Louis is an adult, can go wherever he likes, drop out of uni whenever he likes, fall in love whenever he likes. Also, we don't have Juliet's address. We don't even know her surname, for God's sake. All we know is she attends Lincoln uni. And that's only from what Louis has told us.

So we drive home. Empty.

I leave Mum and Claude eating lunch with the kids, and I walk round to Enid Phelps's house. I'm not hungry, and I'm dehydrated and tired from crying. I need sunshine and fresh air.

It's just off the main road, her cottage. I've walked past it quite often; we have to walk down Canwick Lane to get to the woods. Enid's house is the last in a row of four stone cottages. It's a nice little place, Chimney Cottage, with a small conservatory to one side, and a small Bed and Breakfast sign that's only been there a year or so.

But as I walk up to the old brass knocker, I wonder what I'm doing here. It feels odd. I could just have rung her, which is what I've done before.

I knock anyway.

Enid opens the door with a flourish.

'Rose! How lovely to see you. Come on in, my dear.'

I wipe my feet on the mat and follow her through the dark hallway to the kitchen.

As my eyes adjust, the first thing I notice is the smell. A warm, sweet scent, slightly musky. Frankincense and orange again, I think. Then I spot a cat, a black one, its tail held high, just ahead of me.

'Don't mind Genevieve,' says Enid, smiling. 'She likes to check out our visitors. It makes her feel superior, doesn't it, Genevieve?'

The kitchen is welcoming, with plum red tiles and a bright yellow kettle and toaster. I notice the oil burner on the side, its fumes curling into the air.

Genevieve disappears beneath the table as I sit down. There's a white tablecloth, and a gathering of tea-lights on one side, ready to light.

'Cup of tea, my dear?' asks Enid. I catch her watching me carefully.

'Yes, please, that'd be lovely. Milk, no sugar.'

She makes two cups of tea, then offers me a biscuit from a tin she has on the side. Home-made.

Suddenly I'm hungry.

'Cinnamon shortbread,' she says. 'I make it myself. There's a special ingredient in these that I sometimes use. I can give you the recipe?'

I take a bite. It's soft, delicately-flavoured, melt-in-the-mouth. 'Mm, they're delicious.'

Taking one herself, she beams. 'So, how are you?'

'It's Violette's last school show tonight and we've got tickets. We just wanted to see it again, one more time. And I just wondered whether you'd dog-sit for us, please. I'm helping at a party afterwards, but Claude can take you home, if that's alright. Or you could stay over – we have a spare room?'

She looks at me as if to say, *I like my own bed, thank you very much.*

But she doesn't, she doesn't say it.

Instead, I feel suddenly as if she can read my mind, *is* reading my mind.

She pats my hand. 'Is there a problem, Rose? Something you need to talk about? I can tell you're a bit upset, my dear.'

I burst into tears. Silly schoolgirl sobs that go on and on.

'There, there, let it all out. Just let it out.' She passes me some tissues.

'Sorry, Enid,' I mumble, wiping my eyes and nose. 'It's just – we've lost Louis. He's gone, left the house, not said a word. And now he's not going to uni in September, he's going to ruin his life. And all for some girl he's met. We don't even know her name …'

17

Claude

Sunday July 17th

To the outside world, it looks as though we're a normal family, having fun on a warm, relaxing Sunday afternoon. I drop Violette and Lottie off at Katie's house. She's really Violette's friend, but she always takes Lottie under her wing, so I know she'll be fine. Also, her parents are both head-teachers, pillars of the community.

Unlike us.

Unlike me and Rose.

Oh my God, did Louis find out about us? Does he know about his mother and her ex meeting up? Is that why he's left home?

No. He couldn't know. There's no way he could know.

Anyway, Violette is convinced he's not left voluntarily. I think she's wrong, though. How could anyone take a young, strong, fit man from his bed by force?

No. He must have been planning it for weeks, took advantage of us going to the pub. Which is where we are now, as it happens. I've brought Rose and her mum to the pub for Sunday lunch. To save them cooking, and hopefully to take our minds off things. I say hopefully because, despite the delicious meal of beef lasagne and pint of Doom Bar that's sitting in front of me, I can think of nothing but Louis.

It's my fault, you see. If I hadn't dragged Rose out Friday night, he might have come to me first, to talk. So if I hadn't been so selfish, insisting she tell me the truth, he might not have gone, it might never have happened.

What does all that matter now, though, now we've lost our boy?

It doesn't.

I've tried ringing him, texting him, leaving messages, pleading with him.

Nothing.

No reply.

Rien.

*

Carol insists on staying here with Rose, even though she's booked to go away with friends on Wednesday. They're supposed to be travelling to Rome for a week, all three of them. Thank God it's not Paris or Nice, though, after that awful massacre on Thursday.

Is anyone anywhere safe anymore?

We manage to talk her out of staying. After all, there's nothing she can do. Nothing any of us can do. According to the police, it looks as if he went of his own free will, he's now an adult, and he can do as he likes.

We drive Carol to the station together. There are tears, hugs given and promises made, and she boards the train.

So, except for Bonnie, the house is empty when we return. Devoid. Of children. Of noise. Of love.

All the money we've spent on this house, and it's not brought us happiness. And I've lost interest in it. Time for a change, I think. There's a converted barn in the village centre I've seen. Half a million pounds, it is, I checked on Right Move. We could buy it cash, no mortgage. It's only four bed, but we could always extend onto the side. The kids will be grownup soon, anyway.

Bonnie runs up as we walk in. She looks incredibly guilty and we find a small puddle on the kitchen floor. Right now, though, we're not in the mood for remonstration or fuss. Rose mops up the mess, lets her into the garden, and feeds her. But that's all the attention she gets. We could do with Enid Phelps to come round.

She is a curiosity, that woman. I drove her home last night after watching Violette's show again, which was wonderful, again. For some reason Enid was unusually chatty, asked lots of questions, seemed overly interested in Louis. What is he like towards other people, what are his hobbies, his interests, who are his friends? She is very upset, of course, at his just going off like that. But I got the impression she thought she could help. Very strange. Apparently she's a gypsy, travelled the length and breadth of Britain in a caravan as a child. And I can believe it, with the huge brass earrings and the bangles she wears. She's a nice enough person, though, fusses over the children enormously.

I make coffee for myself and Rose, and spend half an hour in the study working on notes for the accountant. I should spend longer, but I can't concentrate, need to speak to Rose, need to know she's okay.

Saving my work, I go to find her. She's supposed to be in the kitchen, baking; she has a couple of kiddie's birthday parties this week.

But when I look for her, she's not there at all. She's in Louis' room, sitting on his bed, crying quietly. The room is bare, his desk empty, his gingham duvet and pillow neat and tidy. Too neat and tidy. And the clothes and books that usually litter the floor are nowhere to be seen. As if a silent hand has removed him from the world and come back afterwards to tidy up.

I take Rose's hand and pull her away, into the kitchen. The radio is playing an Ella Fitzgerald song. *Ev'ry Time We Say Goodbye ...*

I sit Rose at the table, intending to make tea. But as I fill the kettle a huge sense of loss washes over me. Leaving it, I sit down and take her into my arms.

We weep together.

'We'll find him, *ma chérie,*' I whisper. 'We will find him.'

She pulls back. 'I'm sorry, Claude. I'm sorry, for everything.'

'There's nothing to be sorry for. There is *nothing* to be sorry for.'

'There is, though. I – I thought you didn't love me. I thought you'd stopped caring, were only concerned about your work, your bloody research. Not us, not me and Lottie and Violette and – and Louis.'

She bursts into fresh tears.

I pull her close, stroking her soft hair. 'I'm sorry. I didn't think. I didn't know. I thought you wanted me to be successful. You *did* want me to be successful.'

'I did, of course I did. But not that much. Not so much you forgot about what really matters.'

She looks up at me, her eyes red and swollen. I close them gently with my thumbs and kiss them, one at a time.

She opens them, and they are full of love. 'I didn't sleep with him, you know.'

Gathering her into my arms, I take her to bed.

*

It's nearly eleven o'clock at night. I've been on the laptop for three hours now, trying to find out where he is, where our funny, intelligent, lovely boy is. Lincoln uni has closed for the summer, of course. There is an admin department, but they're only open three days, Tuesday to Thursday. I'll ring them on Tuesday, first thing. And I'll take time off from Oxford. They don't need me, not like the hospital. The *bloody research* can wait a while. I need to find my boy.

On impulse, I've googled *Juliet, Sleaford*, then *Juliet, Lincoln*, and *Juliet, Grantham*. But it just comes up with a load of stuff about Shakespeare. It's an unusual name, so there must be something, somewhere, about her. So I sit. I do everything I possibly can to trace her.

Suddenly there's nothing left, no more I can do. Until the uni opens, we don't even know if she's actually from around here. She could be from anywhere, anywhere in the world.

The thought leaves me stunned.

Rose has been on Facebook and Instagram, searching, getting in touch with Louis' friends, to see if they know who she is, *where* she is. Surely he's told them about her? Surely she's on his Facebook page?

It would appear that Louis himself has not been on social media since Friday night. The last thing he posted was a picture of some boat he'd found. *Three weeks tomorrow until snorkelling, fishing and sailing! Look out, Maldives, here we come!*

He was obviously unaware of this little trip with Juliet at that point, then.

But no. There's nothing anywhere about this Jules, as he calls her. She's a Scarlet Pimpernel, here one minute, vanished the next.

My boy ...

A wonderful vision enters my head. Of Louis running along the beach in Bandol, bucket and spade in hand. Laughing, his eyes sparkling like the sea behind him. Such a beautiful child. The bucket is purple; he specifically asked for a purple bucket. It was his favourite colour for years. Until someone told him it was girly.

No. Violette knows what she's talking about. There's definitely something not right about all of this.

18

Noelle

Monday July 18th

I made sure to visit Valerie and Matthieu last Friday. That dreadful massacre on Thursday really scared me. My God, they could easily have been there, celebrating with everyone else. It just doesn't bear thinking about.

But Valerie was still home, recovering from her fall. It's knocked her confidence a little, but she'll be fine. And Matthieu is enjoying his retirement, fishing and helping out at a beach restaurant in Marseilles. It's owned by an old friend, so Matthieu hangs around most evenings, helping with the food or just chatting and keeping company. He looks happy, with a smile that lights up the world, although he never did marry. Bless him.

So on Saturday I did as Peggy asked and checked on Olivia, at home in Oxford.

Her sister had already left, so there appeared to be little happening. She got up, went shopping, ate lunch, and sat before a huge computer for hours. From what I could see, she still deals in personal injury, dealing with car crashes and the like.

She appeared to be living a normal life, no strange callers, no weird mixing of potions or perfumes. But I hung around until late into the evening, just to be sure.

At ten on the dot, the phone rang.

Emilia.

There was no sisterly chit-chat, no term of endearment, just a quick call to arrange a meeting.

Then I heard something of interest. Great interest.

Olivia began to preen before the mirror. 'I *am* thinking of using the Enhancement Charm, even though you disapprove of it. Well, it's worked before, hasn't it? I got my man. Or should I say Mattie's man?' She laughed maliciously. 'I just never thought Alice – I mean Mattie - would meet up with that Paul Whiting again, the one I suicided in 1942.' She paused for Emilia's reply. 'But I'll make her suffer a different way, just watch me. Tonight.'

Was she talking about Mattie Whirlow, I wondered? Is that why Peggy wants me to watch her?

There was nothing to suggest it *was* Mattie Whirlow, but I had to check. So immediately I transported myself to her farmhouse.

All was calm. All was quiet. I anchored myself at the top of the stairs, listening, watching, waiting. There was no sound, no creaking, just the hourly chirping of a cuckoo clock.

As twelve o'clock turned, all was well. Maybe I'm wrong, I thought. Maybe it's not this Mattie, after all. Maybe I should just continue with my search for Louis.

But then. A noise.

I turned.

Lily was walking along the landing, her nightie pure and white, her eyes closed. I thought she was heading for the bathroom, but no. She carried on, towards the landing window.

A beautiful stained glass window. Left wide open to let in the air.

I watched her climb onto the blanket chest beneath, place her hands upon the sill. I could see she intended climbing up, and out.

'Oh, my God,' I whispered.

She turned as if she'd heard me, her eyes still closed.

She *could* hear me.

'Lily,' I said.

Ignoring me, she pulled herself up. The old windowsill is deep, wide, and she knelt onto it. Reaching out suddenly, her little arm stretched into nothingness.

'Lily!' I called, louder now.

She turned again, but ignored me, again.

I needed something to distract her.

'Lily, why don't you show *Mummy* the pretty window?'

She opened her eyes, stared at me, and screamed.

'Mummy! Mu–mmy!'

Mattie was there before you could say Boo, and despite Lily's insistence that she'd seen a lady on the landing, managed to soothe her with a Peter Rabbit film. She'd obviously heard it all before.

285

I searched the house from top to bottom, but found no malevolences. Even so, I was convinced Olivia had something to do with Lily climbing up to that window. Exactly *how* she'd done it was beyond me.

But I was determined to find out.

And in doing so, I was to discover so much more.

*

I travelled in the car alongside Olivia yesterday. She caught my eye occasionally and blinked, as if she could sense my presence, but never said anything. It did make me smile.

We arrived at Emilia's just in time for lunch.

She'd made a stew, despite it being the middle of summer. They chatted while they ate, enthusing over Emilia's recent trip to her property in Sassari. But as the conversation turned, I realised with horror they were discussing the massacre in Nice.

Emilia shrugged. 'We got him, though, didn't we? No-one suspected the target was just one man. You did well, Olivia.'

'Didn't do so well last night, though, did we? She rescued that child of hers just in time.'

'We can always give it another go. Tori as well. For some reason, we get so far, then they wake up. I don't know what's going on.'

'There's some kind of good spirit hanging around, I think. I sensed it in the car just now. We'll soon get rid of it, though.'

'So what do we do about the boy? She can't keep him there forever.'

I edged closer.

Olivia rolled her tongue around her teeth absentmindedly. The veins beneath it were a cold silvery blue, making me shiver.

'We kill him and throw him out of the car, miles from anywhere. He won't be found for months, years, if we choose the right place. Then when he *is* found, the trail will be icy cold. And Rose will suffer for the rest of her life.'

Her laugh was evil. Evil, mad, and cruel.

I had to find Louis.

*

They set off after lunch, Olivia driving. Twenty minutes later, she was parking up on the outskirts of Lincoln; tall trees, neat sidewalks, shops selling designer fashion.

I followed them into a nearby apartment block, climbing up to the second floor in the lift. To my surprise, as we entered her apartment, a girl dressed in tight jeans and tee-shirt pulled Olivia close.

'Thank goodness you're here, Mum,' she cried.

I remembered. Suddenly I remembered.

Olivia wouldn't drink wine at Claude's birthday party. Not even the champagne we drank to celebrate. She was pregnant. Of course she was pregnant.

So this is her daughter.

'Not long now, darling,' murmured Olivia.

The apartment was neat, tidy, a large suitcase upright in one corner.

'All ready to go, then?' asked Emilia.

'I'll be glad when it's all over, and I can get back to normal.'

'Don't worry,' said her mother. 'Rose and that idiot of a husband have no idea you're here.'

I toured the apartment while they talked. The kitchen, the utility room, the bathroom, and finally the bedrooms.

Louis was in the second one, asleep. I moved closer to make sure. Yes. He was breathing, his chest rising and falling. He looked so angelic, so like the little boy he used to be. So like Claude.

I tried to wake him, whispering in case they could hear me.

'Louis, wake up! Louis!'

He stirred, groaned, but didn't open his eyes.

He must be drugged, I realised.

'Oh, my poor Louis! What have they done to you?'

Then they were beside me, lifting him, loading him into the boot of the car. But Olivia drove off by herself, leaving the others behind, not wanting them involved in his death.

I had to do something.

Peggy.

*

I have never seen such evil, such dark magic. Such power.

Peggy drove like a madman, while Enid in the passenger seat shouted directions whenever they lost the trail.

It took nearly four hours, but eventually we pulled up beside an area of rough moorland.

Olivia had obviously seen us following her at this point. Scrambling out of her car, she ran towards us, shouting as she went.

'You again! I should have guessed!'

'What?' asked Peggy, winding down the window.

'You don't recognise me?' she said. 'What? Then how about this?'

Her face changed slightly, elongating, and her tongue slid in and out. There were no silvery blue veins this time. Just the slippery, slimy scales of a black snake.

Peggy gasped in fear. 'Eva Brunewski!'

Scrambling out of the car, she knocked Olivia to the ground.

On all fours now, Olivia's face contorted into a grotesque sneer. 'How dare you?'

Suddenly the sky was full of crows, big, black, ferocious crows. Circling round and round, lower and lower.

Then Peggy's car began to rock, backwards, forwards, sideways. Screaming with fear, Enid released her seatbelt and fell out of the door.

'Run, Enid!' called Peggy. 'Run!'

I could only stand and watch, could only pray for something to intervene. Something pure and good.

Enid didn't run, her knees wouldn't allow it. So she ambled along, but towards Olivia's car. Pulling open the boot in one swift move, she screamed at Louis.

'Louis! Wake up! Come on – wake up!'

Then Peggy was behind her, and together they pulled him out, lifting him and laying him onto the ground.

'Oh no, you don't!' cried Olivia.

As the crows circled ever lower, Olivia's car engine began to roar loudly, seemingly of its own volition.

'Enid! Move! The car!' screamed Peggy, dragging Louis away.

Enid did move, but only just in time. It missed her by a thumbnail.

By now Olivia was upright, her tongue rolling around her teeth lazily, slowly, as if she had all the time in the world. Raising her arms menacingly, she began to chant. Words that made no sense. That sounded like gibberish. Nonsensical, evil gibberish. But they worked.

Strips of moorland began to lift from the ground, curling into balls and flying towards Peggy. Heavy, sun-dried tufts of heather that caught her in the face, the stomach, the legs. The pain of it caused her to bend double.

'Enid! Go!' she screeched.

But Enid didn't go. Instead, she took hold of Peggy's hand.

'Don't let go. Remember? Don't let go, whatever happens!'

So they stood, holding their ground against everything Olivia threw at them. The crows' beaks, the car, the balls of heather.

For some reason, the joining of forces, the sisterly love they have for each other, bound them, doubling their strength.

'Peggy – the ring!' screamed Enid.

With great determination, Peggy pulled the huge ring from her left hand and threw it high into the air with long, scarlet-tipped fingers.

'Away with you! Let harmony descend! Let peace remain! Away, I tell you. Away!'

Her great, theatrical voice filled the sky.

It stopped. It all stopped. The crows disappeared, the heather settled back into the ground, and the car switched itself off.

Peace. Quiet.

But Olivia rose up, her arms stretching to the sky. 'I call on the powers of the Dim Mak! Rise up and be away with these unbelievers! Kill them! Destroy them! Away!'

'No! Leave them alone!' screamed Louis, suddenly awake, suddenly upright. With a flash of metal, he lunged at her.

Seconds later, Olivia lay unconscious on the ground and Louis stood there, a huge adjustable spanner swinging from his hand.

19

Rose

Tuesday July 19th

They arrived very early yesterday morning. Enid, her friend Peggy, and my Louis. My precious Louis. My son. Safe and sound. Thank God. I had pizza waiting for him, and a warm, safe bed.

But the strangest thing of all. I knew his kidnapper. I recognised her.

Olivia.

*

I do realise there are *more things in heaven and earth*, and so on. But even so, what happened yesterday …

Enid and Peggy stayed with Olivia (or Eva as they keep calling her) in the old stables. Peggy bound her hands together, then fastened her to the reins bar to ensure she didn't escape.

Mattie Whirlow arrived just after breakfast, along with her friend Benjamin Bradstock and a teenage girl called Tori. Benjamin and Peggy brought Olivia across from the stables, and we gathered in the sitting room. The bruise on her head had turned a violent purple overnight, but other than that she was in good form, shouting and struggling against the ropes that bound her. Only after Benjamin had hypnotised her did we release them. He's a professional hypnotherapist, you see, was able to calm her down.

He's also able to regress people to their former lives. Apparently.

I mean, reincarnation?

Then Benjamin counted down, taking Olivia back to her childhood, then back further. Then further. And further.

Until we were in the year 1662. Paris. Versailles, to be exact.

At least, that's what Olivia told us.

The weirdest thing is - she spoke with a French accent. Surreal. The Olivia I knew could barely speak a word of French.

We were all nestled into the horseshoe of large sofas we have, whilst Benjamin and Olivia sat on two dining chairs in the middle where the coffee table would normally be. I'd already sent the children off to the cinema, and had fed and watered Bonnie, fastening her into the kitchen.

And so it began.

Benjamin asked his first question.

'What's your name in 1662?'

'You don't know that, my name? It is everywhere, my name. The scandal, the lies ...'

I was shocked. She didn't sound a bit like Olivia.

'Your name, would you please tell me?' repeated Benjamin, patiently.

She sighed. 'Collette de Savatier is my name.'

'What is it you're supposed to have done, Collette?'

'Ask these women here, these women here with you. Ask them. *Des sorcières, toutes!*'

'Sorry? Could you please translate?'

'You have no idea of what you do. You will regret every second of this ...'

'What do these women have to do with you?'

'My children will see me beheaded, hear me scream in agony, then my body burn.' She turned to Mattie. 'You! I hate you! Always I hate you!'

Mattie, who had been watching with interest, turned suddenly pale, looked as if she might be sick.

'Are you okay?' I whispered, and she nodded.

Benjamin continued. 'Just what is it she's supposed to have done?'

'She and her cronies!'

'Which cronies, Collette? Who are we talking about?'

She looked from Mattie to Tori, and then, finally, to me. 'All of you. You all have a hand in it.'

Confused, we just stared at her. Until finally I broke the silence.

'I did know you years ago, Olivia, but I never did anything to hurt you. We were friends.'

She stared at me as if I were a street urchin, begging for crumbs. 'Why do you call me Olivia? Just what do you play at, Gabrielle?'

Benjamin interrupted. 'Gabrielle? What does Gabrielle have to do with you?' His voice was kind, gentle, and she responded accordingly.

'You really do not know? That Gabrielle is my executioner? And Celeste? Sweet, innocent Celeste?' Here, she stared at Mattie. 'And Hélène, who is my friend?' This was aimed at Tori, sitting beside me.

'What have they done?' he asked.

'They conspire against me, send me to the executioner, have me burned at the stake.'

'But why?'

'They say I am a witch, that I make much money telling fortunes and taking away babies, and use magic to make things happen. But I deny everything.'

Her voice begins to crack with the emotion of it all, so Benjamin taps her arm.

'You are to come forward in time, Collette. Upon the count of three, I want you to come forward, to the next lifetime with your executioners. Tell me what happens.'

*

The next hour was as crazy as it is unbelievable. What I mean is, if I hadn't been there, hadn't actually witnessed it, I would never, in a million years, have believed it.

It turns out that Mattie, Tori and I have all lived before. Unbelievable. Apparently we were all there, in Versailles, in 1662.

Benjamin and I googled the date just this morning. France at that time was rife with witchcraft; there were trials and executions going on all over the place. Collette would only have been one of many sent to be beheaded and burnt at the stake. So what she said may very well be true. Trial after trial found women guilty of witchcraft, of using magic, aborting babies, killing animals and nurturing plants, boiled in secret to create concoctions and remedies that either killed or cured.

But Collette was different. She wanted revenge.

***

Collette's story was slightly muddled, backwards and forwards, to and fro. So here it is, gleaned from Benjamin's scribbled notes, in strict chronological order:

After being beheaded in 1662, Collette was born again as Flora Middlewood in 1737 under the rule of Louis Fifteenth. Under cover of the Seven Years War, she killed two British soldiers in the forest of pine trees that is currently the Bois de Boulogne, thus ending their short lives. Those soldiers are known to us as Mattie and Tori.

Reincarnated as Francine Aubel in 1801, just after the French Revolution, she encouraged an affluent and married socialite to take her own life, after becoming pregnant to her lover. That socialite is now me, her lover Claude.

Collette was born again in 1880 as Joshua Harbison, who in 1914 became a Nazi collaborator. He encouraged and witnessed the raping of Clotilde Dourdos in Paris by German soldiers. Clotilde committed suicide a few months later. We now know her as Tori.

By 1939, Joshua had emigrated to a small Yorkshire village. Three years later, he persuaded Paul Whiting to commit suicide rather than go to war. His girl Alice Webster lost the baby they were expecting, and she died helping the war effort in London. Alice is now Mattie, and Paul her husband Andrew. The baby they lost is their daughter, Lily.

Six years later, in 1946, Joshua became friendly with Elizabeth Salter, a kind, caring mother. He persuaded her to throw herself off a bridge rather than suffer the stigma of divorce. Elizabeth is now Tori.

Joshua took a holiday in Dorset in 1958. He calmly watched as four-year-old Millicent Broadstairs walked into the sea. She never came back. Millicent is now Tori.

Joshua died the year after, but was reborn in 1965. His name? Flora Middlewood. Again. A highly intelligent woman, she reinvented herself as Olivia Brooke in 1986, befriending me at my place of work in Sheffield.

Her secondment in New York allowed her to organise the Paris bombings of 1993 and 1995. She hates the French; it was the Parlement de Paris who sentenced her to death in 1662 after Celeste de Bécherelon (Mattie), Hélène Saboe (Tori) and Gabrielle Auxier (myself) put ourselves forward as witnesses to her evil sorcery.

November 1995 saw Olivia return to Sheffield, when she moved in with me. Her body clock had begun ticking, but she didn't want a man interfering in her sordid life. So she used the sperm of Doug, a married man. Cold, calculating. He never knew. After I married Claude, we lost touch, but she gave birth to a daughter, Juliet, in 1996.

Olivia left Juliet with her sister in 2010. Reinventing herself yet again as Sonia Stephenson, she began an affair with Mattie's husband Rob, causing their subsequent divorce. Sonia left him two years later.

Using the Enhancement Charm to update her looks, she reinvented herself again in 2015, to become Laura Middleton. Known also as Eva Brunewski. All this time dealing in drugs, prostitution, theft and murder, she eventually caught up with Tori, causing her attempted suicide. Thanks to Enid and Peggy, this time around she survived.

A year later, Laura again became Olivia Brooke. This time she tried to kill Tori and Lily, and attempted to destroy my marriage to Claude. When none of this worked, she finally kidnapped our son, with the full intention of killing him.

**

Midnight. Claude is home, the children are in bed, and we're gathered in the stables. Collette is again entwined within her ropes.

Benjamin has told us what's going to happen. He will hypnotise Collette so she'll believe she's a white witch, a good witch, then he'll tell her to leave and never come back. He has also warned us that it won't be a pretty sight, and there may be danger.

So, having fed everyone jacket potato for lunch and pasta bake for tea, I finally sit down on the hay bales to watch. Claude takes my hand, kisses it, and smiles.

I smile back. Happy.

We point our torches towards the centre, towards Benjamin and Collette. Benjamin counts down, and she falls into a deep sleep.

'There's a well-known saying, Collette, and it is this. For evil to flourish, it only requires good men to do nothing.' He pauses for dramatic effect. 'What Mattie, Tori and Rose did all those years ago was what any right-minded, good person would do. They should not be punished.'

Collette's eyelids move, but she says nothing.

'You've spent centuries punishing them for what they did. Life after life you've ruined for them, using witchcraft, deceit, evil ...'

He looks up as the old, unused, barn-light hanging above Collette begins to glow. Brighter. And brighter still. Suddenly it's so bright we have to shield our eyes.

'Sorry. I'll tone it down a bit,' says a voice, and the light becomes a person, a woman wearing a white cloak and clutching a yellow badge.

Claude stands up, amazed. 'Mamie!'

She smiles. 'Bless you, Claude!'

It's as if the sky is in the room, as if the sun is shining. Clouds of dust motes fill the air.

Mamie's stardust. Tears fill my eyes as they dance around.

'There are others,' she says.

An old sailor-type appears beside her. He bows towards us, his scruffy flat cap dripping with water.

'*Bonjour*, Great Uncle John,' she says. 'Now where did Grandma Beattie get to?'

Grandma Beattie walks in through the door behind me, singing.

'*There's a yellow rose in Texas, that I am going to see ...*'

Mattie rushes forward. 'Grandma Beattie - I don't believe it ...'

There isn't a dry eye in the house.

As Grandma Beattie drifts away to stand beside Mamie and Great Uncle John, we watch expectantly.

Mamie removes her cloak, which is so bright I can hardly bear to look.

Grandma Beattie and Great Uncle John help Collette to sit upright, and Mamie places the cloak around her shoulders. She is still asleep.

Mamie looks down at her. 'This cloak is full of love. It will help you to forgive. It will aid your renewal. So you can return, refreshed and ready to start again.' Soft tears fill her eyes. 'I have been waiting for you since Versailles, *ma chérie*. For you were my daughter, and I love you.'

The hush is palpable. Never-ending tears rolling down my cheeks.

Mamie, her hands upon Collette's shoulders, looks around and smiles.

'I've finally discovered the tool with which to help you, my child. It is the cloak of everlasting love. We should all wear it from time to time. We should all forgive. No more hatred. No more fighting. No more destruction. It doesn't have to be an actual cloak, it can be a mere figment of your imagination. But let it *be* real, let it *feel* real.' She pauses. 'So thank you, all of you, for helping us. You are blessed.'

The room fills with more light, a different light. Exploding shards of light that hurt our eyes and force them shut.

When we open them again, they have all gone. Mamie, Great Uncle John, Grandma Beattie, and Collette.

But the room is awash with stardust.

Not dust motes this time, but sparkling sprinkles of starlight.

The Epilogue

Saturday July 23rd

The garden party is going with a swing. The sun is shining, my cake stall, which Mattie and Tori are handling, is making a packet, and Enid's apple and sultana pies have already sold out. Peggy's running the coconut shy, and Louis, bless him, is running up and down the garden with children on his back at fifty pence a time. He must be exhausted after his ordeal.

Lottie's in the orchard, having great fun face-painting, Violette is in the marquee reading stories to the kids, and Justine has come down from Sheffield to read the cards. I'm rushed off my feet making tea and coffee, and Claude is here, taking photos for framing and posting.

The place is absolutely teeming with people. But what a wonderful sight.

All in aid of Grantham and Kesteven Hospital children's ward.

I walk past Justine on my way to the kitchen for milk. Enid's sitting at the table, having her cards read.

'The Four of Wands', says Justine. 'You'll be moving house, but it will be a very happy move.'

'Oh no,' says Enid, shaking her head. 'Oh no, that's wrong. I like my little cottage. I won't be going anywhere.'

'The cards never lie, Enid.' She turns the next card. 'Oh, look - the Ten of Cups. How lovely. You'll be married within the year.'

THE END

ENID'S APPLE AND SULTANA PIE

Enid adds lemon balm tincture to her pies. Lemon balm tincture calms the nervous system, lowers blood pressure and soothes digestion.
So I thought you might like the quick version:

Pastry:
225g plain flour
100g butter/margarine/lard
Cold water

Filling:
450g Bramley apples, peeled, cored and sliced
225g Cox apples, peeled, cored and sliced.
75g sultanas
2 teaspoons mixed spice
Teaspoon lemon balm tincture
50g soft brown sugar

You also need:
One egg, separated, and demerara sugar for glazing
Large baking sheet
Preheat the oven to 200 degrees C
Make up the pastry and leave in the fridge to cool while you prepare the apples.

Instructions:
Mix the filling ingredients together in a large bowl.

Roll the pastry into a large circle and draw a 20cm circle at the centre with egg yolk. Fill in the circle with the yolk.

Pile the filling ingredients onto the circle, leaving space around the edge to pull up the pastry and cover the filling.

Brush egg white over the pastry and sprinkle with demerara sugar.

Bake on highest shelf at 200 degrees C for about 35 – 40 minutes.

Enjoy!

Printed in Poland
by Amazon Fulfillment
Poland Sp. z o.o., Wrocław